SPIN A WICKED WEB

A HOME CRAFTING MYSTERY

SPIN A WICKED WEB

CRICKET MCRAE

WHEELER
CHIVERS

This Large Print edition is published by Wheeler Publishing, Waterville, Maine, USA and by BBC Audiobooks Ltd, Bath, England.

Wheeler Publishing, a part of Gale, Cengage Learning.

Copyright © 2009 by Cricket McRae.

The moral right of the author has been asserted.

The text of this Large Print edition is unabridged.

Other aspects of the book may vary from the original edition.

Set in 16 pt. Plantin.

Printed on permanent paper.

LIBRARY OF CONGRESS CATALOGING-IN-PUBLICATION DATA

McRae, Cricket.
   Spin a wicked web : a home crafting mystery / by Cricket McRae.
     p. cm. — (Wheeler Publishing large print cozy mystery)
     ISBN-13: 978-1-4104-1777-0 (pbk. : alk. paper)
     ISBN-10: 1-4104-1777-8 (pbk. : alk. paper)
     1. Women artisans—Fiction. 2. Spinning—Fiction. 3. Murder—Investigation—Fiction. 4. Large type books. I. Title.
     PS3613.C58755S65 2009b
     813'.6—dc22   2009014331

BRITISH LIBRARY CATALOGUING-IN-PUBLICATION DATA AVAILABLE

Published in 2009 in the U.S. by arrangement with Midnight Ink, an imprint of Llewellyn Publications, Woodbury, MN 55125-2989 USA.
Published in 2010 in the U.K. by arrangement with Llewellyn Worldwide Ltd.

U.K. Hardcover: 978 1 408 45682 8 (Chivers Large Print)
U.K. Softcover: 978 1 408 45683 5 (Camden Large Print)

Printed in the United States of America
1 2 3 4 5 6 7 13 12 11 10 09

For G.G., Grandma, and Mom:
three generations of creative women
who came before

ACKNOWLEDGMENTS

I am grateful to everyone who lends their aid, support, and expertise to my books. Among them are my agent, Jacky Sach, and the extraordinary team at Midnight Ink, including Barbara Moore, Lisa Novak, Donna Burch, Courtney Huber, my hardworking publicist Courtney Kish, and the editor who so gently and effectively keeps me in line, Connie Hill. Then there are the cheerleaders who keep me going, among them Kevin (who puts up with me on a daily basis), my parents Ed and Rochelle, my writing buddies Mark and Bob, and my gal pals Mindy, Jody, and Jane. There are so many others; please know how much I appreciate all your kind words and encouragement. Finally, thanks to Jeanette Degoede for information on tulip farms, and to Chris from the Fiber Attic, who taught me how to spin all those years ago — and let me borrow her wheel until I got my own.

ONE

"We have to talk."

Ah, those four magical words. They strike dread into the most manly of hearts, and as a woman, it was an interesting experience to be on the receiving end. Interesting, but not particularly pleasant.

"Okay." I buckled my seat belt. "Talk."

Barr flipped his turn signal, carefully checked both ways, and turned right onto Highway 2.

"There's something I have to tell you, Sophie Mae."

Oh, for heaven's sake, enough with the preamble. I began to regret the super spicy Thai curry I'd had for dinner in Monroe. Barr knew I loved Thai food. Had he been buttering me up?

"Lord love a duck. Will you just say it, whatever it is?"

He nodded. Paused. Opened his mouth to speak.

A flashing cacophony bore down on us from behind. I twisted around to see what was going on as Barr quickly pulled to the side of the road. The screaming sirens and blaring horn nearly deafened us as they passed, and I put my palms over my ears like a little kid. One after another, emergency vehicles raced by: an ambulance, a fire truck, and a Sheriff's vehicle, all nose to tail and heading toward Cadyville at engine roaring speed.

As soon as they were past, Barr floored it. His personal car, a normally sedate white Camry, left rubber on the shoulder of the highway, and we trailed closely behind the emergency entourage.

"What are you doing?" I shouted over the din.

"Finding out what's going on. Whatever it is, it's not good."

A thrill ran through me. I watched, wide-eyed, as Barr maneuvered around traffic at high speed. I grabbed the oh-my-God handle over the door and tried not to grin. I probably should have been scared, but it was kind of fun.

Even if he was avoiding the issue — which I knew darn well he was. What had he been going to tell me?

We veered around a BMW, and the driver

honked. Barr ignored him. A mile later we rounded a curve and discovered the reason for all the emergency equipment. My urge to grin quickly dissipated. Ahead, a car had left the road and traveled fifty feet before crashing head-on into a telephone pole. Dark smoke rose from the vehicle, and uniformed personnel ran toward it.

We parked behind the Sheriff's SUV. Then I saw the light bar on top of the wrecked car. The logo on the side.

I turned to Barr. "Oh, my God."

His door was open, and he was halfway out of the car, looking grim. "It's one of ours," he said and took off toward the gathering knot of people.

I scrambled out and down the shallow ditch embankment, falling behind as the slick soles of my flip-flops slid around on the long grass. More grass poked at my bare legs and grabbed at my summer skirt. Finally, I hit brown dirt and could run.

Panting, I came up behind Barr, but he held his arm out, preventing my further approach. A cloud of chemicals whooshed from an extinguisher as a fireman emptied it over the engine compartment. As the billowing smoke lessened, the pungent tang joined the acrid scents of burning rubber and hot metal. I peered around Barr. The driver's door was open to show part of a man's shiny black boot, but when I tried to get a better look, he turned my shoulder and walked me away from the scene.

"Who is it?" I asked, breathless. "Why aren't they trying to get him out?"

He stopped and closed his eyes. When he opened them, I knew it was really, really bad.

"It's Scott," he said. "He's dead."

"Oh, no." And again, "Oh, no. Who'll tell Chris?" I knew Scott Popper's wife better than I knew him. We were both members of the Cadyville Regional Artists' Co-op, or CRAC, a somewhat recent addition to our little town's growing artsy-fartsy scene.

Barr nodded toward a rapidly approaching pickup. It skidded to a stop on the highway, and Chris got out. She stared toward the wrecked patrol car, hand over her mouth.

He said, "She has a scanner."

Together, we hurried back across the field to Officer Popper's wife.

"Slow down. It isn't a race," Ruth Black said. "Spinning yarn is about process as much as result."

I reduced the speed with which I was pumping the treadle on the spinning wheel.

12

"Sorry. I guess I'm bleeding off some nervous energy."

"Oh, I don't doubt it, after what happened to Scott Popper last evening. But that's the beauty of it," she said. "I find spinning allows me to let go of all the other stuff in my life for a while."

That must have been why she did it so much. And why I was rapidly becoming obsessed with spinning fiber into yarn. Today, Ruth was teaching me how to take the two spools of single-ply wool yarn I'd gradually managed to create over the last three weeks, and spin them together to create a two-ply yarn. A short and spry seventy, Ruth wore her crop of white hair spiked to within an inch of its life. She leaned close, head bent as she watched me work. Her claim to fame at CRAC was fiber art. I'd always known she was an inveterate knitter but had only realized since joining the co-op that she was also an expert in spinning, weaving, felting, and crochet.

"Now, see how your yarn is getting too much twist in it? When you ply the yarns together, you need to make sure the wheel is spinning the opposite direction from the one you used to spin the singles. The first way gives it an S twist. The second utilizes a Z twist so the yarn unspins just slightly as the two strands twine together."

"Um. Okay." I stopped the wheel and tried it the other way. "This is hard after spinning in the other direction all this time."

"You'll get used to it."

We were watching the retail shop on the ground floor of CRAC. It was ten in the morning, and upstairs the supply area and co-op studio spaces were still empty.

Ruth had invited me to join a couple of months earlier. I'd protested that the handmade soap and toiletries I manufactured for my business, Winding Road Bath Products, hardly counted as art, but the other members insisted they did. In truth, they needed as many participants as possible to generate momentum for the co-op, and I was happy to take part. It was Chris Popper who had bought the old library and renovated it into a place for artists of all kinds to make and sell their creations, and she'd been quite enthusiastic about adding me to their roster.

The screen door opened, signaling a possible customer, and Ruth and I both half-stood to see over the cashier's counter. Instead of customers, three of the core members of the co-op entered. First through the door was Irene Nelson. Mousy. There was just no other word for Irene. Thin hair, colorless eyes, nondescript features, wearing

14

beige on beige on beige. I had yet to hear her say more than a dozen words in a row, though I saw her nearly every time I came to the co-op. Her sculptures were what I thought of as "menopause art" — lots of chunky naked women shown in varying positions of prayer and/or power. We are women, hear us sing.

Dr. Jake Beagle loomed behind her. Tall, broad, and coarse-featured, he looked more like a lumberjack of old than an MD who specialized in family medicine, but I suspected Jake's real passion lay in the nature photography he considered a hobby. He was certainly talented. But art didn't often pay the bills, and though I didn't really know her, his beautiful second wife, Felicia, looked expensive.

Trailing behind Jake was Ariel Skylark: blonde, small-boned, tan and supple as only a twenty-three-year-old can be. She had big brown eyes, pillowy lips, and a bizarre winsomeness that men seemed to find irresistible. Her oversized canvases, all of which sported untidy splotches of black and white and red paint, took up most of one wall of the co-op.

The only missing member of the core group was Chris. Barr and I had managed to get her home the evening before, and Jake had come over, as both friend and doctor. He said he'd prescribe something to help her sleep, but she'd refused to call anyone to stay with her.

The screen creaked open again, and Irene's twenty-something son, Zak, entered last. His Doc Martens thudding on the wooden floor, he was all elbows and knees ranging under long, stringy dark hair and an intriguing arrangement of hoops pierced his lips and nostrils. He managed to look bored and uncomfortable at the same time.

As everyone gathered in front of the counter, Zak and Jake both seemed hyper-aware of their spatial relationship to Ariel, situating themselves near her, but not touching. Irene watched her son's antics with a look of unadulterated disgust. I was surprised that he didn't seem to notice. Ariel did though, and smiled broadly at Irene, who turned quickly away.

"I just checked in on Chris," Jake said.

"How is she?" I asked.

"Holding up. It's hard."

"She knows we're all here for her," Irene said.

Ariel waved her hand in the air. "Oh, she'll be fine. My parents died when I was sixteen, and I'm okay."

We all stared at her.

"What? I'm just saying, people get over stuff, you know? It doesn't help anyone to make it into a big deal."

"Time is indeed a great healer," Ruth said, ever the diplomat.

Wow. I mean, some people called me insensitive and tactless, but those people had apparently never met Miss Ariel Skylark.

"Sophie Mae, watch your tension," Ruth said, and I turned my attention back to my yarn.

Two

Scott Popper looked good dead.

I mean, he looked good when he was alive, too, but the nice folks at Crane's Funeral Home really did a fantastic job. Crashing his car into a telephone pole at high speed could hardly have been kind to his face, but two days later here he was, open casket and all, looking just as handsome as ever.

And only a bit less animated than usual.

Now, that was mean. I'd spent little time around Scott, and even that in fairly large groups. That wasn't really enough to form a studied opinion regarding someone's social skills. Maybe he wasn't always as dull as he'd been in my presence. Maybe he was just shy. Even if they don't always deserve it, I do try to give the dead the benefit of the doubt.

In the pew beside me, Barr's attention flicked from face to face, ever watchful, more out of habit than for any other reason.

Scott lay in peaceful repose at the front of the church. Low music seeped out of speakers hidden behind tapestries in the apse of St. Luke's Catholic Church, the droning organ underscoring whispered voices and the rustle of clothing as people settled into their seats. Summer was only two days old, and the warm June air smelled of greenery and Murphy's Oil Soap. I eyed the gleaming wood pews. It must take hours to wipe them all down.

I sighed inwardly. This probably wasn't the best time to ask Barr what he'd been going to tell me before Scott's accident. I watched him out of the corner of my eye, admiring how he looked in his dress uniform while trying not to look obvious. I loved how his chestnut-colored hair was streaked gray at the temples, how his slightly hooked nose looked in profile, how his dark brown eyes could be warm and inviting when he looked at me, but hard as obsidian when the occasion called for it.

He frequently darted looks at Scott in the glossy walnut casket, then jerked his gaze away as if it were painful to look upon the dead for long. His eyes rested on Scott's wife, and the muscles of his jaw slackened; he'd been clenching his teeth. Raw pity flashed across his face for a moment, then

19

was gone, replaced with his usual mask of easy-going stoicism.

I touched his arm. He squeezed my hand in return.

Chris was a decorative blacksmith. You probably don't have to be a big-boned, muscular gal in order to form the elaborate metal pieces that she created, but it couldn't hurt. Nearing six feet in height, with shoulders like a linebacker, her exposed arms rippled with muscles. She wore a simple black sheath to her husband's funeral, and her straight, peanut-butter-blonde hair hung lank on either side of her wide cheekbones, framing an expressionless face that was notable more for its precise symmetry than for classic beauty. Her blue eyes stared forward, unseeing.

Remembering how I'd felt when I'd attended my own husband's funeral almost six years previously, I could understand the confused numbness that must have swamped her. My heart ached with empathy. At least with Mike's lymphoma, I'd had a little time — far too little, but still — to prepare for his death. But dying in a car accident is a sneak robbery, an unexpected blow to those left behind for which there is no preparation. Suddenly, the rest of Chris Popper's life looked different than she ever could have imagined.

She was surrounded by Ruth Black, Irene and Zak Nelson and Jake Beagle. Jake's wife, Felicia, perfectly coifed and dressed to the nines, stood a little ways away, talking with Ruth's ninety-year-old Uncle Thaddeus.

But someone was missing. "That disrespectful little wench," I whispered.

Barr glanced over at me. "Who?"

"Ariel. Ariel Skylark. From the co-op. Tiny, blonde, sticks blobs of paint on great big canvases, then calls it modern art? She's not here."

He shook his head. "Sorry. Have I met her?"

"I guess not." I was pretty sure any man who met Ariel remembered the occasion.

Her absence was conspicuous, though. CRAC was closed for the funeral, so there was no need for anyone to mind the store. It was downright rude of her not to show up.

The door to the street slammed shut. Daylight winked out save the dim glimmer of the stained glass windows arching above. The last viewers turned away from the coffin and found seats on the aisle as the funeral director quietly lowered the coffin lid. The priest appeared, and the funeral began.

When we walked out of the church my dark linen suit smelled so smoky I felt like I'd been in a casino bar. Father Donegan had not stinted with the incense, and if the idea was for the rising tendrils to raise Scott's soul up to heaven, he was already well ensconced. Barr, a closet Catholic, had explained some of the service to me. I had to admit, I really liked the ritual aspect of it. My parents being dyed-in-the-wool, intellectual agnostics, I hadn't grown up with any formal religious training. I could see how it might be nice in situations like these.

I sniffed my sleeve and wrinkled my nose. "What's in that stuff, anyway?"

"I never thought to wonder. Frankincense and myrrh?" Barr guessed.

"I think that might just be for Christmastime. Gifts of the three wise men, and all that."

"Mm hmm."

"You okay?"

"What? Oh. Sure. Yeah. I'm fine." He watched a squirrel in a yard across the street snake onto a tree branch and then down the chain to raid a rustic wooden birdfeeder.

I cocked an eyebrow at him. Of course he was upset about his friend's sudden death.

But there was something more. I waited.

He took a deep breath, then turned his attention to me. Brown eyes, intelligent and discerning, met mine. "If I say this, promise not to make it into something."

"What's that supposed to mean?" Was he finally going to tell me why "we have to talk"?

"Just promise," he said.

I took a deep breath. "Okay."

"I was just thinking how odd it was for Scott to die in a car crash."

Oh. Not about me. Go figure.

"Because he was a cop?" I asked.

"Well, that, for one. He had a lot of formal training for sure. But he was also an amateur racer. Stock cars."

"Really? I had no idea."

"Almost every Sunday he was out at the fairgrounds speedway, racing with his buddies."

"So he knew a ton about cars. And driving."

"Yes. Both."

"Do you think the crash was something besides an accident?" I asked.

His head swung back and forth. "No, no. Don't do that. You said you wouldn't make it into anything if I told you what I was thinking."

I shrugged. "Okay. You're the detective, and he was your friend."

He reached over and tousled my hair. I ducked away from his hand, nearly twisting my ankle in my brand-new three-inch heels, and he grinned. I still wasn't quite used to my short bob, after having hair down to my waist for most of my adult life.

"I need to get going," he said.

"You're not going to the reception?"

Crap. In the last two days I'd asked him twice what he'd wanted to talk to me about, but he'd sidestepped me each time, telling me it could wait. Maybe it could, but *I* couldn't.

"Robin's holding down the fort back at the cop shop with a lone cadet," he said. "She offered, since she hasn't been in the department all that long, and she knew everyone would want to go to Scott's funeral. But she shouldn't have to handle everything herself for too long."

Detective Robin Lane: Barr's new partner. She was also, I might add, drop-dead gorgeous, a fact he pretended not to notice. It was even more irritating because she didn't seem to realize it, either.

"I want to make an appearance at the reception and have a quick word with Chris," I said. "And Meghan's booked with massages all afternoon, so I need to pass on her sympathies as well." Meghan Bly was my housemate and my best friend.

We said goodbye, and Barr walked away down the sidewalk. I watched him go, noting the lanky, confident stride. I was pretty sure he was The One, but even though he kept pushing me to move in with him, I'd resisted so far. Lately, I'd been thinking about it more seriously, about actually sharing his address on the edge of town.

The thought sent a bolt of perfectly balanced thrill and terror through my solar plexus.

THREE

I went back inside and down the worn, carpeted stairs to the church basement where the reception was already underway. A long table against the far wall sagged under an abundance of food and more food, the traditional buttress against grief. It was almost lunchtime, so I sidled up to take a look. Fried chicken, sandwich makings, and crusty rolls started off the procession of platters, followed by a steaming casserole of macaroni and cheese with ham and a crock pot of bacon-laced baked beans. Then came the pasta salad, the German potato salad, the Parmesan-laden Caesar, and an enormous fruit plate. Strawberry rhubarb pie, chocolate cake, and raisin oatmeal cookies topped off the menu. I inhaled, slow and deep; it all smelled heavenly.

About thirty people milled about, several in dress uniform, most with loaded plates already in hand. I picked Chris out across the room, talking to Irene Nelson, and wove my way through the knots of murmured conversation toward her. Irene broke off mid-sentence when she saw me approaching, and both women turned toward me.

"Chris. How are you?" I asked.

She smiled, though it didn't quite reach her eyes. "I'm doing all right. Thanks for coming." Her pupils were dilated — no doubt Jake's tranquilizers at work.

"Of course," I said. "Meghan couldn't come, but she wanted me to tell you that her thoughts are with you."

"Tell her thank you for me."

"I will." All this felt very stilted. I took a deep breath. "I lost my own husband a while back. I know how hard it can be. If you need to talk, if you need anything, I hope you'll call me."

Chris blinked, and her smile faded. Her head bobbed once. "Okay."

Jake Beagle came up to us then, so I gave Chris a quick hug and left them talking. I passed Zak Nelson, who stood chatting with his boss, Dusty, from the Fix-It shop. Zak's hair was pulled back into a ponytail, and he wore a decent sports jacket. It looked like he'd even burnished his various piercings, but no matter how shiny and scrubbed he was, he still couldn't get the black grease entirely out from under his fingernails.

After I piled a few bites of everything on offer on a flimsy paper plate, I teetered over to a metal folding chair in my heels and managed to adopt a sitting position without spilling anything. Carefully holding the cardboard disk that was the only thing between my lunch and my lap, I took a hesitant bite of baked beans.

Oh, Lord. They had onion and green pepper and little bits of sausage mixed in with the bacon, as well as a healthy dose of molasses and spices. I took another tiny bite, trying to make it last.

Ruth Black plopped into the chair next to me.

I swallowed. "Hi, Ruth. Do you know who brought these beans? They're amazing."

She looked pleased. "I did, actually."

"Oh, gosh. Could I get the recipe from you?"

"Of course, dear. It was my mother's, and always seems popular at gatherings." She looked at Chris, still talking with Jake, and sighed.

"I know," I said. "It seems wrong to have what amounts to a party right after the funeral."

"Oh, no. It's good to do this. It gives people a chance to talk about Scott." She lowered her voice. "Of course, if Scott had been a real Irish Catholic, we'd be whooping it up big time for days. I just love an Irish wake." Her eyes twinkled.

"I've never been to one," I said.

"Well, if you ever get a chance, you should take it."

I almost laughed. "I'll make a note."

She smiled and changed the subject. "I haven't been out to Caladia Acres lately. How is Tootie doing these days?"

"Oh, you're not going to believe this," I said. "Tootie's on a cruise. The Caribbean."

"Really? With her arthritis? I wouldn't have thought her health would allow it."

"Ninety-five or not, Tootie has taken a turn for the better. In a big way. And his name is Felix."

Ruth's eyebrows climbed her forehead. "You don't mean . . ."

"Oh, yes. I certainly do. Tootie Hanover has a new boyfriend, and they've gone on a cruise together."

"Good for her." Ruth looked at me out of the corner of her eye. "Now I just need to find me one of those."

"A cruise?"

"No, silly. A boyfriend."

"I'll keep a lookout," I said.

She laughed again. "Be warned: I'm pretty

picky. Now, are you coming over to the co-op this afternoon for your lesson?"

"I figured we'd skip it today, what with the funeral and all."

"No, let's keep going. You're doing so well, and each day you get a little better."

When I began spending time at CRAC, I found Ruth was there more often than not, spinning away on her wheel or giving lessons to a variety of students. I kept watching, fascinated, and one day she let me try. From then on, I was hooked. So far I'd been spinning sheep's wool, which was wonderful, but I itched to try some other, more exotic fibers, as well.

"Well, okay," I said. "I'll be there."

"And I think you should take the wheel home, so you'll have it to practice on."

"But what will you use?"

"Oh, I have a new one. You can borrow the old one until you get your own." She said this matter-of-factly, but I could tell she was pleased as punch about the new wheel. Some women love shoes. Some love jewelry. Ruth loved fiber and all the tools to work with it.

"That'd be great," I said, a little too loud. A couple of heads turned toward the enthusiasm in my voice. I hunched my shoulders and studied my plate.

"I have to drop Uncle Thad home, and then I'll be over," Ruth said.

"How is Thaddeus?" I craned my neck and saw him, grizzled and serene, leaning on his cane by the buffet table.

Ruth smiled fondly at him. "He's going to outlast me." She stood. "I'll see you in a little while." She moved to where Felicia Beagle stood alone, nibbling on a piece of cantaloupe and watching her husband. Felicia smiled at Ruth's approach, holding out a be-ringed hand in greeting as if they were old friends. For all I knew, they were.

I had to dash home and change out of my hot dressy clothes into something casual, comfy, and cool, so I bolted my food, said goodbye to Chris and left early. As I drove away from the church I thought about Ruth's offer to let me borrow her wheel. Maybe I shouldn't. It might distract me too much at home.

Nah. Surely I could keep my new obsession under control.

I arrived at the co-op before Ruth. She'd be at the reception for a while longer, I was sure, but I wanted to take another look at a hand-painted bamboo roving begging for me to spin it into beautiful, luxurious yarn. It was awfully expensive, though, and I wasn't sure I was ready to work with it yet.

The co-op was housed in the old library at the end of First Street, which Chris had bought for a song — and several thousand dollars — after the town had constructed a brand-new, state-of-the-art facility across from the police station. The ancient building reflected the important role logging had once played in Cadyville, built as it was of enormous Douglas fir trunks painstakingly chinked together. Inside, gleaming wood paneling graced the walls, tongue and groove floor boards creaked underfoot and wide, rough stairs worn visibly thinner in the center from more than a hundred years of footsteps curved up to the second level.

The first floor no longer held children's books, but instead offered various arts and crafts for sale. Upstairs, a collection of supplies and crafting tools dominated what was once the fiction section of the library. Toward the rear of the building, the former nonfiction and periodicals section had been divided into a half dozen small studio spaces for use by CRAC artists.

Heavy floor cloths painted in earth tones delineated functional areas, and light spilled in from well-placed windows. Chris had asked me to develop a signature aromatherapy blend to add to the atmosphere,

32

and the mild fragrances of sandalwood, lavender, and orange subtly permeated the air, welcoming all who entered.

Thank goodness Ruth had wanted to continue my lessons despite the funeral. I really did walk away from those spinning sessions more calm and refreshed. With keys in hand, I hurried up the river rock path that led from the parking lot.

A few feet away, I paused.

The heavy wooden door was already ajar a few inches. I pushed it open, expecting to find someone manning the retail shop, but the interior lights were off. Someone must have come in to use the studio space upstairs and neglected to lock the door behind them. Cadyville wasn't exactly crime central, but risking robbery like that was downright irresponsible.

I looked back over my shoulder at the parking lot. Three vehicles besides mine were slotted into the diagonal spaces in the parking lot, but people unassociated with CRAC were always parking there, especially in the summer. The Red Dog Antique Mall took up most of the block across from the co-op, and customers frequently used our parking lot despite the signage threatening that they'd be towed. Daydreaming about spinning, I hadn't paid much attention to the other vehicles. Now I squinted into the sunlight. A powder-blue Ford Focus peeked out from behind a monster-sized king cab pickup.

Ariel Skylark's car.

Between her unkind words about Chris the other day, her absence at the funeral, and now leaving the door to the co-op open so anyone could wander in, it was well past time someone gave that snotty little prima donna a dressing down.

Pressing my lips together, I went inside and flipped on all the overhead lights. I strode through the eclectic displays, around tables piled with sculpture, art glass, jewelry, my Winding Road bath products, and a myriad of other items. Past those horrid black-and-white-and-red-all-over paintings and Jake's photographs hanging on the walls. Up the stairs, past shelves packed with supplies, barely glancing toward the section devoted to various fiber arts. The bamboo roving could wait.

That girl was going to get what-for, and the words for giving it to her formed with each step I took.

The smell of oil paint and turpentine attested to some of the activity in the studio. The area was divided into sections by move-able six-foot walls on wheels, so I could see the light was on in the far corner. That wasn't where Ariel worked; it was where Ruth had her spinning wheel and other equipment set up most of the time. Perhaps she'd arrived before me after all.

My ire lessened. No way was I going to yell at Ruth about the front door.

"Hello?" I called.

If Ruth had beat me to CRAC, then where was the old Buick she shared with Thaddeus? And why was Ariel's car in the parking lot?

"Hello?" I called again, weaving through the labyrinth of wall sections.

Nothing.

I came around the corner. "Ruth?"

And pulled up short, staring at the floor.

My jaw fell slack as my mind struggled to process the information it was receiving. The figure lying on the floor on her back. The open eyes, directed upwards, unseeing. The puff of blue and green and pink fiber curled in her fingers.

The blue lips.

My first skein of homespun yarn wrapped around her neck.

I hadn't even had a chance to set the twist yet.

"Ariel?"

FOUR

I hate finding dead bodies. I mean, I really hate it.

And Ariel was definitely dead. I mustered the gumption to tiptoe closer, kneel down beside her, and feel for a pulse in her neck. Not so much as a flutter under my fingertips. I couldn't even tell whether she was warm or not, my own hands had grown so suddenly cold. It seemed crucial to know. I stood again, half-aware of wiping my palm against my shirt.

I don't like touching dead bodies much, either.

Why was it so important to know whether she was still warm? Something about how recently she'd been killed.

Murdered, actually. No question about it.

And that meant a murderer.

The thought clamped my jaw shut and sent whatever adrenaline I had left shooting through my veins like acid. I jogged to the stairs, pulling my cell phone from my pocket. As I moved, my attention ping-ponged around the room, an animal seeking a predator, fear sharpening my hearing and sight to something nearly supernatural. Air whistled through the ductwork above. Colors took on an eerie glow. One of Irene's sculptures seemed to leer at me as I hurried by.

I had a sudden flash that this could be what it felt like to go insane. Taking a deep breath, I muttered to myself, "This is old hat for you, Sophie Mae. Buck up. You've been through worse."

The 911 operator sounded ridiculously calm, given the fact that I was reporting a murder. She told me to stay on the line, and she'd send help.

"Sorry. I'll meet them outside," I said.

She didn't like me hanging up, but there wasn't much I could do about that.

I stood in the shade of the giant yellow cedar in front of the co-op and placed another call. Thank God, Barr answered his cell phone after two rings.

"I found a murdered woman," I said.

A pause, then, "Could you say that again?"

I took a deep breath. "Ariel Skylark. The one I mentioned at Scott's funeral, the skinny little blonde from CRAC? Well, she's

37

dead. Strangled at the co-op. I've already called 911."

He swore. Loudly. Not at me, of course, but still. Then, "Are you okay?"

"I'm fine. I'm out front."

A flurry of voices in the background. "Hang on," he said.

A pause, more voices, and then he spoke into the phone again. "I have to go. Apparently there's a murder I have to look into."

"See you soon," I said.

He was grumbling something unintelligible as he hung up.

It didn't take long before Barr screeched to the curb in front of where I stood. Like a leggy supermodel at a movie premier, Detective Robin Lane swung out of the passenger seat of the patrol car they'd obviously appropriated. Barr erupted from the driver's side, took four long strides and stopped next to me.

"What happened?" he asked.

"I'm fine," I said again. Actually, I still felt a little lightheaded, but that seemed to be passing.

Detective Lane tossed her thick auburn ponytail and moved to stand beside Barr, notebook at the ready. She seemed to be standing a bit too close, but I pushed that thought out of my mind. Whatever her intentions might be, I didn't have to worry about Barr straying. After all, he kept bugging me to move in with him.

A thought flickered across my consciousness: unless that was what he'd wanted to talk to me about and kept putting off. Had he changed his mind? He sure looked mad right now.

"Where is she?" Lane asked.

"Upstairs in the studio area. You know where that is?"

"We'll find it," Barr said.

"Good," I said. "Because I'm not going back in there. Can I sit in your car while you work your detective magic?"

They exchanged glances. "Sure," he said.

So I sat in the front seat and waited. It wasn't that I was afraid of dead people. Heck, Ariel was the second dead person I'd seen that day. And I wasn't afraid of the murderer anymore, not with Barr and Robin there.

But someone had squeezed the life out of her. On purpose. The palpable violence of it took my breath away.

A knock on the window brought me back from my reverie. Ruth Black stood on the sidewalk, peering at me quizzically. I opened the door.

"What on earth is going on, Sophie Mae? No one will tell us."

I got out of the police car and looked around. All the other core members of the co-op were there. Even Chris Popper, changed into jeans and a T-shirt now, questioned me with her eyes.

"It's Ariel," I said. "She's . . . well, she's dead."

A group intake of breath at that.

I cleared my throat. "She was strangled."

Stares all around.

"In the co-op. I came early for my spinning lesson with Ruth, and found her."

The stunned silence drew out, until finally Ruth said. "You found her?"

I sighed. "Yes."

That seemed to release them, and the clamor of voices rushed over me like water, drowning me with their shouted questions.

A hand reached through them and grabbed my arm. Robin Lane pulled me away, calling out, "We'll let you know when we have more information."

Inside the co-op, Robin guided me to a corner and gestured toward a rocking chair made out of plum-colored wood.

I shook my head. "Can't sit there. It's for sale. Purple maple. Very expensive. See the sign?"

Lane looked disgusted. "What use is a chair you can't sit on? Okay, come over here." And she led me behind the register counter, where we both perched on stools.

Barr appeared at the top of the stairs. "Robin's going to take your statement."

I nodded my understanding. "There might be a conflict of interest for you, huh."

"Gee, you think?"

"I don't have much information," I said. "I found her is all. I don't know her very well or anything."

He came down the stairs, the heels of his cowboy boots sounding a sharp report on each step. He'd changed out of his dress uniform, and now wore mushroom-colored slacks, a blue shirt, and a string tie from his considerable collection. This one had a copper slide, beaten into the rough outline of a leaf.

Leaning his elbow on the counter, he said, "What is it with you and murder victims?"

"Hey," I said. "It's not like I enjoy it. And come to think of it, I didn't have this problem before I met you."

"No. You met me because you have this problem."

Okay. Technically he was right.

"Are you going to sit in?" Robin asked Barr.

41

"If you don't mind."

She hesitated, at war with her affinity to play by the book. "Shouldn't be a problem."

"Why aren't we doing this at the station?" I asked.

"There's still a lot to do here, and we thought you might want to leave. But we need some information before sending you on your way," Barr said.

"Okay. Shoot."

"How did you find her?" Robin asked, pen poised to take down my answer.

I told them, and after that there were more questions about when I got there and how long it took before I called 911. We spent quite a bit of time on the open front door, and why I went upstairs in the first place. I explained that I thought an artist must have come in to work and left the door open. Then we moved on to Ariel herself. What did I know about her? Not much. I told them Ruth Black would probably know more. Ariel had always seemed kind of standoffish around me; my gender probably hadn't helped. Ruth seemed to get along with everyone, though.

"Did you see the yarn around her neck?" Lane asked.

"You mean the yarn she was strangled with?"

She nodded.

"Oh, I saw it all right," I said.

"Do you know if it came from here?"

"I know it did."

Lane looked the question at me.

"It was mine. The first two-ply homespun yarn I ever made, and Ruth was going to show me how to set the twist on it this week."

Barr's eyes widened a fraction, but he didn't say a word.

"I'm sorry," I said.

"What exactly are you sorry for?" Robin asked, her tone suddenly hard.

"For being upset about the stupid yarn," I said. "I really liked it, though. Even if it was kind of lumpy and thick and full of slubs, it was the first time I'd created a decent amount of actual yarn on the spinning wheel."

"Did you touch her?"

"Only on the neck, to see if she had a pulse."

Barr looked worried. Lane didn't look very happy with me, either.

"Oh, for heaven's sake, I can't possibly be a suspect," I said, exasperation leaking into my voice. "What should I have done? Assumed she was dead? What if she hadn't been?"

Robin Lane studied me for a long minute. I struggled not to look away or protest my innocence further.

"You didn't like her, did you?" she asked.

I blinked. "Well, we weren't best friends."

"I saw her name on those paintings." She indicated Ariel's work.

"Yes. She was an artist." I managed to say it with a straight face.

"Did she paint here?"

I nodded. "In one of the studio spaces upstairs. I believe she did almost all of her work here."

"Was she interested in the yarn and knitting thing?" She couldn't keep her disdain for such homey activities out of her voice.

"Not that I know of."

"Where was your yarn?"

I tried to remember. "Last I saw it was right after Ruth showed me how to unwind it from the bobbin onto the niddy noddy. We tied the hank and hung it over the back of her spinning chair. You'd have to ask her whether she moved it later."

She scribbled in the notebook. "Do you know anyone who might have a motive for killing the victim?"

I stared at her for so long she stopped writing and met my eyes. "You want my opinion about who could have murdered Ariel?"

Her smile was wry. "I'm sure you have one."

"I have no idea." A little triumph in my voice, there.

Lane exhaled. "Okay, that's enough for now. You can go."

"Unless it has something to do with the way men reacted to her," I said. Gawd. I just couldn't help myself. It was embarrassing. "I'd find out who she was dating."

"We'll check into it. Thanks."

"But —"

"Go home, Sophie Mae." Barr's tone held quiet warning.

Fine. I didn't want to be here anyway.

Ruth Black was waiting for me in the parking lot, alone. She fell into step beside me as I walked toward my little Toyota pickup.

"Ariel was strangled," she said without preamble, picking up exactly where Detective Lane had rescued me.

"Yes."

"Do they know who did it?" she asked.

"I don't think so."

"Are you going to try and figure it out?" Beside me, her legs scissored along nearly twice as fast as mine, her steps short and quick like a bird's.

I stopped cold, and she drew up a few paces ahead and turned back.

"Huh uh," I said. "I'm not figuring out anything. This is a police matter, and I happen to know the police in question, and they are quite good at their job. There's no need for me to get involved."

She tipped her head to one side.

"No need at all," I repeated. My hand crept up to my recently shorn head, and I ended by rubbing my neck. The last time I'd tried to "figure it out" — and at Ruth's instigation, I might add — things had gotten a little out of hand in the danger department. "And I'm glad of it, too."

Ruth smiled. "If you say so, dear."

FIVE

As I walked into our backyard, Meghan was latching the door of the chicken pen behind her. When she saw me, she turned and held up one small, perfect blue-green egg.

"It's still warm," she said.

I took it from her, holding it gently in my palm. "Molly or Emma?"

Two of our hens were Easter egg chickens, and they laid that unusual color. They hadn't been producing long enough for us to be able to recognize who laid what.

"Molly, I think. Erin says her eggs are a little bluer, and Emma's are a little more greenish. Apparently she can tell already."

Erin was Meghan's eleven-year-old daughter. She was at math camp during the day for the next two weeks, practicing up on being a genius, but she had become the resident expert on the individual idiosyncrasies of our laying hens.

Brodie, Erin's old Pembroke Welsh corgi,

had taken to sitting outside the chicken pen, guarding them from harm whenever she was gone. Now his fox-like face swung my way, and he gave a low woof in acknowledgement of my presence. But he was on the job, and didn't leave his self-imposed post to receive his usual ear scritchin's.

"How was the funeral?" Meghan asked.

I grimaced. "Good, I guess. If you can characterize a funeral that way." I dreaded telling her about Ariel.

"I think you can." Her gaze took in my casual clothes. "When did you change?"

"I dropped by before going over to CRAC. You were with a client." Like me, Meghan worked at home. Her massage room and a tiny office were tucked into a front corner on the main floor, out of the way of our normal household traffic. She wore her warm-weather working togs: soft cotton knit shorts and a sleeveless T-shirt.

"CRAC. Of course that's where you've been." She stopped herself before adding, "Again."

"I've got some bad news," I said.

She crossed her arms. "What?"

"You know Ariel Skylark?"

"I've met her. Lots of attitude, needs to eat a burger?"

The latter statement was something, coming from Meghan who stood at just five feet and barely tipped the scale to a hundred pounds. Add dark glossy curls, a tiny turned-up nose and cupid lips, and she looked more like a wood sprite than a single mother, former lawyer, and currently much-in-demand massage therapist.

I chewed gently on my lower lip and nodded. "That's her." I took a breath. "She was murdered."

Her gray eyes widened, filled with a combination of kindness, concern, and bewilderment. Consternation flooded her voice. "How did you hear about it?"

I closed my eyes for a moment, shaking my head. "You're not going to believe it."

"Not going to believe what?" Her tone was flat. She had an inkling of what was coming.

"I found her." I opened my eyes to find Meghan had closed hers, and had added the telling gesture of pinching the bridge of her nose between thumb and forefinger. Meghan may have hated me finding dead bodies even more than I did.

I plunged on. "After the funeral reception I went over to the co-op for my spinning lesson with Ruth."

Meghan dropped her hand and rolled her eyes at this further evidence of my recent obsession with fiber.

"Anyway, no one was there when I arrived. The front door was open, and I thought someone was working in the studio and had forgotten to lock it. I went inside, but no one was there. At least not downstairs. Upstairs in the studio spaces, I found Ariel. She was . . ." The screen my efficient brain had erected fell away, and my mind's eye filled with the image of Ariel Skylark lying on her back, lips blue, tongue slightly protruding. The tangible violence surrounding the scene. I took another deep breath and forced myself to swallow the lump in my throat. "She was strangled, Meghan. Strangled with my yarn."

Startled, she asked, "What do you mean, your yarn?"

"It was the first skein of yarn I'd completed spinning. Just a plain, off-white yarn, full of slubs and kind of weird looking, but I could have made a hat out of it, or something. I mean, I'm not saying a hat is more important than, well, you know, it's just, it was my first skein, and I'd just finished it a couple days ago, and now it's a . . ." Another dry swallow. ". . . a *murder* weapon."

Meghan sank down on the bench by the picnic table. "Sophie Mae?"

"Yeah?"

"Why is it that you, of all people, managed to find Ariel?"

I shrugged. "Just unlucky, I guess."

She sighed.

"What?" I asked.

"You're not going to do anything stupid, are you?"

"What kind of a question is that?"

"Like what you did when Philip Heaven died."

"Ruth said something to that effect, too," I said. "I don't know why everyone thinks I'm going to wade into a murder investigation. Last time cured me of that."

My housemate didn't look convinced. "That'd be a lot easier to believe if I didn't know how much fun you have when you're poking and snooping."

"I do not!"

"Uh-huh."

"No one else was looking into those other deaths, and somebody needed to find out what really happened. But believe me, Barr and Robin are all over this case."

"Okay. Good," she said. "I have two more clients, and then I have to go pick up Erin. Let's not make a big deal about this tonight, okay?"

"Right. I don't think she ever met Ariel, so we can downplay it however much you want." I gave her the egg I'd been holding. "I'm going over to Barr's, make him dinner tonight, so I might be home late anyway."

She grinned. "I won't wait up."

Meghan went inside the house. I moved to inspect the squash vines to see if the milk solution I'd applied to the powdery mildew on the leaves had been effective. It looked like it had stopped the unsightly white fungus in its tracks.

Fun? She actually thought I had fun investigating Walter's, and then Philip's deaths? Well, okay. Maybe unraveling a puzzle was . . . interesting. At least it wasn't boring. And I was two for two, so I must have been pretty good at it.

Right?

Of course, making Barr dinner came with a not-so-hidden agenda. I was determined to find out what he'd been pussyfooting around for the last few days. His procrastination had no doubt blown the whole thing out of proportion in my mind, and it would probably turn out to be something totally, laughably boring.

At least I hoped so. What's that Chinese curse? May you live in interesting times?

I also wanted to know whether I needed to worry about the fact that my yarn had been the murder weapon. Did Robin actually consider me a suspect?

Barr lived on the edge of town in a small, two-bedroom house, with a spacious yard surrounded by a cedar picket fence. It looked like something right out of a storybook or a song. Blousy antique roses tumbled from the trellis that arched over the front walk, neglected but persistent. Their fragrance, intensified by the warm afternoon sun, curled along the light breeze. On the front porch I inhaled the sweet scent deep into my lungs as I fished in my pocket for my key.

I felt numb, spaced-out, like I'd taken too much cold medicine. The specter of Ariel sprawled on the floor of the co-op haunted the darker recesses of my mind. My subconscious kept dropping a thick veil over my recent experience, making it seem like it had happened months or years ago. Then boom! — I'd remember the whole thing in vivid detail.

My attention veered to the sound of the key chain jangling in my hand. House keys, truck keys, co-op keys, and the key to Barr's house. If this became my home, that last one would be my house key: a painfully obvious yet unsettling thought. I'd continue to rent Meghan's basement as I did now, and work there nearly every day. Barr spent less time on the job than he used to since the addition of a second detective to the force, but he was still gone a lot. Even if I moved, I'd spend almost the same amount of time with Meghan and Erin that I did now.

At least that's what I kept telling myself. But would it work out that way, really? They were my family. The thought of leaving them made my throat ache. On the other hand, Barr and I had been talking about taking this next step for months now. I was the one who continued to drag my feet.

It wasn't that I didn't love him. I did. Not a single question about it.

But I was deeply content living with my best friend and her precocious child. It's different living with females, and the three of us had been together long enough that we'd pretty much worked out the bugs. If I moved in with Barr, I could still maintain the family unit I'd built up with Meghan and Erin. Couldn't I?

In the middle of Barr's living room, I turned in a full circle, taking in the contents and their arrangement with eyes tuned to how my own belongings might fit in. My attention snagged on the coffee table. Mine, a wrought-iron-and-tile affair, graced our liv-

54

ing room at home; it fit there, and it didn't make sense to bring it over here. It wouldn't go with anything of Barr's anyway.

I sighed. None of my stuff would look good with his. I liked metal and bright colors. He liked wood, the chunkier the better, and muted browns and greens in horrible prints. The sofa was plaid, for heaven's sake.

Oh, but that coffee table would have to go. It was made out of some huge spool, like something a monstrous cable had once been wrapped around. Someone had attempted to sand it a little, but you still couldn't set a drink on it without balancing it between the grooves of the wood grain. And it had been shellacked, slathered with a thick coat of clear goo that had dried unevenly, so long ago that the areas where it had been applied the thickest were beginning to yellow.

Gross.

I'd asked him where he got it. He said a friend had given it to him. I asked if the friend lived nearby. He said no. I asked if he loved the table. I was, of course, being facetious.

But he said yes.

Which wasn't the answer I'd been hoping for, believe me. Not even as a dirt-poor college student would I have wanted such a piece.

I wandered through the rest of the house, trying to figure out if I could squeeze into the place. Thank goodness, I didn't have much. And I could leave most of it with Meghan, so she wouldn't have to get anything new just because I bailed on her. The thought left a sour taste behind. But no matter how little I might bring, this wee house would be awfully crowded.

Meghan's house was so nice. Four bedrooms, three levels, right downtown, so you could walk almost anywhere you needed to go. I pushed that thought aside. Barr owned this house. He wanted me to move in with him. If I did decide to make that leap, the two of us would have to make do in this tiny space. And really, how much time would we be spending here, I reminded myself for the umpteenth time. Maybe down the line we'd get a different place, a little bigger, a little closer to town.

Gawd. What a spoiled brat I was. It was a perfectly nice house. I passed by an open window and smelled the roses again. Opening the refrigerator, I studied the contents. Not much there. If I was going to make Barr dinner, a quick trip to the grocery store was in order.

Ariel would never eat again. The thought struck me like a snake, and I sank into a kitchen chair. I wondered what she'd eaten for her last meal.

Loud knocking jolted me out of my reverie. I hesitated, then rose and walked to the door. Opened it.

The woman waiting on the step blinked when she saw me. I'm sure I blinked, too.

It was like looking into a mirror. She had green eyes. Like mine. Blonde hair, exactly my shade. Only hers was still long and worn in a braid down her back. Her features reflected mine. She was my height. My build. She was a tad thinner. And a tad younger. And she possessed the ability to make clothes look good on her. I disliked her immediately.

All this happened in a split second. I smiled. She smiled.

"Hi," she said. "Is Barr home?"

"Um, no. Not right now. Can I help you?"

"Well, could you tell him Hannah stopped by? And that I'm staying at the Horse Acres Bed and Breakfast, on the south side of town?"

"I'll tell him. Will he know who you are?" Meaning, of course, that I wanted to know.

Hannah smirked. "Oh, I think he'll know. I'm his wife, after all."

Six

I never really knew what feeling the term "thunderstruck" referred to until that moment. But it seemed to cover the stomach-swooping, knee-buckling sensation those last words engendered.

Hannah responded to my silence with a perky, "Okay, then. Thanks."

Then she turned and walked down the narrow sidewalk to a nondescript economy rental car and got in. I stood stupidly in the doorway, and she waved at me as she pulled away. Of its own volition, my right hand lifted in response.

I remained rooted there for a hundred years or so, inhaling floral calm, thinking thorny thoughts, unwilling to turn around and go back inside. So I didn't. Ultimately, I walked the rest of the way out, locked the door behind me, and went to my own vehicle.

Doppelganger.

Wife?

Of course Barr would have a good explanation for all this. Maybe she was crazy. I'd picked up a stalker a few months back; maybe it was his turn.

A stalker who looked almost exactly like me, only . . . better.

Sure.

I thought about living in that little house with him. I thought again about leaving Meghan and Erin, Brodie, the chickens only recently housed in the backyard. The chicken project had been my baby. They'd only laid five eggs so far.

What was I thinking? I could leave all that to move in with . . . a married man? Hardly.

Meghan wasn't home. Erin wasn't home. There was no one to tell about Hannah except Brodie, and even he was occupied with his chicken guarding. So I did what I always do when I don't know what else to do: I worked.

As I mixed the dry ingredients for the bath fizzies a local woman had commissioned as favors for a large bridal shower, I waited for the storm. Perhaps I was in the eye. Soon the rain would begin to fall fast and furious.

It never did, though. The bone-crushing

sadness and disappointment remained at bay.

Instead, I got spitting mad.

Barr would have a good explanation for Hannah? And what might that be? Was there such a thing as a good explanation for having your wife show up and leave a message with the woman you were trying to bamboozle into cohabitating with you?

Well, I'd like to know what it was, then.

I considered going to the police station and making a scene.

Nah. I'd only end up looking like an idiot.

My watch showed a few minutes before six o'clock. He'd be home in an hour or so. Why not meet him at the front door like a good little girlfriend? That had, after all, been my original plan. I'd be damned if I'd cook him dinner now, though.

Dusting the citric acid off my hands, I went upstairs to my bedroom. Changed into my favorite pair of jeans, the ones that made my butt look reasonably small. Put on a tank top with a low-cut neckline. A pair of beaded sandals that showed off my pretty red toenails. I sprayed and scrunched my hair into something that looked downright feisty. Then I spent another ten minutes calming it down; no reason to be so obvious.

Meghan opened the front door as I came down the stairs. Erin trailed behind her, reading a book while shuffling up the sidewalk.

"Hey, I thought you were spending the evening at Barr's." My housemate turned and placed a canvas bag of books from the Cadyville library on the bench by the door.

"I'm going back over there. But I won't be gone long."

She whirled to face me. "What's wrong?" Pouncing on something in my tone. Her eyes narrowed as she took in my ensemble.

Erin tripped on the door frame as she entered the house, eyes never leaving the copy of *An Acceptable Time* she held open with both hands. I glanced down as she caught herself and continued past me into the kitchen.

"I'll tell you later," I said.

"She's in another world. Tell me now." Refusing to be put off.

"I'm going back to ask him about the woman who showed up on his doorstep when I was there earlier."

"Woman?"

"Yeah. The one who looks freakishly like me."

She raised one eyebrow.

"The one who says she's Barr's wife."

The other eyebrow joined the first.

"Gotta go," I said, brushing by her. "Jealousy calls."

Outside, I yanked the door of the Toyota open so hard the hinges creaked.

Okay, so I had to admit it: I was hungry. The smell of grilling meat infused the air as I sat on the front step of Barr's little house. My growling stomach did not help my frame of mind, which was good. I needed a reservoir of anger to draw from, strength to face the idea that the future I had anticipated might well be swirling down the drain. So I sat hunched around my dudgeon and waited for him to come home.

End of June in the Pacific Northwest. Red-winged blackbirds called liquidly to each other in the wetland down the hill to the north. It would be light until well after nine o'clock, and the sky still held a high, thin blue. Only a few clouds crouched on the horizon, waiting to erupt into the crazy pastels of the impending sunset: pinks and oranges, peach and yellow, eventually morphing to red against the navy sky. The splash of colors to come reminded me of the bamboo I'd been hoping to try in my lesson with Ruth. The stuff would be like spinning clouds, so the soft colors were more than fitting. I wondered whether the woman who dyed the roving, a local named Thea Hawke, had felt compelled to imitate the sunset as she'd chosen her dyes and lovingly applied them to the ethereal fiber.

Oh, brother, Sophie Mae. Get a grip. Stop musing about spinning and think about what you're going to say to Barr when he gets here.

My stomach growled again. The oblique angle of the light niggled at my memory. This was the time of day that, as a child, was unavailable in the other seasons. After dinnertime, still light enough to play out-side, offering the promise of packing in more activity before parental summons brought you in for bed. Innocent times. Long gone times.

Sometimes being an adult got pretty darn old, I thought. Was there any possible way to account for Hannah's appearance out of nowhere, her looks, her *wifeness?* I couldn't imagine a scenario in which Barr hadn't lied to me. Just flat-out lied.

I hated being lied to. My anger flared again, accompanied by a hot, sick feeling.

My head jerked up at the sound of a slow-ing engine and tires on concrete. Barr's car door opened and cowboy boots hit the ground. He strode toward me. Slowly, I stood.

"What a nice surprise, finding you here," he said. "You're not going to believe it, but we already have a pretty viable suspect."

His arms encircled me, and I stifled the urge to push him away. Instead I stood quietly and waited. Barr pulled back, a puzzled look in his eyes. "Ariel was having an affair with Scott Popper. We think Chris may have had something to do with it." Regret passed over his features, and I couldn't help but remember his obvious pity for Chris at the funeral.

Then he shook his head, and his features smoothed. He smiled down at me. "You look great, by the way. Did you do something different with your hair?"

Chris? Had killed Ariel? Confusion nearly swamped me. "But —" I stopped myself. Concentrate, Sophie Mae, concentrate.

"Anyway, I for one, wouldn't mind a little help from an interested citizen who might be able to get information through, uh, unofficial channels."

Huh?

When I didn't respond, he said, "Hey, what's wrong with you? I thought you'd be happy to be off the hook. Plus, I thought you'd jump at the chance to help out." He tousled my hair.

I jerked away from his hand. "Knock that off. You know I hate it."

Slowly, his arm lowered. "What's going on?"

I started to bite my lip, then stopped myself. "I came by earlier. While I was here, your wife stopped by. Hannah. She wanted me to tell you she's staying at the Horse Acres Bed and Breakfast."

Barr rolled his eyes. "Great. I should've known she'd come scratching at the door about now."

Well, I don't know what reaction I'd expected, but that wasn't it.

"You're *married?*" I asked, appalled.

"What? Of course not."

"Have you ever been married?"

He raised his hands to his face and rubbed his eyes. "Sophie Mae, please, you have to —"

"I don't have to do anything."

He dropped his hands. "You knew I was married." He actually dared to sound irritated.

"I did not!"

"Listen, can we go inside to fight? Or would you rather the neighbors take part?"

Teeth clenched, I stomped into the house. He went into the kitchen and returned with two beers. Twisting the top off of one, he handed it to me and sank into his favorite TV-watching recliner. I sat on the ugly plaid couch and put the bottle on the spool from hell. It nearly tipped over on the rough surface, and I just managed to catch it.

"I hate this table," I said.

"Okay. We can get a new one."

"It's the homeliest piece of furniture I've seen in my entire life."

A flash of amusement crossed his features. "I told you about Hannah," he said.

"Oh. Right. And when exactly did you do that? You tried in the car after we had Thai food the other night, but then we had to go chase an ambulance. And you never had the courage to 'fess up any of the times I've asked you since."

His forehead wrinkled. "What are you . . . wait a minute." His face cleared. "You think that's what we needed to talk about?"

Now I was unsure. "Isn't it?" I took a shaky sip of beer.

"No, no. Nothing like that. Remember when I told you that ten years or so ago I was involved with a woman who works at my parents' dude ranch? That it was a mistake, and didn't work out?"

"Sure."

"That was Hannah."

I gaped at him. "Involved? Getting married is 'involved'? What are we then, acquaintances?"

He sighed. "It only lasted a couple months. It was a long time ago. I wasn't trying to keep anything from you; I really did think you understood that we'd been married for a short time."

Damn it. That took the wind right out of my sails. Barr had indeed told me about that woman. It was just possible I'd misunderstood the level of their "involvement."

He'd neglected to mention what she looked like, though.

"Well, you certainly do like a type, don't you." I felt bitter and defeated at the same time.

"Type?"

"She looks just like me. Or rather, I look like her, since I'm the Janey-come-lately. At least I used to look like her." My hand started to go to my short hair, but at the last moment I scratched my nose.

"God," Barr said. "Sometimes I just want to shake you."

And I just want to shoot you, I thought, but didn't say. A bolt of understanding hit me, a very personal glimmer of how crimes of passion can occur.

"So why is she here?" I asked.

He looked uncomfortable. "I can't be sure, but I imagine she wants to get back together."

Great. As mad as I'd been, as much as I'd already considered that we might be done and over with, that still hit me hard in the solar plexus. "Do you want to get back together with her?"

"Of course not, you dope. I love you."

I took a big swig of beer and considered him. "She still loves you?"

"Maybe. I doubt it. What Hannah loves is money. Always has."

Another swig. My stomach gurgled. "I don't get it," I said. "You don't have money."

Now he looked uncomfortable. "That's what I was trying to tell you."

What the heck? I put the beer bottle back on the table, and it started to tip over again. I caught it and directed another glare at Barr.

But he was looking out the window. "My uncle died earlier this year. It turns out he left some money to my mom and dad, my brother and sister, and me." He looked directly at me now. "A *lot* of money. That's what I've been trying to figure out how to tell you."

My mouth dropped open.

"You have a *sister?*" I practically shrieked

the question.

He looked startled. "Sure. Glory. She and her husband live outside of Missoula."

"You never told me you had a sister!"

"I didn't?"

"No. You didn't. Any offspring around that you also forgot to mention?" I wasn't kidding. All of a sudden, it seemed like a valid question.

He laughed. "No."

I very pointedly did not laugh. "You can't expect me to be happy to suddenly meet some woman who says she's your wife. You can't expect me to move in with you when that same ex-wife is staying in town."

His eyes widened. "Listen, Sophie Mae . . ."

I shook my head so hard my hair whipped across my cheek. "I don't know who you are, Barr Ambrose. I thought I did, but it turns out that I don't."

He tried again. "Listen to me." His voice was reasonable, down to earth, all the things I loved about the guy.

Aargh.

"Hannah must know about the inheritance from my uncle. It would be just like her to think she could get to it through me. Mom will know. I'll call her after dinner."

"Your mother? Why would she know?"

"I told you: Hannah works at the ranch." Barr's parents owned and operated a touristy dude ranch in Wyoming.

"She still works there?"

He nodded. "I'll call her tonight, too. Send her packing. Hannah showing up all of a sudden *does not* mean anything. You can't let this mess up our plans."

"It's not just about your ex, you know? What about the sister I knew nothing about? What else haven't you told me?"

He shifted in his recliner, leaning toward me. "What do you want to know? I'll tell you anything you'd like."

I shook my head. "We've been dating for eight months, Barr. This is the kind of stuff that just comes up. If I have to know the questions to ask to get basic kinds of information like siblings and past marriages, I don't want to ask them."

"Oh, come on, Sophie Mae. Don't be like that. I'm willing to tell you everything."

My face grew hot, then my eyes. *Don't be like that.* If the phrase, "we have to talk" was dreaded by most males, "don't be like that," trumped it for women. Those were words a man says to a woman who is not behaving in a way they find easy or comfortable. *Oh come on. Don't be like that.* It was a horribly typical way of trying to control the situation by making me feel bad for being angry.

"Go to hell."

He blinked. The expression on his face changed to contrition. "I'm sorry. You're right, and I'm sorry. I should have thought about the things in my past that might interest you. It's just that I'm not, anymore. Interested, I mean. Glory and I aren't close, I've moved on from the whole Hannah thing, and I'm not one to look backward. But if you want to know, I'll tell you every detail, starting with, 'I was born on a stormy winter's night' and going from there."

At least he'd apologized, and it sounded genuine. I sighed. "I'll hold you to that."

Was I being stupid, giving in like that? I'd have to wait and see. As for Barr, he was on probation, as of now.

"I'm going home," I said. "To eat dinner with Meghan and Erin."

He didn't look very happy. "Are you sure?"

"Positive."

"Okay. I'll call you later." He knew when to back off.

I stood up and walked to the door.

He followed. "Are you still willing to help me?"

"Help you what?"

"Find out a little more about Ariel Skylark? Just get some people to gossip about her? No one seems to want to talk to us."

"You're kidding, right?"

"Just gossip. Nothing else. You know, no obvious questions," he said. "You can be subtle when you want to."

"I don't get it," I said. "You hate it when I snoop. What's with the sudden change of attitude?"

He looked nonplussed. "Well, you're pretty good at finding things out."

I waited.

Turning both palms to the ceiling, he said, "All right. Here's the thing. Your yarn was the murder weapon, so I can't be the lead on this case even though I have seniority over Robin in the department. So she's the lead, and she loves it. She's good at investigating, but darn it, she questions people like she's killing snakes. Especially when she's excited about getting the answers. Not a lot of finesse, you know?"

I nodded. "Oh, yes. I know exactly what you mean."

Detective Lane and I had had our difficulties a few months back as I tried to convince her to investigate a poisoning. I admired her abilities, and liked her well enough; eventually we'd called a tentative truce. However, the more time she spent in Cadyville, the more pig-headed she seemed to become.

"So will you put some of that Reynolds charm to work for the common good?"

Oh, brother. Talk about charm. Sheesh.

"Maybe," I said.

He inclined his head. "I guess that's all I can ask for."

He kissed me then. Despite the post-fight awkwardness, I still felt the same thrill as always. Damn.

I opened the screen and began walking out to my Toyota. A few steps down the sidewalk, I turned around. He stood in the doorway.

"A lot of money?" I asked.

"Uh huh."

"Just how much is a lot?"

He licked his lips. "Two million," he said. "Give or take."

The blood drained from my face. "Yeah. That's a lot," I croaked.

"Each." He flushed when he said it, as if embarrassed. Knowing Barr, he probably was.

"Right. Uh, well, congratulations. Bye." Dumbfounded, I walked to my vehicle, got in, and started the engine. I drove home like a zombie.

Holy crap. No wonder Hannah was on the prowl.

SEVEN

I followed the sound of voices around to the backyard and found Meghan, Erin, and Ruth Black seated at the picnic table. The scent of lime-and-garlic-marinated shrimp lingered on the still-warm air.

Meghan greeted me. "Hey there. How did it go?"

"It was . . . odd," I said. "Hi, Ruth."

"Hello dear."

"Go get some dinner," Meghan said.

"It smells delicious. I'm surprised there's any left."

"There wouldn't be if I hadn't hidden yours away in the kitchen."

I held up a finger. "Be right back."

In the kitchen I discovered not only crustaceans grilled to pink perfection, but a pile of grilled asparagus and the remains of a gorgeous summer salad. Harvest continues late into the fall in the northwest, but can start slowly due to damp, cool springs. But lettuce, radishes, baby carrots, scallions, and various herbs were abundant in June. Meghan had added sprigs of chickweed gleaned from weeding our organic beds, a few succulent dandelion leaves, and a sprinkling of violas. I could have feasted on how pretty it was. Theoretically, at least. I added a light lemon and olive oil vinaigrette to the salad, piled shrimp and asparagus onto a stoneware plate, and returned to the group sitting in the backyard.

I slid onto the cedar picnic bench. Brodie waddled over and sat by my foot, making corgi noises in his throat. Now that I had food, I was back on his A-list.

Across the table, Meghan leaned forward, anticipation all over her face. "So? Who was she?"

I glanced at Erin, an even more petite version of her mother, and asked, "How was math camp today?"

"Fun enough," she said. "We played with Möbius strips. Mom already told us some strange woman was at Barr's house today, and you went over there to yell at him about it. So don't try to send me inside or anything."

Meghan suddenly became inordinately interested in one of our hens pecking at the tray of oyster shell in their pen. What a gossip, I thought, surprised. Maybe Barr should have asked for her help instead of mine.

"It certainly does sound like you've had a full day," Ruth said.

"That's putting it mildly." I took a bite of salad. Something peppery in there. I peered at my plate. Ah. Nasturtium leaves. I swallowed. "I either won't sleep at all tonight, or I'll sleep like the dead."

Meghan coughed.

"Oh, God. Not like the dead, I mean, you know . . ." I rubbed my forehead.

"Whatever," Erin said. "So who was the lady at Barr's house?"

"We don't want to pry," Ruth said. "But we want to know you're okay."

So Meghan had told her, too. I couldn't blame her.

"I'm fine," I said. "It turns out he did tell me about Hannah — that's her name, Ruth. But I didn't realize they were married."

"He's not actually married now, is he?" Meghan asked.

"No, it all happened several years ago, and apparently only lasted a couple months."

"Then what's she doing here now?"

Between bites, I told them most of my conversation with Barr up until I walked outside his house. Then I found myself growing silent.

"So Barr's rich?" Erin asked.

"I guess," I said, reluctant to talk about it further. Now I understood why he'd had such a hard time telling me about his sudden wealth. The idea of having that much money bordered on the obscene.

Both Meghan and Ruth seemed to sense my unwillingness.

"Are you happy with his explanation?" Meghan asked.

I hesitated, then said, "I think so."

"You know what you should do, to put it to bed once and for all?" Ruth asked.

"What?"

"You should do a background check on him. Then you won't wonder. I bet Meghan's beau would give you a discount."

My lips parted in surprise. Who knew Ruth was so mercenary?

"Meghan?" she prompted.

"Well," Meghan said. "I guess I could ask Kelly about it."

Kelly O'Connell was Meghan's sort of boyfriend. The sort of part was mostly because he lived in New Jersey. They chatted on the phone for hours every night like school kids, and there'd been talk of him moving out to Cadyville once he got his private investigator's license in the state of Washington.

Hmmm. I considered the idea. It really would make me feel better to know for sure, to stop wondering if Barr was keeping anything from me. Call it trust issues if you want to, but I'd never before thought of myself as one of those walking wounded who couldn't get close to anyone. I just didn't want to be stupid.

"Will you talk to him about it tonight?" I asked Meghan.

"Um." Her reluctance was palpable.

"You think it's a bad idea, don't you."

"It's not up to me."

"Yeah, but . . ."

She hesitated, then, "Is that the kind of thing you want to base your relationship on?"

After a few moments, I met her eyes and shook my head. "No. You're right. It's not. I'd hate it if he did something like that to me, and if I went ahead with it, I could never take it back."

She smiled her approval.

Ruth shrugged and changed the subject. "I brought a spinning wheel for you to practice on."

"The one from the co-op?" I was surprised she'd been allowed to remove it from the crime scene.

"No — I had an extra at the house."

"So you have three spinning wheels? Wow."

She ducked her head. "Four actually."

"That seems like a lot. Do you use all of them?"

"Well, not this one, at least not very often. That's why you should keep it as long as you want, until you decide what kind you want to get."

I grinned. "How do you know I'm going to want my own wheel?"

"Because you, my dear, are thoroughly hooked."

Meghan snorted. "I'll say."

Erin wrinkled her nose. "You're spinning yarn? Like in the olden days?"

"Well, yes. I guess so. Only, like so many things we do now, it's more for fun than out of necessity. The people who used to spin in order to cloth themselves never had that luxury."

She nodded. "Yeah, I get it. I guess there are a lot of things like that."

Ruth gestured over her shoulder toward the pen where our four pullets were quietly clucking and making the low moaning sounds that count as conversation among chickens. "Like keeping laying hens."

Meghan and I both smiled as Erin jumped in. "But the girls *are* necessary. How else would we get fresh eggs for breakfast right from our own backyard? Plus they give us fertilizer for the garden, and then turn around and eat all the weeds from it."

"Girls?" Ruth asked, looking amused.

"Well, they are girls, aren't they? Girl chickens," Erin said.

We all liked raising the chickens and keeping them in the backyard, but she was the most enthusiastic. She cared for them exclusively, so the burden on Meghan and I came down to occasionally buying chicken feed, grit and oyster shell. Since "the girls" would likely produce more eggs than we could possibly use in the summer, we'd told Erin she could sell the extras and keep the money for all her hard work.

"Well," I said, spearing a few leaves of chickweed from my salad and holding them up. "At least we get to eat some of our own weeds, too."

Conversation continued, and I concentrated on my dinner. As I chewed, I stubbornly pushed aside the disturbing events of the day and focused on my environment: warm friends, the beauty of the vegetable beds, the bat house mounted on a fence post, the chickens getting ready to roost for the night.

When Ruth touched my arm, I jumped.

"Let's take some of these plates in," she said.

We gathered up plates and utensils, waving Meghan and Erin back when they tried to help. Erin slipped into the hen pen, as she called it, and began murmuring to her girls in a low voice. Meghan watched, smiling.

In the kitchen, I quickly set to washing the plates. I love the dishwasher, don't get me wrong, but when we grilled in the summer there were rarely enough dishes to justify starting it up. Besides, the house still held heat from the day, and it didn't seem prudent to add to it.

Ruth said, "The spinning wheel is in the living room."

"Thanks again for that. It's sweet of you to let me borrow it."

"I want you to do something, though."

I paused in rinsing a plate. "Oh?"

"I want you to go over and talk to Chris Popper."

Oh.

Slowly, I dried my hands and sat down at the kitchen table. I'd been so caught up in my own drama that I'd nearly forgotten what Barr had said about Chris killing Ariel. Now I remembered my insistence that she call me if she wanted to talk, and felt torn.

She'd lost her husband twice, it seemed: once to another woman and then, finally, to an accident. But would she really have killed Ariel over it? Especially after Scott was already dead?

"Barr and that woman detective think she killed Ariel," Ruth said.

There was a note of distaste in her voice when she mentioned Robin Lane. The fledgling detective had tried to bully information out of Ruth a few months previously. Ruth had been flat on her back in a hospital bed at the time and in a lot of pain. Barr was right. His partner had all the people skills of a grumpy badger.

Cautious, I inclined my head a fraction.

"Barr already told you?" Ruth said. "Well, of course he did. Will you talk to Chris before jumping to any conclusions, and make up your own mind? That's all I ask. Because you know how hard it is to lose a husband. Can you imagine how hard it would have been if, in addition to losing your husband, you'd been accused of murdering his lover on the day of his funeral?"

I blanched. Turned out I couldn't imagine it.

Barr had asked me to foster gossip amongst the CRAC crowd, and I had already offered a listening ear should Chris be interested. Complying with Ruth's request was a no brainer.

"Of course I'll talk to her," I said. "Though I'm not sure what good it will do."

She shrugged and reached for a dishtowel. "To be honest, I don't know, either. But do it anyway."

Kind of pushy, I thought. "Or you'll take away the spinning wheel?" I joked.

Ruth smiled gently.

I stared at her placid face. "You're blackmailing me?"

"Don't be ridiculous," she said. "I'm bribing you."

EIGHT

After Ruth left, I took a long shower, dressed in a soft, oversized T-shirt and crawled into bed with one of Gladys Taber's *Stillmeadow* books. Her descriptions of bucolic life in the late-seventeenth-century farmhouse she and her friend Jill had rehabbed in 1920s and '30s Connecticut seemed the perfect continuation of my determined affection for the home life I had with Meghan and Erin.

Meghan came and stood in my bedroom doorway. I put my book down.

"Think tomorrow will be as exciting as today?" she asked with a rueful look.

"I hope not."

"What did Ruth want?"

I pasted innocence on my face.

"Come on. I know she came over specifically to talk to you, and it wasn't just about twisting fiber into yarn."

"She wants me to talk to Chris."

"Oh. Well, that makes sense, since you're a, you know . . . widow."

"Yeah, that and the police think Chris had something to do with Ariel's death."

"What!"

"Ariel and Scott were having an affair. Barr wants me to talk to Chris, too. Well," I amended, "not just Chris. He wants me to talk to other people at CRAC, too. More like get them talking." I'd sort of left that out when I'd recounted my conversation with him earlier.

She stared at me. "He *wants* you to?"

I nodded.

"Well. I, um . . ." Meghan rarely looked as flummoxed as she did at that news. "I guess nothing I say is going to make any difference."

"I'm not investigating. I promise. I'm not asking a bunch of questions or putting myself in danger. I'm just acting as some extra eyes and ears because Robin Lane may be gorgeous, but she has the tact of a sledgehammer when it comes to questioning people about murder."

Understanding settled onto Meghan's face. "Ah. Promise you'll be careful?"

"Cross my heart."

She started to leave, then turned back. "You do lead an exciting life, don't you?"

I snorted. I couldn't help it. "Yeah. Maybe a little too exciting."

She grinned. "Goodnight."

" 'Night," I said, and reached for the lamp. It was only nine-thirty, but I was ready for some shut-eye. I heard Meghan dialing New Jersey as I drifted off.

Fitful dreams punctuated my nighttime and early morning hours, and sunlight began to creep through my window at four-thirty. Days were long on both sides in the summer.

At six I gave up trying to sleep, showered again, and donned a lightweight skirt and T-shirt in response to the weather forecast; the temperature was supposed to advance into the nineties, which was hot for this early in the summer. Humidity curled in the air like a languid animal after a big meal.

Meghan, mom of the world, had breakfast waiting for me when I came downstairs a bit before seven. Fresh strawberries from the farmer's market piled in a bright blue bowl and splashed with cream looked like a Fourth of July decoration as much as something to scarf down to start the day. Chicken and apple sausage, also from the farmer's market, was joined within minutes by eggs scrambled with fresh chives and oregano.

The eggs had probably still been warm from the chickens when she'd cracked them into the bowl. A steaming cup of coffee topped the whole meal off. How could I even think about leaving this?

"Where's Erin?" I asked, between bites of sausage.

Meghan joined me at the table with her own plate. She nodded toward the backyard.

"Already?"

"Not the chickens this time," she said. "I told her if she'd weed bed three I'd take her to the river this afternoon after camp to swim."

"Nice." We only had four small vegetable beds, but they seemed to require constant attention. "I'll weed one today, too."

"Do you have time?" Meghan asked.

"Oddly enough, I'm pretty much caught up, except for the usual order filling. Cyan is coming by tomorrow, so I can have her do some of that." I bit into a juicy strawberry and let out a low moan. "God, these are good."

"Aren't they? Of course, by the time the season is over we'll be sick to death of them."

It was hard to imagine, but she was right. "That's what freezers are for. Do you have any clients today?"

"Two." Her massage business had begun to slow for the summer, too. "At noon and at one."

"I have an errand to run. I'll be home later," I said.

"Sounds good."

I refrained from mentioning the errand involved spending time alone with a possible murderer.

The ranch-style house was located on ten acres of land on the east side of Cadyville, set back from the county road that wound north from Highway 2. A large black dog and a smaller brown one greeted my arrival with joyous barks and wagging tails. Laughing at their enthusiasm, I pushed their cold noses away from my bare legs. A metallic clang sounded from behind the house as I reached for the doorbell.

Chris didn't answer. Another loud reverberation carried through the air, followed by another and then another. A low droning underscored the mesmerizing rhythm. The dogs gamboled around me as I walked around the house to the backyard.

The drone became the roar of an enclosed fire as I neared the source: Chris' blacksmith shop. No walls enclosed the thirty-by-thirty space, but eight thick corner posts supported the octagonal roof. The floor was bare dirt, swept smooth. Her arm, pale in the relative darkness, rose and fell, the clank of the hammer on red-hot metal sparking with each blow. The pounding stopped, and, with a pair of tongs, she transferred a flat, tapering rod from the anvil to the forge.

Chris turned and saw me watching. I raised a hand in greeting.

"Oh. It's you," she said, swiping at the sheen of sweat on her forehead with the back of her wrist. She beckoned me in. "Be careful. Forge's hot."

The air close to the blaze warped and shimmered with heat. The tang of hot iron mingled with the earthy scent of Chris' perspiration. It smelled like hard work.

"Do you want some iced tea?" she asked.

"Sure."

"Oh. Well, there's some in the big thermos over there. Should be some cups by it."

I found the cups and opened the thermos. "Do you want some?" I asked. "You must be roasting in here."

"I'm fine." She sighed. "I'm sorry. I know I'm not being very gracious."

Her hair hung lank, as if she hadn't washed it for days, and it was held back off her face on each side by blue plastic barrettes more suited to a ten-year-old girl. She wore a white tank top that needed an appointment with a washing machine, and faded jeans, frayed at the edges. I wondered whether it wouldn't be safer to wear long sleeves when working with hot metal.

"Don't worry about it," I said. I could hardly recall the period right after Mike died. Mostly I remembered having to put on a good show for all the people who were trying to be nice to me. At the time it had felt almost like an imposition, but now I realized it had been one of the things that had kept me from falling apart completely.

Chris, on the other hand didn't seem to be concerned with putting on a game face. She dipped a sopping bandanna out of a bucket of water near her feet, used it to swab the back of her neck, and then rubbed her forehead furiously, leaving behind a bright pink patch of skin.

"Is there anyone who can stay with you?" I asked, and took a sip of tea. The stuff was strong enough to strip paint, and so cold it made my teeth hurt. I rolled the sweating cup across my cheek.

"I don't want anyone to. I just want to get through this mess." She sat on a bench and waved to the space beside her. I joined her. She grew still, looking at me. Really looking at me for the first time since I'd interrupted her work. "Does Barr know you're here?"

I shook my head. Well, he didn't, did he?

"Do you know about the murder investigation?"

I paused, and her gaze became suspicious. No way to lie here, and probably no reason to, either. Thank God. I was a horrible liar.

"Oh, I know about it," I said. "For one thing, I found Ariel. And, yes, Barr mentioned something about you being a suspect."

For a split second she looked triumphant, before it quickly faded to sadness underscored with a heavy dose of anger.

"So did Ruth," I added.

Chris looked at me curiously. "Is that why you're here?"

"Did you kill Ariel?"

"No!"

"Okay then. I told you after the funeral that I'd lost my husband. I know how rough it is. But . . . can I be frank?"

"Please. I'm sick and tired of people tiptoeing around me."

"My husband died of cancer, not in a sudden accident. He wasn't having an affair. And I wasn't accused of killing his lover. So in my book, this has got to be even harder on you than it was on me. I thought you might want someone to talk to. Or cry on.

Or yell at."

She stared at me, and for a moment I thought I'd gone too far. Then a smile tugged at her lips.

"I'm available. That's all," I said.

"Noted," she said. "I think I'll have some tea after all."

I poured frigid brown liquid out of her thermos into a plastic cup and handed it to her.

"Why do they think you did it?" I asked.

Barr hadn't told me much, and I was curious. He was no dummy, after all. Maybe she really had killed the girl. I eyed her bulging biceps.

She sighed. "You already know that Scott and Ariel were having an affair."

"How did the police find out?"

"I told them."

"You knew about it before the accident?"

"Oh, yes. I knew. He knew I knew. She knew I knew. Everyone concerned knew. Hell, the cops he worked with probably already knew before I told them."

"I don't think so," I said. "Barr seemed pretty surprised."

She stood and grabbed the tongs, used them to remove the flat bar of metal from the forge. It glowed a high, bright yellow that was almost white at the tip. She lifted the hammer. Slam! I jumped at the burst of sound.

"But he didn't want to stop seeing her. He was going to leave me." Fury rode her tone. She shifted the angle of the bar on the anvil. Bang! I jumped again, even though I'd seen it coming.

A trail of perspiration trickled down my side under my T-shirt, and I leaned back, away from the heat. No wonder Barr and Robin thought she had a good motive if she'd acted like this when they'd talked to her. Naked anger rolled off her in waves.

"I told them all of that," she said. "I wanted them to know what kind of man they worked with. I wanted them to know he wasn't as perfect as they seemed to think he was."

She clenched her fists around hammer and tongs so hard they turned white and began shaking. For the first time I felt a trill of fear, and I shivered in spite of the heat.

Then her eyes filled with tears. "I didn't even realize why they were here. I thought it was a condolence call. I handed myself to them on a platter." She was choking out the words now.

She put the tools down with studied care, and I jumped up and led her back to the bench. The sobs that followed sounded like they were being ripped out of her chest against her will. I took a chance and left her, running to the back door and into her kitchen. I rifled quickly through her cupboards. There. I grabbed the bottle of Hornitos and ran back out to the smithy. I tossed her iced tea on the grass, replaced it with a shot of tequila and set it on the seat beside her. Then I patted her on the back, and waited.

It took a while for her to run down, but when she did, she slammed the shot in one swallow with a grateful glance my way, shuddered once, and was quiet.

"Wow," she said. "That's the first time I really cried about it."

I wondered whether "it" referred to Scott's death, or his affair with Ariel — or both.

"Believe me," I said. "It won't be the last time. But it will get better."

I still couldn't get over the affair between Scott and Ariel. They were so mismatched: he, a rough-and-tumble, racecar-driving cop who was at least twenty years her senior, and she, an airy, unfocused artist. He'd been good-looking enough, but I didn't get what she'd seen in him beyond that. Maybe she'd had a daddy complex?

Yuck.

"There's something I don't really understand," I said. "Why would you kill Ariel three days after Scott's accident?" It wasn't the most tactful thing to say, I know. But geez, how else was I supposed to put it? Talk about closing the barn door after the horse is long gone.

"They think I was so mad that I didn't care."

"That's nuts," I said.

"They think I'm nuts. Anyone who kills someone else out of jealousy is nuts. If I'd actually done it, I'd agree with them."

I couldn't help it. I had trouble thinking about Ariel and Scott without my doppelganger nibbling constantly at the edge of my attention. Of course it was nuts to kill someone out of jealousy. But there was a tiny part of me that could understand going nuts in precisely that way.

"How long had you known?" I asked.

"About three months. I found out shortly after it started." She looked longingly at the bottle of tequila, sitting on the ground.

I poured out another and handed it to her. "Were you angry at Scott?"

She gave me a look, then downed the second shot. "No, I thought it was great that he was seeing a woman who could have been his daughter, and didn't seem to give a damn whether I knew it or not. What's to

95

be angry about?"

"Yeah, okay. Sorry. Stupid question. Do you have any kind of an alibi for when the murder occurred?"

"I might."

I looked the question at her.

"Detective Lane asked me what I was doing between eight and ten, night before last. If that's when that little bitch was killed, then I'm home free."

I readjusted my idea that Ariel had been killed the morning of Scott's funeral. Apparently her body had been at CRAC for hours before I found her.

"What were you doing?" I asked.

"Ruth and Irene were over here. Jake was, too, for a while. They were here from a bit before seven until after ten."

I took in the blue half moons under Chris' red-rimmed eyes, the tiny tremor in her hand even after knocking back a couple shots of tequila. Could she handle an arrest, a trial, the scandal that would result in a town this size?

"So let's hope Robin asking you about that time means that's when the murder occurred. Then they'll have to look elsewhere," I said. As long as Robin didn't turn her attention back to me.

Chris' eyes flicked up at me and then away

again. "I know that department. Scott worked there for fifteen years. They know what they're doing. It's just that right now they're going down the wrong track." She stood and nodded toward the house. "Do you want something to eat? People have given me so much food, and I don't have much of an appetite right now. I think I'm done beating up on metal for this afternoon."

"No, thanks. I have to be going. But Chris?"

"Yeah?"

"The offer to talk still stands. If you want to be left alone right now, that's fine, but if you change your mind, well . . ."

"Okay. Thanks. I'll keep it in mind."

NINE

"So what are we going to do with her art?" Jake Beagle asked. "We can't just keep displaying it at the co-op. What if someone wants to buy it?"

"Fat chance," Irene muttered.

Jake, Irene, Ruth, and I had gathered around a small rickety table in the corner of the Beans R Us coffee shop to talk about how to keep the co-op from going under. All of Cadyville knew a woman had been murdered in the studio, and the yellow crime scene tape strung over the exterior doors provided a constant reminder in case anyone forgot. No one was allowed inside, so we couldn't retrieve any of our belongings or any of the artists' stock or supplies.

Behind the counter, the barista, Luce, fussed with bags of coffee beans and craned her head so as to best hear our conversation.

"Making money off someone's death isn't

right," Jake said, still talking about Ariel's big splotchy paintings.

"Isn't that something we should worry about later?" I asked. Irene was right; no one was likely to buy Ariel's art right away. After all, no one had bought any of it yet. "Right now isn't the main problem getting back into the building?"

Irene flicked a quick sidelong look my direction.

"Detective Lane told me we'd be able to get back in tomorrow afternoon, at least downstairs. The crime scene people may be done with the upstairs by then, too." Ruth said.

All eyes turned to me, as if I should have already had this information. I looked at the floor. Barr and I had only spoken briefly on the phone since he'd dropped the triple bombshell of ex-wife, sister and fortune on me the previous afternoon.

"So, it is pertinent, what we do with Ariel's art." Jake again. "If we're going to re-open .CRAC."

Irene scowled at him, then quickly transferred her gaze out the window. Ruth sat quietly and watched all of us. Chris had said she'd rather not join us, and no one blamed her. Ruth had invited me along, just as she had invited me to join the co-op in the first place. I'd jumped at the chance to be in on the discussion, but now I felt like an interloper.

"You may be right," I said. "She must have some family."

"Just a brother, I think," Ruth said. "Up north, around La Conner. I don't know his name." She looked the question at all of us, and we all shook our heads.

"There can't be that many Skylarks in La Conner," I said.

"I believe he has a different last name. Ariel changed hers to Skylark," Ruth said.

"Really?" Jake asked, bushy eyebrows climbing up his forehead.

Irene rolled her eyes. "Don't tell me you're surprised."

"What about friends around here?" I asked.

Everyone shook their heads.

"No one?"

"Us," Ruth said. "And she had a roommate."

"I wasn't her friend." Irene's tone was flat. "But I guess Jake was." She gave him a little wink, which looked downright weird coming from her.

He looked out the window.

Sheesh. What was wrong with these people?

"Tell you what," I said. "I'll go talk to her roommate, see if I can find out more about her brother. Maybe we can just ship the art off to him."

Irene pressed her lips together, as if to keep from saying something. Jake nodded his approval.

"That would be nice," Ruth said with a slight look of triumph on her face. "Now, what do we do about the bad publicity?"

No one responded. Sighing inwardly, I stepped up again. "I've got to say, I don't think it's a problem for business. People are weird, and they'll want to see where the murder happened. We need to change the lock on the doors and implement some rules about being safe when working there, but for the most part, I bet we get more traffic than ever."

Jake leaned his rather squarish chin on a meaty fist. Eyeing his spatulate digits, I reflected that it was a good thing he hadn't chosen gynecology as a specialty. "You may be right," he said.

We finished our coffee drinks and shuffled out, squinting, to the hot, bright street. Through the window I saw Luce reach for the phone, but there wasn't anything we'd said that was a big secret.

Go for it, girl. Gossip on.

■ ■ ■ ■

"I thought you said you weren't going to investigate Ariel's murder," Meghan said, tying up an heirloom tomato plant with strips cut from old pantyhose.

I looked up from where I was sowing another section of slow-bolt cilantro. "Oh, for heaven's sake. I'm not investigating anything. Only checking with her roommate to find out where to send her art."

"Sure you are." She walked over to the large wicker basket on the ground between us. "The zucchini plants are going nuts. I'm going to strip some of the blossoms."

Yum. I'd been waiting for a chance to add squash blossoms to a light stir-fry, or stuff them with fresh mozzarella and chopped pumpkin seeds, dust them with chipotle chili powder and flour and fry them all golden and crispy.

Finished with the cilantro, I began harvesting the outer leaves of the lettuce. "We have a ton of this red-leaf. How about wilted lettuce and stuffed squash blossoms with some grilled lamb tonight?"

"Now you're talking," Meghan said. "You should invite Barr over."

I sat back on my heels and let my fingers

sift through the dirt at my feet. "Oh, all right."

It felt like Meghan was playing matchmaker, which was pretty weird since I'd dated the man in question for several months already.

She bent over the tumbling vines. "Do you think she did it?"

"Who?"

Her look told me to stop being stupid. "Chris."

"I don't know. I doubt it. It sounds like she has an alibi."

"So you went over there today?"

I nodded. "I told you Barr asked me to keep my finger on the pulse of the CRAC crowd."

"I knew you'd get involved one way or another." She finished tying up another tomato plant and stood upright, stretching her back. "At least you have permission from the police this time."

Well, maybe not *all* the police. Robin would pop a vein if she knew Barr had asked for my help.

"I'm going to run over and talk to Ariel's roommate now, while I'm thinking about it," I said.

One side of Meghan's mouth turned up. "Okay. See you when you get back."

■ ■ ■ ■

As I guided my little Toyota pickup down the street toward the address Ruth had given me, I pondered the exchange at Beans R Us. Irene — mousy little Irene — had been downright nasty at times. It was obviously she'd disliked Ariel intensely. Ruth had been uncharacteristically taciturn. Jake, on the other hand, had been vociferously insistent that Ariel's art was well taken care of. He seemed quite upset by her death. Oh, don't get me wrong; her murder was horrible. It was just that something about his reaction made me think it was a little more personal for him than even, for example, me — the woman who had actually found her body.

Lordy, what was the deal with the CRAC members? They were like a dysfunctional family. I bet they had a few dirty little secrets hidden away, too.

Blue and red lights flashed in my rearview mirror: a silver Impala, the "undercover" prowler of the Cadyville police department. At least Barr had shown a little subtlety and kept the siren off.

The siren chirped.

Nice.

I wondered what he'd do if I didn't stop. Arrest me?

The siren chirped again.

Perhaps not the best time to find out. I turned onto a residential street and pulled over.

Barr got out. I stayed where I was and rolled down the window. Our conversation on the phone the night before had been short and slightly uncomfortable. When he stopped beside me, I silently offered my license and registration.

He ignored it. "Are you still mad at me?"

Hmmm. "I don't think so. Why, has something else happened?"

"I talked to my mother," he said.

I raised my eyebrows.

"She said Hannah took a week off. My brother, clever bear that he is, told her about the money from my uncle." He rolled his eyes. "Randall, who's seven years younger than I am, by the way, has a bit of a crush on Hannah. Mom thinks he was trying to impress her."

"So she's here for the whole week?" I asked.

He shook his head. "No. I called her over at Horse Acres. Sent her packing in no uncertain terms."

Wow. "Really?"

"Really."

"That seems kind of mean," I said.

He grinned. "I can call her back and tell her to stay. We could all go out for dinner, if you'd like."

"Nah. That's okay."

"Thought you might say that," he said.

"Listen," I said. "I'm on my way to talk to Ariel's roommate about where to send her CRAC art. Do you know about Ariel's brother?"

He nodded. "His address was in her things."

Of course. I knew he and Robin would've already gone to Ariel's apartment, but I felt a little deflated anyway.

"His last name isn't Skylark?"

"Nope. Kaminski."

"Ruth said Ariel changed her name," I said.

"Apparently so."

"Why?"

He lifted a shoulder. "She liked the sound of Skylark better than Kaminski."

"Did you learn anything else interesting?" I asked, a note of frustration creeping in.

"From the roommate? Not much." He looked regretful. "Robin, well . . ."

Ah.

"Come over for dinner tonight," I said.

106

"We're having lamb."

His eyes widened. "Grilled?"

"Of course."

"Count me in."

"See you then." I rolled up my window.

He placed his right hand against it, the pattern of his palm pressed against the glass. With one finger, I traced his love line. My eyes lifted and met his. I bit my lip.

We both smiled.

TEN

Ariel had lived in an apartment on the second floor of a lone twelve-plex on the corner of Maple and Pine. Someone had purchased and rehabbed the old building and painted it a sumptuous apricot with green and maroon trim. Planter boxes lining the tiny balcony railings dripped purple verbena, blood-red geraniums and lobelia in deep rich shades of sapphire. A rack in front supported a row of bikes. To the right, an expanse of asphalt hosted a series of compact and economy cars, most of them sporting parking stickers from the neighboring college. These were primarily digs for students, and nice digs at that.

I climbed the stairs, my sandals scuffing on the wooden steps, and rapped on the metal door with my knuckles. Rustling sounds came from inside, and then slowly the door opened.

"Yes?" A tall woman in her early twenties

grinned down at me. Her hair was blue black, the kind that has to come out of a bottle, and it fell unfettered to a pair of impressive — and unharnessed — breasts. She was so tall I found myself staring straight at them. My face grew hot as I realized what I was doing, and I craned my neck up to look into a wide pale face with amused green eyes.

"Hi," I said. "I'm Sophie Mae Reynolds. I'm a member of the artist's co-op Ariel belonged to."

The smile faded. "Oh."

"She lived here, didn't she?"

The woman nodded.

"I'm sorry. You must be pretty shaken up by what happened."

"Yeah. I mean, well . . . yeah." She stepped back and held the door open. "I'm sorry. Please, come in."

I stepped into an herbal oasis. There were potted plants everywhere, at least fifty of them, clustered around every window, tucked into corners and onto bookshelves under grow lights, lining the kitchen counters. Every one of them had some kind of culinary or medical application, and sometimes both. There were lavender and rosemary, sage, oregano, and a variety of thymes. Mints were interspersed with feverfew, calendula, scented geraniums, and chamomile.

"Wow," I said. "This is amazing. Is that borage?"

She nodded, obviously pleased. "I grew it from seed. Would you like something to drink? I have some iced tea."

"That would be great, thanks."

I wandered around the little apartment in wonder. All the plants were incredibly healthy, not a yellow leaf nor leggy one among them, despite being crammed into the tiny living space.

She returned and handed me a sea-green concoction that smelled of mint. "I'm studying horticulture."

"Well, you've got the green thumb for it." I sipped from the tall glass, condensation already forming along its sides. Mint and a myriad of other herbal infusions. "This tea is lovely, um . . . I'm afraid I don't know your name. We only knew that Ariel lived here and that she had a roommate."

"Oh! I'm Daphne. Daphne Sparks."

"Nice to meet you. Were you and Ariel close?"

She hesitated, then seemed to make a decision. "Not really. We weren't even friends. I found the apartment, but couldn't afford it by myself, so I advertised for someone to share it with me. That was almost a year ago. Ariel answered the ad, and at first I thought she'd make a good roommate."

"At first?"

She blinked and looked away. "It doesn't do any good to talk bad about her now."

"No, you're right. Listen, the reason I'm here is because there's a bunch of her art over at the co-op, and we don't know who to give it to."

"I don't want it."

I laughed, then quickly covered my mouth.

Her lips twisted in wry response. "Sorry. I guess it just isn't my style."

"I understand."

"But you know, I think she had potential, and if she'd been willing to learn more, Ariel might've been pretty good. That's how I met her. She was going to school, like me, only she was in the art department."

"I didn't know that."

"She dropped out. Too many classes she thought were boring, too much homework," Daphne said.

"Did she have a job?"

A half shrug. "She was a part-time hostess at The Turning Point."

"Hard to make a living doing that, even if it is the fanciest restaurant in town," I said.

111

Daphne snorted. "She didn't. Make a living, that is. She owes me almost two grand." She looked at the floor. "Or *owed* me, I guess."

Not exactly peanuts. I took a drink of cold tea.

She continued. "Ariel kept saying she was going to go back to school, then get a really good job. But really? She was determined to meet a rich guy who'd want to marry her."

"How was that working out?" I asked.

"Lots of dates, lots of overnighters she'd bring here. Not a lot of marriage proposals from what I heard. Probably didn't help that she had a thing for men who were already married." She looked at the floor. I could tell she felt bad talking about Ariel, even though she'd obviously taken advantage of Daphne. "She was also hoping her art would take off and support her. Being accepted into the co-op was the first step in proving to the art world that she had real talent, she said."

The Cadyville Regional Artists' Co-op? Related in any way shape or form to the "art world"? I almost snorted. Instead, I asked, "Did she have any particular boyfriends?"

A shrug. "She was gone a lot. I was gone a lot. When we were both here we got so we avoided each other."

"She had an affair with the husband of a friend of mine. It caused a lot of pain," I said. Well, Barr had said to gossip, hadn't he?

We'd been standing as we talked, and now Daphne sat down on the overstuffed sofa. I moved to a window box and ran my fingers through the thick, gray-green leaves of a French lavender in bloom. The intense fragrance curled around me like a hug.

"Maybe your friend is the one who called," Daphne said.

I turned. "Called here?"

She nodded. "I answered. She sounded furious."

Chris hadn't mentioned calling Ariel, but that didn't mean she hadn't. And if she had, it was a sure bet she'd sound furious.

"Did she tell you her name?" I asked.

"Huh-uh. She told me to stay away from her husband, then hung up on me after I said I was Ariel's roommate."

"It must have happened quite awhile ago," I prompted.

"Nope. Just last week."

I thought about asking her what day, but that seemed to be pushing it. She already looked uncomfortable talking about Ariel's affairs as it was. Heck, between the phone calls and bringing men home all the time, I was surprised Daphne hadn't killed Ariel herself.

Of course, I couldn't know for sure she hadn't.

I fingered a tiny rosemary formed into a spiral topiary. "This is exquisite."

She gazed fondly at the little plant as if it were a child. "Thank you."

"How long had you and Ariel lived together?"

"Almost a year. The lease is coming up, and either she was going or I was, or both."

"You'd already talked about it?"

"Not really. Ariel wasn't the easiest person to talk to, so I kept putting it off."

"Not easy to talk to," I repeated.

She shook her head. "Kind of . . . volatile. Hard to reason with if things weren't going her way."

I finished my tea. "Thanks for this. I'll just put the glass in the kitchen, and get out of your hair."

"You're welcome." She stood.

The kitchen counter served as a half-wall separating it from the living room. More plants spilled over the window sill.

"About the art: did Ariel have any family?" I asked over my shoulder as I put my glass in the pristine sink. "I heard about a brother. Maybe he can tell me what to do with it."

"Yeah. He lives up north. His name is Rocky Kaminski. I don't know the address or the phone number, though. The police were here earlier today, and they took her address book."

I walked back into the living room. "Did they take anything else?"

Another shrug. "Some paperwork. They may've taken some things from her room; I didn't go in there with them. They just told me not to get rid of the rest of her stuff until they call me. I sure hope it's soon, because I have to find someone to share expenses right away if I'm going to stay here." She walked toward the door.

I followed. "Do you mind if I ask how her bill with you got so high?"

Daphne fidgeted with a fingernail. "It's kind of embarrassing, actually. It happened bit by bit, falling behind on this bill, and then that one. And she always had a good reason, a story about how she couldn't pay me right then, but the money was on the way. And she did come through with money sometimes. Just not all of it."

Ariel sounded like the roommate from hell.

"Good luck," I said. "If I hear of anyone

who'd be interested, I'll send them your way."

"Hey, thanks. I appreciate that."

Back in the cab of my truck, I thought about the address book. Barr and/or Robin Lane would be contacting Ariel's brother. Well, of course they would; he was her next of kin. But I'd better be careful not to appear to Robin as if I was trying to interfere with her investigation. Maybe it'd be better to have one of the other co-op members contact Rocky Kaminski about taking Ariel's art.

But who? Irene wouldn't do it. Jake probably shouldn't do it. And Ruth didn't even like to drive outside of town.

That was when I realized I wasn't thinking about calling Rocky Kaminski at all. I was planning a trip to La Conner.

I didn't want to give the task of following up with Ariel's brother to anyone else. I wanted to go up there, not only because I was curious about what her brother might be like, but because I wanted to get the heck out of Dodge.

The murder and Barr and his ex-wife woes were enough to escape from temporarily, but now that I thought about it, I hadn't taken even a single full day off from my business in almost a year. I wanted a mini-vacation. If I happened to find out more about Ariel's murder, so be it.

I just had to tread carefully.

On the way home, I kept expecting — even hoping — to see Barr behind me again, curious about what I'd learned from Daphne Sparks. But I didn't see the Impala.

About halfway home, however, my constant monitoring of the rearview mirror did net a nondescript economy rental car that looked an awful lot like the one Hannah had been driving. I took a few extra turns, but she stuck with me. As I parked on the street in front of the house, her car pulled up even with my truck. She glared at me for a few seconds, then slowly and deliberately smiled. It wasn't a nice smile at all. As she sped away, I resisted giving her the ol' one-fingered salute.

Apparently Barr had not, as he put it, sent her packing.

ELEVEN

I plunged into a frenzy of housework. Unfortunately, I'm wired to clean and tidy before venturing away from the home fires. It was only a day trip to La Conner, too, which shows how pathetic my life had become.

Besides, the harder I scrub, the less I think about things that are bothering me. And between Ariel and Hannah, I was plenty bothered.

Two loads of laundry, a sparkling clean refrigerator, stove, and kitchen floor, a swept front step, tidied mudroom, two scrubbed toilets and a dusted living room later, I fell into a kitchen chair, drank a glass of iced coffee and contemplated the pile of lettuce I'd taken out of the fridge and put in the sink.

Time to get back to work.

There is something about rinsing every square inch of every leaf of lettuce to rid it of dust and make sure no crawlies make it onto the dinner plate that is back-breaking. We hadn't even reached the time of year when we did most of our canning and pickling, but I was getting that stuck-over-the-sink feeling already. I'd never do it if it weren't for the fact that I absolutely love how a big pile of lettuce wilts into a manageable, delectable mound when tossed with crumbles of bacon, a little hot bacon grease and warm cider vinegar mixed with a little salt, pepper, and sugar. It wasn't food you could get in a restaurant, and besides, for me, it was one of the definite signs that summer had arrived.

Cleaning takes a certain amount of concentration; rinsing lettuce does not. My mind was now free to obsess about Hannah.

My second view of her today confirmed it: she looked a lot like me. But men are well known to find a certain type of woman attractive.

Of course, women have their preferences, too. Which was entirely beside the point.

I wondered if she was a nice person. Well, she would be, wouldn't she? I mean, Barr wouldn't go and marry someone who ate kittens for breakfast or yelled at old ladies. Because I had to give him credit for his taste in women, or else what was I saying about me?

Oh, B.S., Sophie Mae. She followed you around town and gave you the stink-eye right in front of your own house. She's been told to go home, but she wants her ex-husband's money. Face it. She's not nice at all.

Two million dollars. Some women would do a lot for money like that.

Like what? Beg, steal . . . kill?

Oh, man. This was nuts. I reached for the kitchen towel, dried my hands and went out to the hallway for the phone. My heart went ka-chunka ka-chunka as I waited through the rings for Barr to answer.

He picked up.

"I thought you might like to know your ex-wife followed me home."

"Hell," he muttered under his breath. "Okay. I'll take care of it."

"Is she violent?" I asked.

"What? No, of course not."

I wondered whether he really knew.

"Sophie Mae? Can we talk about this tonight? I'm kind of in the middle of something."

"Sure. I'll see you later." I pushed the off button on the cordless handset and replaced it in the cradle. I went back to my pile of lettuce, thoughts roiling.

When I was nearly done, Meghan came in and offered to take over.

"That's okay. But I wouldn't mind some company," I said.

She flipped on the kitchen light. I hadn't realized how dark it had become with the sun on the other side of the house.

"Okay. When you're done I'll stuff the squash blossoms," she said.

I'd almost forgotten. The thought made me feel a little better.

A very little.

I heard a faint clicking noise and looked over my shoulder to see Meghan knitting peach-colored cotton yarn into a rectangle.

"What are you doing?"

"Making a purse for Erin. Apparently Zoe got one for her birthday, and Erin feels left out." Zoe had been Erin's best friend since first grade.

"Those two haven't been hanging out as much this summer," I said.

"I think it's the math camp," Meghan said.

"I didn't even know you knitted."

"My mother taught me. I haven't done it for a while, but all your talk about spinning and fiber inspired me. It is kind of fun."

Well, of course Meghan would already know how to knit, would be able to pick it up after years and years and create some-

121

thing totally funky and cool like that little bag. I sighed, thinking about how I struggled with the twin needles, preferring a simple crochet hook and only a few loops of yarn to worry about at a time.

"I called Barr," she said. "He told me you'd already invited him to dinner."

I finished the last leaf of lettuce, tossed it in the drainer and turned around with the dishtowel in my hands. "Do you know what he did today?"

"Uh, no."

"He pulled me over on Cedar Street. Lights, sirens, the whole bit."

She laughed. I scowled.

"Then what happened?" she asked, sounding far too delighted and knitting away faster than anyone who hasn't done it for years has a right to. She didn't even look at her hands while she was doing it.

Suddenly, I remembered the image of Barr's palm against the truck window, and a wave of emotion washed through me.

"Sophie Mae?"

I waved the dishtowel and took a deep breath. "He was just checking in."

She laughed. "What, he can't call your cell phone?"

"Oh, gosh. My cell phone. It's still in the truck. I'd better go get it." After finally joining the rest of the wireless world, I kept forgetting I had the dang thing.

As I came back in the door the hall phone was ringing. "I've got it," I called to Meghan. Twisting my mouth at the irony, I put my cell phone down and answered the land line.

"Is Sophie Mae Reynolds there?"

"Speaking," I said.

"This is Cassie Ambrose. Barr's mother. My knucklehead son's told me quite a bit about you. Sounds like he's really stepped in it, and I thought perhaps I could help."

Ohmygod. "Mrs. Ambrose. How nice to hear from you. Barr's told me a lot about you, too."

"Oh, has he now." She laughed. "That's not what I heard. I heard he's been a regular horse's patootie about telling you about his family and his past. And please, call me Cassie." Her voice was strong and deep, with a homey inflection I took to right away.

"Did he ask you to call me?" I asked.

"He did not. In fact, he asked me not to. But I thought it was high time we got ourselves acquainted. After all, he said you two are talking about living together."

Oh, dear. "Does that bother you?"

"Not at all. Much better than jumping into a marriage like he did with Hannah. It

123

would have been better for all concerned if they'd found out ahead of time that they disliked each other so much."

"Disliked? Then why did they get married in the first place?"

She snorted. "Lust. Pure lust."

I coughed. "I see."

"It happens to all of us, of course. The question is what do we do with it?"

I couldn't believe I was having this conversation with Barr's mother. "So you think living together is a good idea?"

"Sure. Especially if there's still all that lust. You can't make a good decision about the rest of your lives if your brain's all clouded with love chemicals."

"Ah," I said.

"And I don't think you're interested in my son because he's loaded now. Right?"

"Uh, no. Of course not. I only found out about the inheritance from his uncle yesterday. Was it your brother who passed away?"

"My oldest brother. He was a clever sort, played his cards right in the oil fields."

"Well, I'm sorry for your loss. Barr didn't tell me."

"See, there you go. He's a knucklehead, thinking you wouldn't be interested in knowing a relative had died. You're a nice girl, I can tell."

"Um," I said.

"Hannah isn't being too much of a pain, is she?"

"Well," I said.

"Because she's really a very nice girl, too, only you know, kind of crazy."

"What?" Crazy? What kind of crazy?

"Not crazy crazy. Just, a bit unpredictable. Don't you worry. She'll come on home here in no time. Barr will see to it."

Right. So far that hadn't worked so well, but I refrained from mentioning that to Cassie Ambrose.

"Well, dear, I'm glad we had this talk. I sure feel better, and I hope you do, too. The dudes are coming in from a ride and will be wanting their dinner, so I'd better go light a fire under the kitchen staff. You take care now, bye."

And just like that, she was gone.

Holy cow, I thought. So that was Barr's mother. I wondered what his father was like. Probably quiet. How could he not be, if that was any example of Cassie's conversational style?

Knuckles rapped on the frame of the front screen, and I looked up to see Barr standing on the step.

"Your mommy called," I said, opening the

door for him. "She thinks you're a knuckle-head."

Shaking his head, he glanced skyward as if invoking the heavens. "I told her not to."

"I got the feeling that wouldn't make much difference," I said.

"Obviously."

"I like her."

"Good, because you're stuck with me, and that means you're at least partially stuck with her. Now, where's my grub, woman?"

I laughed and led him into the kitchen.

TWELVE

The lamb was rare, the stuffed squash blossoms delicately crunchy on the outside and creamy good on the inside, and the wilted lettuce savory and sour and sweet and salty all at once.

Taking advantage of the warm weather — the rain would return soon enough — we once again ate at the cedar picnic table in the backyard. Erin was having dinner at her friend Zoe's house, so we could talk freely about Ariel's murder.

"Chris told me she thought she had an alibi," I said. "She said that Robin asked her about a specific time the night before the funeral when the murder probably happened."

Barr nodded. "I wish Robin hadn't given that away up front, but yes, Chris says she was with at least two other people during that time."

"You don't sound convinced," Meghan said.

"Well, at least one of them had a dislike of Ariel that bordered on hatred, from what I can tell."

"Irene Nelson?" I asked.

"That's the one." He took a bite of squash blossom. "Say, these are pretty good."

"But the other person was Ruth, right? She never seemed to feel one way or the other about Ariel," I said.

"So it looks like Chris is clear," he said. "Especially because there are two people who vouch for her, and not just one."

"What about Jake?"

"He was also at Chris' home that evening, but he left before the time of the murder."

"Which was between eight and ten at night?"

He nodded. "See, you do find things out."

"Well, here's something else I found out. Ariel's roommate told me today that a woman called the house and threatened Ariel, told her to stay away from her husband."

"You think it was Chris?" Meghan asked.

"Probably. Daphne — that's the roommate — answered the phone. The caller hung up as soon as she realized she wasn't talking to Ariel."

Barr looked thoughtful. "Any idea when this might have been?"

I finished chewing a mouthful of wilted lettuce and swallowed. "Last week. I couldn't narrow it down further without being obvious."

"That's good enough. Nice job."

Meghan grinned at me.

I tried not to fluff my feathers. "I'm going to La Conner to see Ariel's brother."

Barr paused with a forkful of lamb halfway to his mouth. "I don't know about that."

"CRAC has to do something with all her art. I might as well take it up there. At least I assume he'd want it. I'll call first and find out. But cross my heart and hope to die, I won't step on your toes or do anything to hurt the investigation."

He rested his elbows on the table, long fingers dangling a goblet of wine. "Robin is going tomorrow. Can you wait a day?"

"Sure. I have to get all the canvases packed up anyway." I turned to Meghan. "Come with me. We'll shop in all those kitschy little shops along the waterfront. I'll buy you dinner."

"I have clients scheduled."

"I have work, too. Rearrange some things."

"There's Erin."

"Bring her with."

"Math camp."

I still couldn't believe Erin was spending two weeks of her summer attending math camp on *purpose.* "Have her stay at Zoe's," I said.

"Sophie Mae, I can't just pick up and leave like that."

I sighed. "Neither can I, usually. I really need to get away for a little while."

Barr frowned. "Does that have anything to do with Hannah?"

"Honestly? I don't like her following me around town."

Meghan looked alarmed, and I hurried to reassure her. "Don't worry. It was only one time, and she was probably just curious about me. After all, I'm curious about her."

Next to me, Barr looked uncomfortable. "I don't know why women are like that."

"Well, we are. And I bet in the same situation, you'd be like that, too."

He shook his head. "She's probably already on her way out of town. I called Horse Acres again after you said you'd seen her, and she'd already checked out."

"Just because she's left the bed and breakfast doesn't mean she's left town." I clamped my mouth shut, ashamed of how shrill my voice had become.

Meghan, bless her heart, quickly changed

the subject. "The members of CRAC should put together something for Ariel's brother. Maybe some nice flowers."

"I like it. But how about a gift basket? I could give him some toiletries, and . . . oh, I don't know. Maybe he wouldn't want any of that stuff."

Barr said, "He's married, you know. And has twin boys. They live on a tulip farm outside of town. They seem more rural than arty."

"Do your parents like art?" I asked. "Or do they prefer to decorate with dead animal heads?"

"I don't think you want to know the answer to that question."

"Oh."

Meghan laughed.

"But yes," Barr said. "There is some very nice art in the lodge, wedged in among the elk antlers and Indian blankets. Point made. I'm sure Rocky Kaminski and his family would appreciate anything the CRAC crew wants to give them."

I laughed.

"What?" Meghan asked.

I shook my head. How could I explain the image of one of Irene Nelson's menopausal ladies that had danced across my mental screen? No doubt Ariel's brother would just

131

love one of those sculptures.

Better to stick to soap and the most ubiquitous comfort offering of all: food.

I was fast asleep the next morning when my cell phone began blaring "Sympathy for the Devil" on my bedside table.

"That's it," I mumbled as I groped for the offending noise. "I'm getting a mellower ring tone. Hello?"

"Get up, get out of bed. Get up, you sleepyhead," Barr sang into the phone.

I peered at the clock. Seven a.m. "Don't you know it's impolite to call before the civilized hour of nine a.m.?"

"That's why I didn't call the house phone. Besides, you're always up this early."

"Make a note: not always." I didn't mention that the evening before I'd begun reading a mystery by Jane Isenberg and couldn't go to sleep until I'd finished it.

"Okay, grumpus. You want me to call back later? Or do you want to know what I found out about the nasty phone call Ariel's roommate told you about?"

I pushed back the covers and swung my bare feet to the floor. "You've already checked phone records?"

"Hey, the cadets have to have something to do during the graveyard shift."

"What a resourceful man. So? Was it Chris?"

"No. She didn't call Ariel's cell phone, because we already checked that. And she didn't call the house, either. At least not from her cell or home."

"Hmm. Well, a negative isn't very useful."

"However, there was a call to the apartment last week which is curious."

I perked up at that.

"And this is where you come in," he continued. "The call was from Felicia Beagle's cell phone."

"Oh, wow. Ariel really got around. I suspected something was going on from the way Jake acted."

"Maybe you're not the only one who suspected something was going on. And maybe someone else at CRAC knows for sure. You're going over there today to pack up Ariel's art, right?"

"I have to call some people, but that's the plan."

"Well, my dear, I will await your report."

"You know you're getting downright scary about asking me to do your snooping, right?"

"We talked to Jake and Felicia, and got nothing. Complete stonewall. A few rumors here and there never hurt a police investigation." His voice changed then. "I want this killer, Sophie Mae. So does Robin."

I thought of Ariel, small and broken and lifeless. I didn't even like her, and it turned out a lot of other people didn't either. But I had to agree with Barr; I wanted her killer brought to justice, too. No one deserved what had happened to her.

"I'll call if I find out anything."

I used to dream of traveling. I used to, at the very least, go hiking in the Cascades a couple of days a month in the summer. Now, with my own business to run, there wasn't time. At some point work had simply taken over my life.

And, of course, I fell in love with a man who worked even more than I did. Was it possible that Barr and I hadn't spent enough time together in the last eight months to really get to know each other? In my basement workroom, I shook my head, resisting the notion. I did know him, despite the mix-up about his having an ex-wife.

Enough. I had things to do.

I called my teenaged helper, Cyan Waters, and told her to take the next day off. She didn't mind a bit. Then I googled Rocky Kaminski and found the website for the tulip farm he and his wife, Gabrielle, owned near La Conner, Washington. I printed out the directions on how to get there. The phone number was on the website, so I copied that down, too.

Gabrielle Kaminski answered the phone when I called. I explained who I was and that I'd be in La Conner the next day. Would she and her husband like for me to bring Ariel's art up with me?

"That'd be awful nice of you, if it's not too much trouble." The shouts of children in the background then, and she said, "Hang on a sec." Muffled voices and the distortion of a palm over the receiver. "You boys take your lunch outside and eat on the porch. And no throwing food, you hear?" A pause, and then to me, "Okay, I'm back. When do you think you'll be here?"

"In the early afternoon, I should think. Is that convenient?"

"That'll be just fine. We'll see you then."

Then I called Ruth, Irene, and Jake. Ruth assured me that the police had given her permission to go back inside, and the co-op would reopen the next day. Apparently Chris had influence with someone who pulled a few strings with the police, hurrying things along. Not surprising; after all, her husband had been a cop and she had an alibi for Ariel's murder. When I told everyone what I wanted to do they agreed to meet me that afternoon at CRAC — even Irene said she'd come. We'd all sign a card for the Kaminski family, and they'd help me load Ariel's paintings into the covered bed of my small pickup.

Before heading over to the co-op, I filled a gift basket with soaps that looked like quartz crystals and smooth river rocks, a few lip balms and lotion bars, an eye pillow filled with flax seeds, two jars of homemade raspberry jam and a jar of pickled asparagus. It was a bit much, but I wanted to do something nice.

The gift basket took longer than I'd anticipated, so I got there late. I rushed in to find Ruth and Irene, hands on hips, silently looking at the big stark canvases that leaned against the front counter. Empty spaces gaped on the wall where they'd hung.

Ruth greeted me, smiling with her eyes. She held out a sympathy card. "We've all signed it. Did you bring the blankets?"

I took the card and uncapped a pen. "Thanks for picking this up. The blankets are in the bed of my truck."

"Zak," she called. "Jake?"

"She's here?" They clomped down the stairs.

"Hey, you two. Thanks for helping out," I said.

"No problem." Jake said. Beside him, Zak nodded silent agreement. "We'll just take these out for you, pack them up."

"Okay, thanks," I said, and bent over the card. "Mine is the gray Toyota with the topper. The back is open, and there are blankets to pad the paintings."

Each took a big canvas and carried it out the door. I turned to Irene and Ruth. "Do you think we should do something more than just pad them in blankets? Something a little more professional? And I was going to keep them in the truck overnight, leave first thing in the morning."

Irene scowled. Ruth said, "The paintings will be fine. I'm sure her brother will be grateful."

"Yeah, I guess they'll be all right. As concerned as Jake was about Ariel's art, I'm sure he'll pack them well."

This time Irene snorted. I raised my palms. "What? Did Jake have a thing for her or something?"

She stared at me for several seconds, then without a word turned and strode to a display of her sculptures on the other side of the room and began rearranging them.

Ruth watched her with sympathetic eyes.

Zak and Jake came in and grabbed a couple more paintings. When the door had closed behind them, I turned to Ruth, "Did I say something wrong?"

"Not really. You see, Jake did have feelings for Ariel, but I think they were of a fatherly sort more than anything."

I'd seen how he looked at her. Fatherly, my ass.

She saw my expression and insisted, "He was very protective of her."

"What did Felicia think about that?" We were talking in low tones, and Irene steadfastly ignored us, fussing with a statue of a squat dancing woman with flowers in her hair.

Ruth hesitated. "Felicia may have misunderstood. Apparently she found some e-mails Jake had sent Ariel, and found their tenor a bit too, er, intimate."

"Ah," I said. "But his motives were pure, eh?"

"I like to think so," Ruth said, holding my gaze.

"So do I," I said, since that seemed to be what she wanted.

She nodded, and I had to wonder if Felicia's possible motive for killing Ariel was lost on her. It was the same motive Chris supposedly had, after all. But did Felicia have an alibi?

In no time, Jake and Zak had loaded and wrapped the paintings. I thanked them again, and Jake left, saying he had to get back to the office. I'd been surprised he'd been able to get away from his practice at all on such short notice; more evidence of his feelings for Ariel.

We all went outside. Irene stalked over to Zak, who was standing in the parking lot by my truck, and pointed to her car. He shook his head. She said something, and he shook it again. She opened her mouth, then snapped it shut again. Yanking her car door open, she got inside without looking at any of us and roared out of the parking lot.

"What on earth is wrong with Irene?" I said. "Did I make her that angry with that comment about Jake?"

Ruth sighed. "She's been through a lot, Sophie Mae. Her husband left her nine years ago for a younger woman. The divorce was not in the least bit amicable, and now he's started a whole new family. Irene was deeply hurt."

"I had no idea. No wonder the idea of Jake being attracted to Ariel hit a raw nerve. Did she know Ariel was having an affair with Scott Popper?"

A pained expression pinched Ruth's features. She nodded.

"How is Chris doing? Have you seen her?" I asked. "I went by and talked with her like you asked, but I figure the ball is in her court now."

"I spoke with her on the phone yesterday," Ruth said. "I think your visit helped. She seems to want to mourn alone, though."

Chris had a strong independent streak, and was a bit of a loner. "That might be okay," I ventured. "As long as it's not for too long. She might simply need time by herself to process everything that's happened."

"Indeed. And I'm keeping an eye on her, don't you worry. Now you give our best to Mr. Kaminski and his family, and I'll talk to you when you get back. It's very nice of you to do this, you know."

"Oh, I welcome the chance to get out of town, if you want to know the truth."

"It's a nice drive," she said. "Enjoy." She went back into the co-op building, her pace brisk and businesslike.

Zak stood by my pickup, apparently waiting for me.

"So you're going to see Ariel's brother," he said as I approached.

I nodded. "He has a tulip farm in Skagit County."

"Um, I put a note on one of the paintings I want to buy. Is that okay? Do you think he'll let me?"

Oh, wow. "Uh, I don't know. But I'll make sure he knows you want it."

"I'd appreciate that." He sounded so much more grown up than he looked, with the barbed wire tattoos on his biceps and the metal sprouting out of his face. And he'd never be able to fix the damage from those rivets in his ears.

Then his eyes welled up with tears, and he turned quickly away. Raising a hand in farewell, he practically jogged down the street.

Ohmygosh. What was that all about? Ariel had had the most amazing effect on the male of the species. How did she do it?

THIRTEEN

Barr and Robin had talked to Jake and Felicia already, to no avail. I didn't know her very well, but perhaps I'd have better luck talking to Felicia Beagle than they had. For one thing, I was a woman, and I'd found women tended to talk more readily to another women. And then there was also the fact that I wasn't Detective Robin Lane.

Jake had gone back to the office. If Felicia was at home, she'd likely be alone.

The Beagles lived in a new McMansion in a recently developed neighborhood on the east side of town. Their house had a turret, for heaven's sake, and enormous columns flanked the stone steps. I felt like a poor cousin as I parked my old truck in the driveway and got out. There were no vehicles in sight, but there wouldn't be. These were not people who parked on the street.

The doorbell reverberated inside, a long musical tone that would have driven me nuts after a month. Maybe they didn't get many visitors. Maybe Felicia was tone deaf. She opened the door almost immediately, and I wondered whether she was expecting someone.

"Hi," I said. "I don't think we've formally met, but I'm a member of the Cadyville Regional Artists' Co-operative with your husband."

"Of course," she said. "Ms. Reynolds, isn't it?"

"Sophie Mae, please."

"And I'm Felicia. Won't you come in?"

"Thank you."

The interior was decorated expensively, but still felt comfortable and welcoming. The furniture — lots of leather and dark wood — was oversized, which probably suited Jake just fine. Several of his framed photographs adorned the walls, along with a variety of drawings and simple watercolors. The intense, almost cloying perfume from a gardenia in the hallway drifted around us as we walked by, the sound of our footsteps echoing back faintly from the vaulted ceiling.

Felicia herself, perfectly coifed as always, wore white capris and a white T-shirt with a short white jacket. Her manicured toes were painted deep red, and housed within thin, white strappy sandals.

"Can I get you anything to drink?" she asked as she led me into the living room.

"Thanks, but I'm fine. I hope I'm not disturbing you," I said.

"Oh, no," she said. "I'm taking the day off today."

On my days off I wore sweats or shorts and a T-shirt. Heck, I wore the same things when I was working. I sat in a wingback upholstered in butter-soft red leather. No chair should be allowed to be that comfortable. Visitors would never leave.

"Where are you working?" I asked.

Her chin lifted. "I volunteer for a variety of organizations in both Cadyville and Seattle. I'm particularly interested in the theater." She settled gracefully into the matching leather sofa.

I cocked my head, recognition dawning. "You were an actress, weren't you? I recognize you now. What were you in? Let me think . . ."

"I like to say I'm still an actress, though, truth be told, I haven't been paid for it for years." Her voice was smooth and pleasant, her manner warm.

I held up my palms. "I'm sorry. I can't remember where I know you from."

"Most people don't recognize me at all. I

did a few commercials, years ago. And I played Malissa Harris on *Mountain Time* for part of one season."

"Of course! I watched *Mountain Time* when I was in college. It was one of the first prime-time soaps, and since I lived in Colorado I loved that it was set in Vail. You," I pointed at her, "were a very evil lady."

She laughed. "I was indeed. Downright ruthless. I loved playing that character. I only wish it could have lasted longer. But Malissa was written in specifically with the intention of killing her off."

"So why don't you act more now?"

Shrugging, she said, "Cadyville is pretty far from the center of things. I don't need to work. Heck, Jake doesn't even need to work, but he enjoys his practice, and I wouldn't want to take that away from him. Maybe one of these days we'll move closer to the city, but for now we like living here."

I wondered. Felicia, self-possessed as she was, seemed isolated. It didn't seem to bother her, but then again, she didn't seem like the type to let you know if something bothered her. And she was nicer than I'd anticipated. Someone I'd like to have dinner with.

"Enough about my defunct acting career," she said. "Was there a particular reason you dropped by?"

"Well, as I mentioned, I'm part of CRAC, and I know Jake. You know about the murder there, of course."

She nodded. "Of course. Jake's been very concerned about the other co-op members." Her hand flew to her mouth. "Oh, and weren't you the one who found her? How silly of me. You're here to see Jake, aren't you?"

"No, I'm here to see you. Like Jake, I'm worried about how this terrible incident has affected the co-op members. I'm really here because I wanted to check in with you about how Jake is taking it."

Her eyes narrowed. "Why would Jake be taking it worse than anyone else?"

I shrugged. "He seemed more upset about Ariel's death than some. He's a very caring man."

She held my gaze for a long moment. "Meaning?"

I licked my lips. "Nothing. Only . . . you know . . . he's a nice guy."

"Particularly to Ariel."

Thin ice here. I could feel it beginning to crack under my feet. "I don't know. Was he?"

Felicia stood. "I'll let Jake know you stopped by."

"Oh. Um, okay. Thanks." I rose to my feet as well.

She walked me unceremoniously to the front door and opened it. "Thanks for stopping by, Ms. Reynolds. 'Bye, now."

"Um," I said, nonplussed by how smoothly she'd kicked me out. The door shut in my face.

No wonder Barr and Robin hadn't gotten very far questioning the Beagles.

Meghan met me at the front door. "Hannah came by."

My eyes widened, and I began looking wildly up and down the street for Barr's ex or her rental car.

"Oh, she's gone now," Meghan said. "I don't think she looks *that* much like you."

I grabbed her arm and pulled her inside the house. "What did she want?"

She gently pulled out of my grip and studied me. "To talk to you, of course."

"About what?"

Another long look. "About Barr, I expect. I don't know for sure because we didn't chat all that long."

"Did she seem . . . you know?" I swirled my finger by my head.

"Bonkers?"

I nodded.

Meghan's shoulders relaxed, and she laughed. "She seemed like a perfectly reasonable woman, certainly nice enough. When I said you weren't here she said she'd try again tomorrow."

"Ha! Well, I won't be here tomorrow. And come to think of it, she's not supposed to be, either. Did she say where she's staying now that she's checked out of the Horse Acres B&B?"

She shook her head. "No. And I asked if you could call her, but she said she didn't know when she'd be near a phone."

"Probably doesn't want Barr telling her to leave town again."

Meghan said, "That'd be my guess."

"I'm sorry she bothered you," I said. "And it sounds like she's going to do it again tomorrow."

"Will you relax? It's not a big deal. And you said she only took a week off from her job in Wyoming, so she's going to have to leave town pretty soon, anyway."

As long as Hannah didn't quit her job at the Ambrose ranch altogether, thinking she'd soon be swimming in money.

"She came by the house, Barr. What does she want from me? Why isn't she bugging you?" I was clenching the phone so hard it

148

hurt. One by one, I forced my fingers to relax.

He sighed. "I don't know, hon. I really don't. I've asked the patrols to keep a look out for the car she listed on the registration at Horse Acres, but no one has seen her. I'm doing my best to get her out of your hair."

I felt guilty for making a big deal out of it. He had better things to do. "Oh, heck. It's okay. I'm going out of town tomorrow anyway."

"Have you already gone over to CRAC?"

"Yessir. And that phone call Ariel's roommate picked up was probably from Felicia Beagle. Ruth told me Jake had 'fatherly feelings' for Ariel, but his wife misunderstood them."

Barr snorted.

"I agree. She probably didn't misunderstand at all. Apparently Felicia found some e-mails Jake had written to Ariel, and she didn't care for what they said."

"I wonder when she found them," Barr said. "Recently?"

"No idea. I even dropped in on her, thinking she might open up to me."

"Any luck?"

"None at *all*. Does she have an alibi for the time Ariel was killed?"

149

"I'm afraid she does. Jake said he was home with her."

"Oh."

"Don't worry. We'll figure it out. Listen, I need to go. Call you tonight, okay?"

"Okay." I hung up feeling disgruntled.

For one thing, I didn't know if I bought the idea of Jake providing the alibi for his wife. And secondly, it had been several days since Barr and I had spent the evening together, and he'd only offered me a phone call later.

A phone call? That was it? Sheesh.

FOURTEEN

That night I was putting a few things away in my workroom when Erin came down to say good night. She hugged me for so long that I asked if anything was wrong.

She shook her head against my shoulder.

"You sure, Bug?"

A nod, then, "Do I act all snotty about being smart?"

I pulled back so I could look her in the face. She wasn't crying, but she looked pretty miserable nonetheless.

"No. You do not act all snotty about being smart. Who said you did?"

She looked at the floor.

"Zoe?" I guessed.

"Uh huh."

"Do you know why she said that?"

"No." Erin's voice was sullen.

"So when did this come up?" I asked.

"At dinner last night. I was telling her about some of the stuff we did in math camp yesterday." She turned her face up toward mine. "Do you know anything about Fibonacci numbers?"

"Nope. Never heard of them."

"Well, they're this really cool series of numbers that represent the ratio of all sorts of things in nature — the spirals in sea shells and sunflower seed heads and pinecones and — you know about phi, right?"

"Uh . . . sort of."

Her face fell.

"I'm sorry, Bug. I'm just not into math. But you're obviously getting pretty passionate about it, and that's great. No, really," I said, seeing her skepticism.

"Well, when I told Zoe about it, she said I was being all conceited about being smart. She's smart, too, you know. It's not my fault her mom makes her go to soccer camp instead of math camp. So I told her she was being snotty about being a big jock."

"You guys don't usually fight."

She shrugged and looked away. "Yeah."

"Feel pretty bad now, huh," I said.

"I guess." She ground the toe of her flip-flops into the poured concrete floor.

"I bet she feels pretty bad, too. Why don't you give her a call?"

". . . maybe."

"Tomorrow. After you've both slept on it

a little longer."

She hesitated, then nodded. "Okay. G'night, Sophie Mae."

" 'Night, Bug."

At the stairs she turned around. "Are you going to move in with Barr?"

Oh, gosh. Deep breath. "I don't know."

"Well, I hope you don't," she said. "I want you to stay here."

I could only manage a nod.

Planning to leave early the next morning, I called it a night at ten o'clock and went to bed, but for some reason I couldn't settle down. I lay in bed feeling twitchy and itchy and wide, wide awake. Finally, I gave up and went down the hall toward the stairs. Through Meghan's closed bedroom door I could hear her murmuring, talking to Kelly out in New Jersey. As I walked past Erin's open door, Brodie raised his head, his big pointed ears silhouetted against the night-light.

The spinning wheel Ruth had brought over still sat in the living room. She'd also brought two paper bags of fiber for me to practice on. I retrieved a straight-backed chair from the kitchen, set it next to the wheel, and added two small pillows from the sofa to provide back support while I perched on the edge. Chairs actually designed for spinning had very shallow seats, more like stools with tall, narrow backs to enable the spinner to freely pump the foot peddle that rotated the wheel. Carefully, I oiled the moving parts of the wheel to reduce friction and wear and tear. This was a traditional wheel made by the Ashford company. I wondered if something like this was what I would ultimately choose for myself. There were many reputable wheel manufacturers and different designs of wheels. There were even portable ones that folded up and had a handle for carrying.

Of course, the most portable way to spin was the drop spindle, a device that looked like a stick with a perpendicular disk near one end. You stood and spun the spindle, which twisted the fiber attached to the top into yarn. Gravity provided the draw for the yarn. As the spindle neared the floor, you wrapped the yarn around the stick and began the process again. Of course, for me this was all merely theory; as fascinated as I was by the idea, Ruth hadn't taught me how to use one yet.

Expecting to find more of the natural wool I'd used to make what turned out to be a murder weapon, I opened a bag. Instead, I found a luscious rolled batt of Thea Hawke's hand-painted bamboo fiber in sunset hues — the exact thing I'd been so excited to try when I went in for my lesson and instead found Ariel. I'd mentioned how much I liked it to Ruth, and she'd remembered. What a sweetheart. I'd pay her back for it.

Oh, but how it felt, smoothly gliding through my fingers, the colors twisting together to make a gorgeous, variegated yarn that looked good enough to eat. As the spool gradually filled, the tension in my shoulders abated, my breathing deepened, and one by one the thoughts racing around in my head fell still. After awhile, I wasn't thinking about anything at all, the act of spinning fiber into yarn capturing my entire attention. I'd tried to meditate before, but never with an ounce of success. This had to be the most Zen-like thing I'd ever done.

When I ran out of raw fiber, I came back to myself enough to look at the clock. I'd been sitting there, pumping my foot up and down for over an hour! Better than any sleeping pill; I'd drop right off now. Plus, several yards of incredible yarn filled the spool. I'd have to find something marvelous to make with it. Heck, anything I made with it would be marvelous.

I removed the tension from the brake band and slipped the drive band off the wheel, then stood, stretching my palms up to the ceiling to work the kinks out of my back.

Oh, yes, I was addicted. I definitely needed to start shopping for a wheel of my own.

La Conner was located fifty miles northwest of Cadyville. When I left at 7:00 a.m., the air still held the sweetness of dew caressed by the early sun. Sipping coffee from a travel mug, I admired the increasingly pastoral view as I drove north on Interstate 5. At exit 221, I ditched the main highway and headed west through Conway and Stanwood on a series of roads that wound through lush farmland.

For twenty-five years, spring tourists had descended upon La Conner and the surrounding towns of Stanwood and Mount Vernon for the annual tulip festival. Buses took folks out to admire the profusion of multicolored blooms in the fields, where they could ooh and aah like spectators at a fireworks show, take pictures to their hearts' content, and buy more bulbs and tulip-themed geegaws than you could shake a stick at.

It was a lot of fun, granted, but I was glad the festival was over for the year and I'd only have to navigate the usual summer crowds.

Meandering through the bucolic June morning, I reviewed what I knew about Ariel so far. She was a bad artist, but didn't seem to know it. She was too lazy to get the training she needed to improve. Didn't want to deal with college because the expectations were too high, and she'd have to take classes she didn't like in order to get a degree in something she did like. She mooched money from her roommate. Jake Beagle had either a fatherly or carnal interest in her, though there was no evidence she'd been interested in him one way or the other. She wanted to marry money, but she had an affair with the husband of someone she knew.

Scott Popper was at least twenty years older than she was. I mean, that's not the worst thing in the world, but it made no sense in this situation. He wasn't rich, and his wife could have broken Ariel in half if she'd found out.

That thought gave me pause. Chris really could have, physically, strangled Ariel. And she admitted that she knew about the affair. It was a good thing both Ruth and Irene could vouch for her.

What would I have done in Chris' situation?

I frowned at a field of alfalfa and shook my head. I wouldn't want a man who didn't choose to be with me. Maybe Chris had also been unwilling to fight for Scott. Had it been the first time he'd had an affair? And never mind what Ariel got out of the affair — what about Scott? What the heck was wrong with him, to even get involved with her in the first place? Was it simply because she was so pretty?

Maybe. Men could be awfully stupid about physical beauty.

So I thought and drove and drove and thought. Traffic was light, and I made the trip in good time. In La Conner, I stopped at the Wild Radish Cafe and treated myself to breakfast. Then I went for a walk along the waterfront. Visible across the water was Fidalgo Island, home of the Swinomish Indian tribe. Gulls swooped and called, cormorants lurked, and the occasional seal frolicked in the Swinomish Channel.

Looking at my watch, I found I'd managed to waste the whole morning. How decadent!

At a waterfront restaurant I snarfed a quick cup of clam chowder, anxious to meet Ariel's brother and his family. I got back in

158

my pickup and gave up my early bird parking spot. The town was already filling up with day-trippers from Seattle.

FIFTEEN

An unexpected thrill of excitement fluttered through my solar plexus at the thought of learning more about Ariel from people who really knew her. No one I'd talked to so far had been all that close to her. The picture I'd developed was largely one-sided, and less than flattering. Maybe she was kind to animals. Maybe she mentored troubled teens. Maybe she helped out on the tulip farm every year without fail.

I mean, it was possible, right?

A few miles southeast of town, a brightly painted sign advertising Kaminski Tulip Farm hovered over a mailbox covered with stencils of tulips. The arrow at the bottom pointed down a recently graveled drive, toward a house easily visible across the fields. It was white with dark-blue trim, and a big covered porch wrapped around from the eastern-facing front door to the south side of the house. A windbreak of tall poplars, straight and precise as the pickets of a giant fence, marched along to the north. As I drove closer, I saw the impressive vegetable garden sprawled to the south, separated from the porch by a narrow strip of emerald green lawn.

It was an oasis in the brown dirt of the newly harvested fields, but in the spring, floating in the sea of daffodils and tulips of every color imaginable, the tidy and welcoming farmhouse would fade into the background.

My tires crunched up the driveway, and a huge German shepherd came barreling around the corner from the direction of what looked like a barn. Fitting the idea of Ariel into this rural background was beyond difficult. Maybe the family had originally lived in town. Perhaps Rocky was the anomaly, not his sister.

I parked behind a dark blue Suburban, opened my door and reached to pet the dog. He promptly raised his hackles and growled low in his throat. I jerked my hand back. Froze. Tried not to look him in the eye. Of course, I can't hide my emotions from humans, so I don't know why I thought I could hide them from a dog. He advanced slowly, a continual rumble issuing from deep in his chest.

"Tut! Tut, you leave her alone. Get in here." The speaker stood in the shadow of the front porch.

At first I thought she was saying, "tut, tut," bad doggie, but soon realized Tut was the monster's name. He obeyed with alacrity, bounding up the steps to the porch, tail wagging, seemingly the embodiment of man's best friend.

The woman stepped into the light and waved at me. "Don't you worry, he's all right. Come on in!"

I grabbed the gift basket and ventured up the walkway, noting the neat rows of white alyssum, yellow daisies, and purple allium that lined each side of the flagstones. Enormous baskets of fuchsias hung over the porch railing. Half a dozen bird feeders swung from giant iron hooks driven into the ground around the yard. The beneficiaries of this abundance flitted in from the poplars. Beneath the feeders, Oregon juncos and varied thrush grubbed at the fallout. The shouts of children playing carried from behind the house.

"I'm Sophie Mae Reynolds," I said. Tut watched me, but his gently waving tail signaled more of a welcome. "Are you Gabrielle Kaminski?"

The woman came down the porch steps.

"That's me. Everyone calls me Gabi."

She was in her late twenties, buxom, with light brown hair drawn back into a simple pony tail. The sunlight glinted off the smoothness of it. My hand ran through my own short mop when I saw it. Gabi had brown eyes and a sprinkle of freckles across her cheeks and nose. Her lips were surprisingly pink against her tan, and they parted to reveal a slight overbite. She was taller than me, and gave the impression of bulk, mostly because of her chest.

A farmer's wife who looked like a farmer's wife ought to.

I held out the basket of soaps and preserves to her. "I'm Ariel's friend." A slight exaggeration. "I called yesterday about bringing her art up from Cadyville?"

She took the basket and smiled broadly. "Oh, look at all these goodies! That is just so nice of you."

"It's from everyone at the co-op," I said, exaggerating again.

"Well, you just tell everyone thanks, then. It's such a sweet thing to do." She turned back toward the door, still talking. "Now, I've got iced tea brewed, or there's cider from last fall. Or would you rather have a cup of coffee? I can warm some up from — oh, that's silly. I might as well make us up a fresh pot, don't you think?"

"Cider sounds delicious," I said.

I followed her inside. To the left, toys littered the living room. Straight ahead, a spacious kitchen in yellow and white. A basket of peas dominated the middle of the trestle table, and another large basket of produce sat on the counter: beets, Swiss chard, and a few early cherry tomatoes among the greens and onions. Though I'd traveled north, there was more sun and fewer trees here; a microclimate that allowed a longer growing season.

I pointed. "All that from your garden?"

She nodded as she poured out cloudy amber liquid and returned the chunky stoneware pitcher to the refrigerator. Ice cubes hissed and cracked as she handed the glass to me. I breathed in the sweet tang of apples before taking a sip of the cold homemade cider.

"Hope you don't mind if I shell some peas while we talk," she said. "We're having them for dinner, and it takes awhile to work through a big pile, you know?"

"I'll help." I sat down at the kitchen table and reached for a handful of pods.

She smiled, revealing more of the overbite. "Thanks! Just toss the empties in this pail."

"Ariel's artwork is in my pickup," I said.

"Rocky'll unload it later."

"Is he at work?" I asked, a little disappointed.

She nodded. "Putting a new transmission in Ollie Swenson's old Le Baron."

I'd told Gabi when I hoped to arrive, and received the impression Rocky would be there, too. But I didn't want to ask how long he'd be. I could stay for a while. After all, I was on vacation. In the meantime, Gabi seemed quite willing to talk to me, and she had a pile of peas to shell.

I pressed a pod between the pad of my thumb and the side of my forefinger. It opened with a popping sound. "Gabi, I'm so sorry about what happened to Ariel."

"Thanks." Her tone was light.

I looked at her out of the corner of my eye. She didn't seem all that broken up over her sister-in-law's death.

She glanced up at me without raising her head from where her hands worked rapidly over her dishtowel-draped lap. "Were you a close friend of hers?" Ping! A handful of peas bounced into the stainless steel bowl.

"Not what I'd call close, no," I said. "I only recently joined the co-op, and we hadn't had a chance to get to know one another very well. She seemed like a nice girl, though."

I was telling the truth. Until I'd heard about her mooching and affairs, Ariel had seemed like a perfectly nice girl, if a bit of an air-head who lacked empathy.

Gabi smiled uncertainly. She probably wondered why some woman who barely knew her sister-in-law had driven to La Conner to offer her sympathies. Her hands never slowed, though, and the bowl of shelled peas began to fill. The German shepherd wandered into the kitchen, black toenails clicking on the vinyl floor. I eyed him, still leery.

"Don't worry about Tut," Gabi said. "He's territorial — that's why we got him — but once he knows you're okay, everything's fine."

Still, I didn't plan on making any sudden moves. I glanced at my watch. "Does Rocky come home for lunch?"

"Oh, he'll show up pretty soon. He's out in the shop."

"I thought he was putting in a transmission," I said.

"Sure. He's a mechanic. No way could we make it on what the flowers bring in. So he has a shop around the back where locals bring anything with four wheels — and some things with two — for him to work on. Would you like to see it?"

"Yes, I would."

"I thought Rocky'd see you're here and come into the house, but he gets so involved he may not have noticed. I don't usually bother him while he's working, but he's been out there long enough. Let's go."

We got up, leaving the peas, and went out the back door. Three boys raced around the yard, yelling. One of them was waving a stick at the other two, but no one seemed to be in actual danger.

"All of those yours?" I asked.

"Only two." She pointed. "That one's Evan, and that one's Noah. They're both six. Evan is seven minutes older."

"I bet they're a handful."

She laughed. "Justin's the tall one in the red shirt. Belongs to the neighbor down the road. He might as well be mine, though, as much time as he spends here."

The shop was in what I'd thought was a barn. No horses, just horsepower. Inside, the concrete floor was pristine. Three cars awaited Rocky's attention, and the fourth hunkered over a pit in the middle of the floor.

"Dang it!" a male voice said from somewhere. "Gabi, that you? Grab that clutch spring compressor and bring it over here."

She smiled at me and went to an array of

tools on a bench along one wall, searching with her eyes. "I don't see it. Oh, wait a minute, here it is." She hefted an awkward and arcane-looking contraption and walked around to the far side of the pit.

"Hey honey," Gabi said. "Ariel's friend from the co-op is here."

Rocky came around from the other side of the car, eyebrows raised. He was about five-ten, with dark, prematurely thinning hair and a hooked nose. Muscles roped through his arms and across his bare chest and abdomen.

"Hiya," he said, holding out a grimy hand. Then he flushed, pulled it back and began wiping it on a greasy rag. "Sorry. Occupational hazard."

"No problem," I assured him. Fishing in my oversized tote bag, I found the sympathy card. "I brought the paintings Ariel had on display at the co-op. And this." I held out the envelope.

He took it, carefully drew out the card, and opened it. He looked at it for a long time. His eyes moved from one signature to another, and back again. At last he looked up, and his face was wet.

"I didn't know she had so many friends. Thank you."

I swallowed, feeling like a big, fat liar.

"You're very welcome."

A quick glance at Gabi. She was focused on her husband, face pinched with distress.

"Ariel was the artistic one," Rocky said. "She was the one in the family who got all the talent. I just know how to fix things." He looked at the ground and shook his head, smiling.

I was at a complete loss as to what to say; any response was bound to come across as insincere. For the gazillionth time I wished I was better at prevarication.

Luckily, Gabi stepped in. "You're a better mechanic than your sister was an artist, and you always were."

"Don't talk about her like that, Gabi." Grief laced the words. He turned to me. "She was a wonderful artist. And she was just as good as me at fixing cars and stuff. We were restoring that '69 Cougar there, together." He gestured to a maroon street rod in the corner. "Hadn't had much of a chance to work on it in the last year or so. She couldn't come up to visit much, and I only work on it when she's here."

We all spent awhile looking at the half-finished vehicle on blocks, pieces and parts arranged precisely on the tarp around it. I had a sudden flash that the car would become a mechanical shadow of Miss Haversham. I saw it a hundred years in the future, in exactly the same place, rusted, covered with dust and cobwebs, waiting for Ariel to come back and help her brother put it together again.

Rocky walked a couple steps away, as if unable to look at the Cougar anymore. The movement shook me out of my daze.

"I had no idea Ariel was mechanically inclined," I said.

His small smile didn't reach his eyes. "She didn't look like that kind of girl, she was so little and pretty, but she could take an engine apart and put it back together, have it running like a kitten in no time."

"Was it just the two of you?" I asked. "Any other brothers or sisters?"

"Nope. Just us. For years we only had one another, after both of our parents were killed in a car wreck."

"That must have been horrible. How old were you?"

"I was twenty-one," Rocky said. "Ariel was sixteen."

Right. She'd mentioned that when she more or less said Chris should just get over Scott's death. "That must have been especially difficult for her, so young," I said.

"It was hard on both of us. But I took care of her, and we got through it." The last words were clipped, and he moved farther away.

His nerves were already raw, and in my enthusiasm to understand Ariel I'd apparently overstepped the bounds of tactful behavior once again.

"I'm sorry," I said.

He smiled and shook his head. "That's okay. It's kind of hard to talk about right now, is all."

"Of course."

He took a deep breath, closed his eyes, and then opened them again as if making a decision. "Do you know who found her?"

Oh, God. "Um, yeah."

He waited.

"I'm afraid it was me."

His eyes widened. "Oh!"

Sixteen

Well, I have to tell you, I'd be hard pressed to find a more awkward moment than that. We both looked anywhere but at each other.

Finally, Rocky said, "Well, maybe it's not good to speak too much of the dead."

Not quite what I'd been hoping for this trip, but understandable. He seemed like a genuinely nice guy, and it was obviously too soon to quiz him about his sister.

"A police detective came yesterday, with all kinds of questions. Horrible questions. I can't do it anymore." He mopped his face with the grimy rag. "I mean, how could anyone have done that —" His voice cracked, and he turned away.

"I'm so sorry," I said yet again.

He nodded, silent.

Gabi indicated the door with a jab of her chin. Once she and I were outside again, she said, "He doesn't like people to see him so upset."

"Of course," I said. "Maybe you could help me unload Ariel's art, and I'll be on my way."

"Why don't you take it back to the co-op and sell it and then send us the money," Gabi said, her voice laced with bitterness.

I'm sure my surprisc showed on my face.

"She owed us a lot," Gabi said in a confiding tone.

So much for not speaking about the dead.

"Well," I said. "You might be able to sell one of the pieces. There's a note on one of them from someone who's interested in buying it."

Rocky's voice came from behind us. "I want that art. Every single piece if it. Just show me where it is."

Gabi shook her head and walked toward the house. I led him around to my truck and opened the topper. I reached for a painting.

"I'll take care of them. You go ahead in the house and have Gabi gct you something to drink," he said.

I didn't mention his wife had already plied me with cider, but obediently turned around and walked toward the front steps.

"Miz Reynolds?"

I turned.

"I'm sorry if I sounded rude. I want you

to know how much I appreciate you driving these all the way up here."

"No problem at all," I said. I watched him fumble with one of the large canvases for a moment, but couldn't think of anything to say that would make any difference at all. I turned and went into the house.

I found Gabi sitting back at the kitchen table, working away on the pile of pea pods. Her face was red, her hands a blur.

I sat down and reached for another handful. "I'm sorry if I upset your husband."

"Oh, heck. I'm the one upset him, not you. I have a hard time keeping my mouth shut about that sister of his, even now. He wouldn't stand for it when she was alive, either." Her expression was strained with worry. "I guess now we'll never see that money."

I looked around the kitchen. The parts of the house I'd seen so far were clean, but well-worn. The vinyl in front of the sink was torn and the curtains were faded. I didn't know how much land they were able to devote to the tulip bulbs, or how much Rocky was able to bring in with his mechanical work, but the budget here seemed pretty tight.

"If it helps at all," I said, "I don't think keeping the art at the co-op would do much good. It wasn't exactly flying out the door. I doubt that you'd have seen much money from it, anyway."

Gabi's laugh was sharp. "Well, that figures. Ariel and Rocky were the only ones who ever thought she was any good."

"Well, I'm not saying she was bad," I hedged. "Just not, you know, popular with the buyers. It's possible she'd have sold more if the prices hadn't been quite so high."

The look she gave me said she didn't believe me. "Let me tell you a little something about Ariel." Another handful of peas rained into the bowl. "She was a slut."

I paused in my pea shelling, jarred by how she grated out the word.

"Oh, I know. I'm not supposed to talk about her like that. But if you knew her at all you'd know I'm telling the truth. Are you married?"

I shook my head.

"Boyfriend?"

"Yes."

"Well, I sure hope you didn't let him spend much time around her, because men were idiots whenever she was around, and that girl knew how to take advantage of it."

"I'm not sure what you mean. Oh, I know she was pretty popular with the male of the species, but how did she take advantage?" I caught myself starting to lean forward in eagerness and forced myself to sit back in my chair.

"Every which way she could," Gabi said. "I've known that family forever, grew up on the place next to here."

"Rocky married the girl next door."

She smiled. "Yep. We were meant for each other from the start."

"So you knew his sister very well."

"Too well. Here's an example of what I mean: in high school, she had an English teacher, name of Randolph Owens. Made the kids read, lots and lots, as part of his class. Ariel didn't like having to read a lot — too boring, too much work, and she sure didn't like being told exactly what she was supposed to read. So she didn't do it. Tried to fake it in class, got some CliffsNotes, you know the drill. But she wasn't clever enough to pull it off, and everyone in class knew she hadn't done any of the reading, including Mr. Owens. Heck, she even talked about it."

I glued an interested look on my face and shelled faster. So Ariel was lazy. That wasn't exactly a news flash.

"But she got an A in that class," Gabi continued. "She and Mr. Owens had an 'arrangement,' if you know what I mean. He lost his job over it."

Well, that *was* news. "That's terrible," I said.

"Now don't be thinking she was some kind of victim. She seduced him, and she did it because his class was hard, and she didn't want to do the work in order to get a good grade. And she needed the good grade in order to up her GPA and get into college. Not that it did much good, since once she got into college she just turned around and dropped out. Maybe the professors there weren't as easy to manipulate.

"She was a user. She used people to get what she wanted, and if that meant she had to sleep with them, well, that didn't seem to bother her one bit. Didn't have much use for women in general, since her charm was somewhat lost on them. But still, there were those who saw how little and cute she was and wanted to mommy her, take care of the little thing. She wasn't above using that, either."

"But she didn't fool you," I said.

"Not for long. But her brother, my darling husband, who is just about the sweetest man on this planet in my opinion, well, she played him like a fiddle their whole lives. He's five years older'n her, but she managed him like I manage this mangy mutt here." She chucked the German shepherd under the chin as if it were a child.

"That's sad, in a way," I said. "People like that don't usually have a lot of friends. I imagine she was pretty lonely."

Gabi blinked. "I never really thought about it that way, but I guess you're right. 'Course she had that friend from high school. Lindsey. Thick as thieves then, and I know they're still in contact."

"Lindsey," I repeated. "I think she might have mentioned her." A bald-faced lie, that, but Gabi didn't seem to notice.

"Lindsey Drucker. Still lives here, just down Bowers Road. She's married now. She and Ariel were awful close, but they sure took different paths in life. Lindsey seems happy enough with the one she chose."

The back door opened and the kitchen filled with loud boy voices clamoring for a snack. Gabi rose and fetched a gallon of milk and a cookie jar packed to the top with old-fashioned chocolate chip cookies.

"All right, you heathens. Go out and eat on the porch, where I can just sweep up after your mess." Loading each child with a plastic glass of milk and a handful of cookies, she shooed them out of the house. They seemed content enough to go, taking Tut with them.

"Don't you feed that dog any cookies," Gabi called. "If he eats chocolate he'll die."

She sat back down and gave me a sheepish grin. "I know it would just make him sick, as much chocolate as is in those cookies, but I've learned by now that boys don't do so well with subtle differences like that. Here, have a cookie."

I looked at my watch. "Gosh. I didn't realize it was so late. I need to get going."

"Oh, stay for dinner, Sophie Mae."

"I'd love to, but I can't." I felt a little grumpy, realizing I'd spent so much time with the Kaminskis and had learned so little. The story about the high school teacher was interesting, but likely didn't have anything to do with Ariel's murder. If I hurried back to La Conner, at least I could fit in a solitary seafood dinner before having to drive back home.

"We're grilling out," Gabi said. "Got a nice fresh salmon yesterday from a friend who fishes, these peas, and there are some baby potatoes ready in the garden to cook up with them."

Hmmm. That sounded a lot like a seafood dinner right there. And, the thought niggled at me even though I tried to ignore it, I might still learn more about Ariel.

"Please? Heck, you can even spend the night. No reason to drive all the way back tonight, is there?"

Surprised by the invitation to stay overnight, I realized this woman, who didn't seem to work outside of the house, was quite lonely. The prospect of remaining longer grew on me. Maybe I could assuage Rocky a little. I even liked the energy of the boys, now clustered on the front porch playing some quieter game.

But the meal offer clinched the deal. Fresh wild salmon and produce from the garden.

"That dinner sounds terrific," I said. "I'd love to stay, thank you. But I do need to get back to Cadyville this evening."

Gabi looked pleased. "Come out and keep me company while I get us some potatoes."

I put the bowl of fresh peas on the counter, and Gabi hefted the heavy pail of shells, heading out the door to the garden. "These'll go straight into the compost pile."

"May I use your bathroom?" I asked.

"Down the hall there." She pointed through the living room to a hallway that ran behind the stairs to the second floor. "Ignore the boys' room; it's a disaster."

I peeped into the room in question as I walked to the bathroom. Disaster, heck. It looked like a superfund site.

On my way back out to join Gabi, I stopped cold. Tucked away in the corner of the toy-strewn living room sat a spinning wheel. It wasn't one of those cutesy decorative ones either; it looked a lot like a Schacht I had considered buying. A pile of seductive rovings and rolled batts overflowed a basket next to it, and the spool still on the wheel held a tasty variegated yarn in chocolate, red, and orange. The tuft of the batt left to be spun looked shiny and soft, maybe cashmere, or even silk.

Resisting the urge to plunge my hands into the basket of fiber, I hurried out to join Gabi. I found her gently digging into hills of purple potatoes, teasing out the tiny new offerings near the surface. The skins of the potatoes were iridescent in the sunlight when I rubbed off the dirt. Unlike purple beans, purple potatoes kept their color when cooked.

"These are going to be gorgeous with the bright green of the new peas," I said.

Gabi grinned. "I know. Rocky doesn't realize it, but that's one of the reasons I grow this variety. I just love the way they look with other food on the plate."

"I saw your spinning wheel in the house. Wouldn't a combination of those colors in a two-ply yarn be amazing?"

She sat back on her heels and stared at me with delight on her face. "Sophie Mae, do you spin?"

I nodded, then shrugged. "I just started, but I can't see stopping now. Never imagined something so mundane could be so addictive."

"I've been doing it for years, but it's hard to find the time."

"Years? I bet you have quite a stash of fiber and yarn." Spinners, like knitters and quilters, were known collectors of the basic "ingredients" of their craft.

She laughed. "Rocky would die if he realized how much."

"Would you show me some of it?" I asked, kneeling beside her and digging my fingers into the dark lush soil piled up around the potato plants.

"I'd love to!"

She stood and lifted the pail, which now held the delicate baby potatoes, and we went back into the house.

Rocky came in from the shop and sat at the kitchen table sipping hot coffee as Gabi and I got things ready to steam and grill. His stoicism had returned in full measure, and I was glad to see any lingering rancor between him and Gabi had vanished. Tag-teaming each other and finishing each other's sentences, husband and wife told me a bit about how the tulip farm worked. Then the boys came in, and we were treated to a recounting of the day's adventures while Gabi whipped up a pie crust. She sent the twins out to cut rhubarb and pick strawberries; by the time we had a big salad together they were back with their booty and we assembled the pie.

We ate under an apple tree out back. It wasn't until after dinner and dishes were done that I got a dose of Gabi's fiber stash.

SEVENTEEN

As I started for the basket in the corner by the spinning wheel, Gabi called from the kitchen that we were going down to the basement. The sky was still light, but the sun would set soon. Rocky offered to get the boys into bed, and Gabi took him up on the offer.

"I'll be getting myself off to bed then, too," he said. "Long day tomorrow, and it starts early. Sophie Mae, it was nice to meet you. Thanks for bringing the paintings all the way up here. I sure appreciate it."

He still didn't say Ariel's name.

"It was no trouble. I'm glad I could help. And what a treat that dinner was!" I said.

He nodded at that. "Sure was." He gave his wife a peck on the cheek, bid us goodnight again and went to round up the twins.

Gabi led the way downstairs, bottle of merlot in hand. I followed with two glasses. The basement was unfinished, but in one corner she'd created an area devoted to crafts. A little natural light came in from two window wells on that side of the house. She augmented that with a combination of fluorescent and incandescent lights, so the space was bright and cheery even as the sunlight faded outside. A sewing machine dominated a long industrial-looking table, with a set of half-finished curtains heaped beside it. Behind, shelves held an assortment of fabrics, and a folded quilting frame leaned against another wall. Apparently, when it came to crafting, Gabi was more than a one-trick pony.

With a flourish, she opened a wide, deep cabinet in the corner, revealing a rich assortment of sensuous fibers and neatly wrapped balls of yarn stacked in baskets. The colors ranged from delicate baby-blanket pastels to deep, saturated jewel tones vibrating with exuberance. They all begged to be touched, and I happily complied.

"Oh, wow," I said. "This is some stash. Did you spin all of these yarns?"

"Not all of them. Sometimes in a yarn store or a knitting shop you just can't resist picking up something new, you know?"

"Yeah. It gets awfully expensive, though, doesn't it?"

"I've gathered this stuff over years and years, and I have friends who raise sheep and alpacas. That means a lot of very cheap fiber if I'm willing to clean it, card it, and dye it myself."

I looked at her in amazement. "You do all that?"

She looked at the floor, modesty prevailing. "When I can. It's hard with two boys and a husband to take care of. Sometimes, though? I stay up most of the night spinning, and Rocky doesn't even know it, he's such a sound sleeper. I'm tired the next day, but somehow calmer, too."

"I know what you mean." I stroked a particularly silky royal blue and teal roving. "What's this made of? It's not alpaca, is it?"

"Oh, no. Hmm. Let's see, I think it's soy." She dug out a tag I hadn't noticed. "Yep, soy fiber. I ordered it online last year, curious about how it would spin up, but I haven't had a chance to get to it yet."

We spent the next hour exploring the offerings of her extensive fiber stash and talking about the different flavors. In addition to soy — and if you could make yarn out of bamboo, why not make it out of soy, for heaven's sake — she had silk "handkerchiefs," a variety of sheep's wool from coarse to fine, fluffy alpaca, angora, cashmere, mohair, even a tuft or two of musk ox.

"Musk ox? You've got to be kidding," I said.

"Oh, no. You can even get camel hair to spin, and some people spin up the hair from their dogs."

"I bet that smells great if you use it to make a sweater and then get caught in the rain."

She laughed. "Then there are the plant fibers. You've seen the bamboo and soy, but of course there's also corn and cotton and hemp and flax."

"Flax?"

"That's what linen is made out of. Some people say in the fairy tale, Rumpelstiltskin spun flax into gold for the miller's daughter, not straw."

"Huh. Now how did I manage to live this long without knowing that?"

We finally exhausted ourselves, as well as the wine, and returned upstairs. It was dark outside, and I was surprised to find the clock read almost eleven-thirty.

"Uh-oh," I said, and dug my cell phone out of my bag. Sure enough, Meghan had left me a message.

It began, "Why do you even have that thing if you don't turn it on, Sophie Mae?"

I sighed. Just because I was starting to remember to turn on my cell phone didn't mean I was used to actually carrying it around on my person all the time. She should be happy I had it at all.

The message ended, "Are you coming home tonight or not?" In between there was a lot of stuff that sounded a tad too much like nagging from my housemate. I hated being nagged, but I had to admit that in this case I pretty much deserved whatever I got.

I deleted the message and hung up the phone, sighing. "Better go. I'm in trouble at home."

"Was that your boyfriend?"

"Worried housemate," I said.

"Oh, gosh. You can't go now," Gabi said. "It's way too far, and you've been drinking."

Well, true enough, but I'd only indulged in a glass at dinner and another in the basement. I'd be okay having ingested ten or eleven ounces of wine over five hours. However, the wine bottle was indeed empty, and now that I really looked at Gabi, I could see she was flushed and a little tipsy.

"I'll be all right," I said, though the truth was that I felt bone weary, and the thought of the drive didn't hold much appeal.

"Besides, I didn't bring an overnight bag."

"Oh, don't worry about that," she insisted. "I can set you up with everything you need. You just call home and let her know you'll drive back first thing in the morning."

I made a decision. "I'll see if I can get a hold of her. If I can, I'll go ahead and stay."

"Oh, goodie," Gabi said.

That gave me pause. Oh, goodie, indeed. But the idea of waiting to drive home in the morning was still mighty appealing. I called home, and Meghan answered on the second ring.

"Are you okay?" she asked.

"I'm fine. Things kind of got away from me, and now it's late, and I'm going to stay up here."

"You're still in La Conner?"

"Close enough. I'm at Ariel's brother's house. We got to yammering, and his wife? Gabi? She's a spinner, so we got kind of involved in talking about . . . well, stuff. You know."

Meghan sighed. "I know."

"I've had a couple of glasses of wine, too, and Gabi invited me to stay. It seems like a good idea."

"I guess you'd better then."

"Tell me I didn't wake you."

"No, I was talking to Kelly. Did you find

189

out anything about Ariel?"

"Not much. I'll tell you about it when I get home."

"All right. I'll see you tomorrow."

Gabi was delighted to learn I'd be staying, all oh goodie all over again. "While you were on the phone I put out a nightgown in the guest bedroom, and I had a spare toothbrush and some other things. You'll have to share the bathroom with us upstairs, but at least the little beasts don't go in there, so it's clean."

I thanked her, and turned toward the stairway to the second floor.

"Oh, wait," she said. "Let's sit out on the porch now that it's cooled off and have another glass of wine before bed."

"I think I've had enough," I said. "It's been a long day."

"Please?"

Oh, Lord. I was beginning to regret staying, but I was stuck now. "The bottle's empty."

"I opened a new one." She held up a fresh bottle of white zinfandel like a trophy.

Taking a deep breath, I said, "Okay. One glass, and then I'm off to bed."

"Okay."

On the porch, I had to admit the cool air felt nice. It smelled of vegetation and dust, occasionally cut by the sweet scent of a hardy jasmine planted in a pot in the corner. I could make out the tiny, white star-shaped flowers wending up the porch railing.

I took a sip of wine, which was enough to confirm I still detested white zin.

Gabi said in a suddenly quiet voice, "I know Rocky's reaction must seem odd."

I tried to switch gears from our previous light-hearted conversation. "He's grieving. Everyone does that differently."

"There was a policewoman here yesterday."

"He mentioned that."

"She asked a lot of questions."

"Well, that's her job," I said.

She shifted in the chair beside mine. "Some of the questions were a little harsh. Put Rocky on edge. She almost acted like it was Ariel's fault she got killed."

Nice, Robin. Real nice.

"But he answered the questions, didn't he?" Of course I itched to know what the questions — and answers — were, but I resisted. "Because he wants to find out who killed his sister, too."

"Oh, sure. Of course. It was just kind of hard on him, you know. He loved Ariel, but she's caused him a lot of grief over the years. At least this will be the last of it."

"The money?" I asked.

"And the men."

I took a chance. "You know, she was having an affair with the husband of one of the other artists at the co-op."

Gabi shook her head. "Another married man? Of course she was."

I shrugged. "Maybe they fell in love. It happens."

"Oh, she wasn't in love." Gabi sipped her wine. "Ariel didn't know how to love, not really. Trust me, she benefited in some very practical way."

"How sad."

Gabi was silent for a moment. "And dangerous."

Maybe it was the hour, maybe the wine, but the conversation was taking a baffling turn. "Dangerous how?"

"Their parents. She didn't get along with them. Always felt like they were too hard on her."

I waited.

Gabi leaned in, the cloying smell of cheap wine rolling off her. "The car wreck. I saw Ariel doing something to their car before they left that day." She sat back.

It took me a moment. "Are you saying she caused the crash that killed their parents?"

Light leaking out of the window from

inside illuminated the fear on Gabi's face when she realized she'd said too much. "Oh, heavens no. It's not like that."

"Then what did you mean?" I asked.

Gabi looked toward the screen door and lowered her voice even more. I could hardly hear her as she said, "Just forget I said anything, okay? It doesn't matter now anyway, does it? She's dead." She put her hand to her forehead. "I guess I just can't hold my wine. Please don't say anything to Rocky."

"He doesn't know?" I asked.

She shook her head again, her chin swinging back and forth in an exaggerated way. "There's nothing to know."

EIGHTEEN

I was awakened by the distant sound of a rooster the next morning, crowing at the brightening hour of five a.m. Too early to go downstairs, and no way was I going back to sleep. I'd been half thinking, half dreaming about what I'd learned about Ariel so far, and now that I was fully awake the thoughts were clamoring too loud to allow further rest. Plumping my pillows and sitting up in bed, I took in the details of the Kaminski's guest room. I'd been too tired the night before to do much more than change into Gabi's kind offer of a nightgown, turn out the light, and climb into bed.

Looking around in the dawn light, I saw cream-painted walls and a ceiling so pink it was almost fuchsia. Next to the louvered doors of the closet, an old-fashioned white dressing table dominated one corner, the surface noticeably empty of girlish potions and unguents. Opposite the window hung two giant posters, both velvet textured and brightly colored so they'd glow under a black light. The first showed a rather petulant-looking fairy with elaborate, luminous wings; the second depicted a winding road to an imposing castle that could have been either romantically gothic, or frighteningly Bram Stoker. I found both of them a little creepy, and was glad I hadn't noticed them before dropping off to sleep the night before. A battered dresser, gauzy pink curtains, and the double bed — dressed in pink and white gingham, for heaven's sake — rounded out the furnishings.

With two boys in the house now, and the fact that the Kaminski children had grown up here, there was no other reasonable explanation: I was in Ariel's girlhood room. The thought gave me a bit of a turn, then made me curious. After my interesting evening with her family, especially Gabi, my mental picture of Ariel was beginning to fill out. Still, I had to remember that, while the information I was getting from Gabi didn't really contradict anything I'd learned earlier, it was still just one source.

Swinging my legs over the edge of the bed, I reached for my shorts, now in a crumpled heap on the floor. I must have been too tired to fold them. Wouldn't Barr love living with a slob like me? He should count himself lucky I'd put off moving in.

I dressed, happy enough to add the hooded sweatshirt Gabi had given me to wear the night before to my early morning attire. It was chilly in the new dawn, and likely to stay that way until the sun had a chance to work her magic. No one seemed to be moving around in the household yet.

I eyed the closet.

The louvered doors didn't open smoothly, but I managed to make a minimum of racket. It was stuffed with clothes, most of them winter garb that looked like it belonged to the entire family. Gabi made good use of Ariel's old closet for storage. Well, what did I expect? A shrine to the departed sister? Hardly. I wondered whether Ariel had resented her space being taken over like that.

Quietly pawing through the items hanging on the rod, I found two dresses in the back that were certainly not suitable winter wear. They were too skimpy for most summer temperatures, and even then only if you were going for a certain look. I took one out and held it up to the window, noting the outline of the corner of the barn roof outside through the flimsy material.

Wow. There was a part of me that was

slightly scandalized, and part of me that admired anyone with the chutzpah to actually wear something like that in public.

More rooting around revealed a few more pieces of barely-there clothing items: tiny halters, short short skirts, and the like. But nothing of real interest. So Ariel had dressed like a hooker when she lived at home — what bearing did that have on her murder? Whenever I'd seen her she'd been dressed provocatively, but nothing like this. It appeared her taste in clothing had matured a little.

I closed the doors to the closet and began opening drawers. I mean, after all, if you put someone in a room for the night and say it's the "guest room," it's not exactly surprising if they open a few drawers, right?

The dressing table held precisely nothing. Not even dust. Thoroughly cleaned out. The small bureau held two utterly empty drawers, but the third, bottom drawer, was full of high school annuals. Some of them were Rocky's, and some were Ariel's. The siblings had been five years apart in age, so their high school careers hadn't overlapped; eight annuals altogether.

Settling myself cross-legged on the floor, I pulled out the first one and thumbed through it. Rocky's, when he was a junior.

He was nice enough looking now, but the school picture had captured a gleam in his eye that seemed to be missing in the man I'd met yesterday. He'd been one of the more active kids in school: on the football, basketball, and wrestling teams, as well as belonging to Future Farmers of America and Future Business Leaders of America. The abundance of friends and teachers who had signed his yearbook, and what they wrote, indicated he was well-liked by a variety of people. In fact, he'd been quite the big fish in the small pond of the La Conner school system. I flipped through a few more pages and found Gabi's picture. She was a year younger than Rocky and sported a very short haircut. She had a big happy grin pasted on her face. No doubt a ridiculously well-adjusted teenager.

All his annuals had the same flavor, but when I got to his sister's, they told a slightly different story. The pictures of Ariel as a freshman and a sophomore showed a gawky girl, first slightly gap-toothed, then second with braces presumably to correct said gap. All light-brown hair and hesitant smile, she looked skinny and awkward and very, very uncomfortable about having her picture taken. Frightened, tenuous, unsure; it was shocking how different that little girl in the pictures was from the young woman I'd known.

Something must have happened in the summer between her sophomore and junior year, though, because the Ariel pictured in the last two yearbooks was quite different. She'd dyed her hair blonde, loaded on the eye-liner, lowered her neckline by a degree that no doubt tempted official school reprimand, and gazed at the camera with a hard, determined smile.

Ariel had been sixteen when her parents died. My bet was that it happened between those two yearbook photos. Could her transformation have been a reaction to losing her mother and father?

The new and improved Ariel was certainly sexier in a crass kind of way, and, if the story about the English teacher was true, she'd put it to immediate use. Could Gabi have been jealous of her sister-in-law? Or did she just dislike her? What I'd learned so far about Ariel painted her as the kind of person who demanded instant gratification, took shortcuts to get what she wanted, and was not willing to wait. Impatient. Owed.

In fact, Ariel was beginning to sound like a bit of a sociopath. Could you be a bit of a sociopath? Or was that like being a little pregnant? She was charming as the dickens up front, but as you got to know her those charms faded. A social parasite, taking advantage of the people around her — and especially taking advantage of the particular weaknesses of men — to get what she wanted.

Except she wasn't all that good at it. At least not yet. Still young. And possibly becoming more effective with time.

What had Scott Popper offered her? What practical benefit, as Gabi put it, had Ariel reaped from the affair?

Scott Popper, ready to leave his wife to be with Ariel.

Who died in a car wreck.

Lifting the books to place them back in the drawer, I nearly dropped them.

A good driver, a semi-professional driver, for that matter. Certainly well trained as a police officer. Scott Popper, who died in a car wreck.

Just as his lover's parents had.

His lover, who, whatever she might have wanted from him, might not have wanted his city-salaried self on her hands full time.

His lover, the girl who was such a good car mechanic.

NINETEEN

I managed to return the high school year-books to the dresser drawer. When I pushed the drawer back in, it shrieked as if in agony. Slowly, I pulled it back out and tried to re-align the gliders. This time it slid on the track with only a low moan, but wouldn't go all the way in. I removed the drawer completely and, on my hands and knees, peered into the dark recesses under the dresser.

Something on the floor, way back there.

I leaned in, cheek to the floor and butt up in the air, and scrabbled among the dust bunnies with my fingertips. Finally, I grasped hold of the edge of whatever it was and dragged it out to the light of day.

A book, fabric covered, with one corner all bent up from having the drawer jam into it. It was filthy, and one edge had yellowed after obvious water damage. I opened it and recognized Ariel's spiky handwriting from the few times I'd seen it at the co-op.

Footsteps in the hallway paused outside my door. I froze.

An eon later, they moved on and went downstairs. Hurriedly, I pushed the drawer back in. It moaned like a wounded animal again. Standing, I took the book and stuffed it into the bottom recesses of my tote bag. Then I pulled the covers up, tidied the bed, grabbed the toothbrush Gabi had given me the night before, and opened the door.

Noah and Evan hurtled past me and down the stairs, calling, "Hi!" and "Hello!" over each other. And then, from the kitchen I heard, "Hey Mom, can we have pancakes?"

I turned to see Rocky come out of his and Gabi's bedroom. He paused when he saw me, surprised.

"Good morning," I said, trying to sound cheery.

"Uh, morning." He walked down the hall barefoot, carrying a pair of tube socks in his hand. "Everything all right?"

Meaning, why are you still here?

"Oh, sure. Time just got away from us last night, talking yarn and stuff, and Gabi offered to let me stay." His face remained impassive. "So, I took her up on it," I finished in a more subdued tone.

"I see. Well, I hope you slept well." He

didn't wait to find out if, in fact, I had slept well, but walked past me and down the stairs without another word.

Maybe he resented my spending the night in his sister's bed. I had to admit it was a little weird.

I strode down the hallway to the bathroom where I splashed water on my face, brushed my teeth and futzed a little with my hair. It looked like I'd just rolled out of bed, which I had, but it always looked like that now, so there wasn't much help for it. I grabbed my bag and followed in Rocky's footsteps.

In the living room, I paused. Even with the gluttony of fiber caressing and fondling the evening before, we'd never looked at the wonderful stuff spilling out of the basket by Gabi's spinning wheel. The rattle of pans and clamor of voices carried out from the kitchen. I tiptoed over to the basket, went down on one knee, and plunged both hands into the beautiful fluffy goodness.

I just wanted a quick hit, and would have stopped there, but when I separated the batts and slivers waiting their turn on the wheel, I saw the familiar sunset pastels of my new favorite fiber.

It wasn't mine, of course. It was Gabi's. But it was the same hand-painted bamboo Ruth had left for me when she brought her wheel over to the house. The same delicious softness that had soothed my soul in the middle of the night and made me completely forget about Barr, Hannah, and Ariel et al. And right next to it, another batt with Thea Hawke's label attached, this one an ethereal mixture of blue and green and pink.

Gently, I ran my fingertips over it and smiled. Something tickled my memory. Hadn't I seen this color combination before?

"What are you doing?"

My head jerked up and I saw Gabi, looking disheveled and tired, standing in the doorway to the living room.

"I, uh, never got a chance to look at what's in here," I said. "Sorry. Didn't mean to presume."

Gabi flushed. "No, I'm sorry. I didn't mean to snap. I guess I'm a little cranky this morning — not used to late nights, especially not involving wine."

Standing, I said, "Oh, gosh, that's okay. I sure appreciate you putting me up for the night, but I'll go ahead and get out of your hair."

I was dying to see what Ariel had written in that book.

A book I was essentially stealing. Not good. If there was anything important in there, I'd bungled things. Would it be admissible in court? Maybe I should put it back. But then no one would know what was in it, important or not. Could Barr and Robin get a warrant for an old journal? Unlikely. I couldn't think of another way to see what Ariel had written. Swallowing my doubt, I decided to take the chance.

I pointed to the basket. "Isn't Thea's stuff great? I just finished spinning a few ounces of it. Amazing."

Gabi frowned.

"The pastel bamboo."

She came over and stood beside me, and I reached down and pulled the batt out, to show her what I was talking about.

"Oh, that. Yes, it's pretty, isn't it? I think I got it online."

"Uh oh. Don't tell me that. I could develop a serious Internet shopping illness for this kind of stuff," I said.

"Every once in awhile I can't help but order something." She bent her head. "Pretty self-indulgent, I know."

I handed her the batt. "Good for you."

She stroked it a couple times, as if it were a baby animal, and returned it to the basket. "What would you like for breakfast?"

"Oh, no. Nothing for me. I can't impose on your wonderful hospitality anymore. Besides, I have to get back."

"Are you sure?" But she couldn't quite hide her relief.

"I'm sure." I stripped off the sweatshirt and handed it to her, then went over and leaned into the kitchen.

The twins sat at the table, slurping their orange juice and making play plans for their day. Beside them Rocky listened with a half-smile and sipped coffee from a mug advertising the Skagit Valley Tulip Festival from six years before.

"Goodbye," I said. "And thanks for everything."

"Bye!" the twins said in unison.

"You drive safe now, Sophie Mae," Rocky said. "And thank you for bringing up the pictures."

"I'm glad I could help. I'll be thinking about you."

He inclined his head in acknowledgment.

As I turned to pull the door closed behind me, I saw Gabi pop a couple of aspirin in her mouth and chase them with a swallow of coffee.

I wanted to go home, actually feeling a little homesick. Maybe it was silly to feel that way after just one night, but the atmosphere at the Kaminskis in the cold light of day made me miss my morning routine with Meghan and Erin. And if I missed it after one pleasant evening out of town, how much would I miss it if I moved? Would it be so bad, not moving in with Barr?

He'd understand.

Wouldn't he?

But homesick or not, I was starving, not to mention intensely curious. I stopped at the Calico Cupboard Bakery in La Conner, mouth watering the second I hit the doorway. A serving of their famous bread pudding and large cup of coffee in hand, I sat at a little table by the window and dug the handwritten book I'd found in Ariel's room out of my bag.

It smelled like old library books do, the ones in the back room that no one ever checks out. Musty and dusty. I took a bite of pudding and opened it to the first page.

I hadn't dared to hope, sure that would jinx it, but there it was, right in front of me. An honest-to-Pete diary. Ha! Elation hit my bloodstream at the same time as the caffeine, and I had to keep from grinning to myself so the locals wouldn't think they had a raving lunatic in their midst.

Ten pages later, I sighed. It was the most boring diary I'd ever seen. Oh sure, there were things in it that were telling. She recorded every single thing she ate, complete with calorie content. She also wrote down whenever anyone said anything about her weight, good or bad. I remembered wondering what her last meal had been before she was killed; now I tried and couldn't remember ever seeing her eat. Maybe she hadn't had a last meal at all.

She also kept track of things that the other students did and said at school, musing on the reactions they engendered in other people. It was as if she were creating a road-map of behavior, with a particular effect as the goal. Her writing voice was cold, almost mercenary. As I read on I was struck by the lack of information about Ariel's own feelings, which I found odd given the usual teenaged girl's abundance of angst about everything from a broken fingernail to world hunger.

I munched and sipped and read on, skimming a lot of the content. But when I reached the final entry, I swallowed and slowly returned my cup to the table.

Today I lost a button on my shirt, and I caught Mr. Blankenship looking at the side of my boob. At first I was embarrassed, but then he seemed more embarrassed than me. So I let him do it some more. He didn't turn away. He kept looking. And that was when I realized that all those girls with the fancy clothes and snotty attitudes weren't going to get their way. They're too scary. But if you're not scary, if you smile and are nice to men, they start getting all stupid and let you do anything. I read once boys think about sex every seventeen seconds and that men think about it almost that much. When Mr. Blankenship was looking down my shirt I finally got it. And now I'm going to get whatever I want.

The rest of the pages in the book were torn out. A part of me was glad I couldn't read them. I sat and looked out the window at the tourist traffic beginning to parade down the street outside of the bakery. Sadness mingled with distaste as I digested what Ariel had written about the discovery of her sexual power.

It could be a dangerous thing, to intentionally manipulate with that power. I hoped it hadn't burned her, as she apparently brandished it, no doubt awkwardly, in her teen years.

And then later? As a young woman, somewhat more refined and practiced? Had it been the reason she'd been murdered?

TWENTY

Things had certainly become complicated, I mused as I maneuvered along the country lanes leading back to the interstate. Had Ariel killed Scott Popper? I mean, she was the murder victim, right? It was ridiculous to think that she might have actually killed a policeman.

Even if she'd somehow caused his car crash, what good did knowing that do? As Gabi had pointed out, it hardly mattered what Ariel might have once done, now that she was dead.

Unless . . . did Chris Popper know more about her husband's death than she had let on? Did she think Ariel killed him? That could be a significantly stronger motive than an affair.

But no matter how strong the motive, Chris had an alibi. My brain hurt. Nothing was making any sense. Instead of having too little information, I suddenly had more than

I could fit together, as if someone had added a few extra pieces from another box to the jigsaw puzzle.

I opened my window and inhaled the morning breeze. A high haze of cloud cover cast a veil between the sharp summer sunlight and the verdant greenery below. Soon it would burn off, and the ambient temperature would again begin to rise. Above, hawks circled and dove, hunting the small things that crept in the fields on either side of the county road.

Ahead, a sign warned that I was approaching a four-way stop. Bowers Road.

The road Ariel's high school friend lived on.

I sighed. Even if there were a few sections from another puzzle box thrown in, I obviously didn't have all the pieces of the original jigsaw, either. However much I wanted to return to my own happy home, how could I resist making this slight detour? I tossed a mental coin and turned west. Three miles later, I turned around and went back, crossing my original path and tried east. I had no idea what Lindsey Drucker's address was, or even whether her name was still the same; Gabi had said she was married. This was a stupid way to try and find her.

Almost ready to turn around again and give up, I saw it: Drucker & Sandstrom. The names were spelled out in reflective letters on the mailbox in front of a sprawling, single-level house painted dark green with wine-colored trim. A long, low barn surrounded by a series of paddocks and pasture indicated that they kept livestock, but I didn't see any horses or cows. Then the driveway curved, and I saw alpacas clustered and dotting one of the large fields. Recently sheared, they looked like teddy bears crossed with oversized poodles. There must have been a hundred of them, in shades varying from cream to brown, with a few gray and black ones thrown in.

The woman who answered the door had short red hair and wore navy shorts with a plain white cotton T-shirt. The expectant look on her smooth tan face invited me to introduce myself.

"Hi. Are you Lindsey Drucker?" I asked.

"Yes."

"I'm Sophie Mae Reynolds. I knew Ariel Skylark."

She tipped her head to one side, considering. "I see." Without another word she stepped back and opened the door for me.

Inside, sunlight streamed through the windows that made up the back wall of the

212

main living space, and through a large skylight overhead. At least I thought it was the main living space, because it looked more like an artist's studio. A huge loom dominated one side of the room, with an elaborate rug in progress. The interlocking geometric design in red, cream and light brown was reminiscent of traditional Native American art, but somehow possessed a modern flair. Three easels took up the other half of the room, each displaying a landscape painting in a different stage of completion.

"Coffee?" Lindsey asked.

I shook my head. "I'm full up. Thanks, though." I walked over to the loom. "Are you the weaver?"

"I am." Her voice was deep, confident, her manner easy and unhurried.

"And the alpacas?"

"I raise them for wool and sell them for breeding."

Gabi had mentioned that she could get sheep and alpaca wool locally. Lindsey was probably one of her sources.

"My husband's the painter," she said. "He's out of town at a gallery show right now."

"It practically vibrates with creativity in here."

She smiled. And waited.

"I understand you were a good friend of Ariel's," I said, wondering what this self-possessed woman had in common with Ariel — and what Ariel got out of it. "I'm very sorry for your loss."

"Thank you." Sad about her friend's death, certainly, but not grief stricken. Serene. But how could I presume to know how she expressed sorrow?

She looked down, her face suddenly pinched. "We all have to go eventually, but no one deserves to die like that. The venom, the hatred behind such an act of violence. It's inconceivable."

And yet, inconceivable as it was, this was the third time I'd been involved in a murder in our little town. A woman could get a real complex about something like that.

"Everything all right?" Lindsey's concerned voice brought me back to earth.

I shook my head. "I find what happened to her upsetting, too." I'd started feeling downright sorry for myself there for a second. "Had you known Ariel for a long time?"

She took a sip of her coffee and considered me. "How did you know I knew her at all? Did she mention me?"

"Um, no. Her sister-in-law did, though. I was there last night."

"You stayed the night at the Kaminskis?"
I nodded.

"Friend of the family?" Obvious intelligence shone from her eyes. No way I'd get away with lying to her.

"Not exactly." I took a deep breath. "Ariel and I belong . . . belonged to the same artists' co-op. I drove up with her paintings, to give to her brother. One thing led to another, mostly because Gabi and I hit it off and have a common interest in spinning. I ended up staying the night. She mentioned you and Ariel were friends in high school, and what road you lived on, and when I was driving by on the way home, I sort of . . ." I trailed off, lame as could be.

She squinted. "I guess I still don't quite understand why you're here."

Why indeed? "Um. Well, I keep finding out things about Ariel that I hadn't known before. I thought you might be able to tell me more."

"You're simply curious, then."

I grimaced.

Lindsey laughed, which disconcerted me further. "It's okay. Ariel was an odd little thing."

"But you were friends."

"In high school. Since then it had devolved to exchanging Christmas cards. At least most of the time. Once in awhile she still called when she needed to."

Something about the way she said that. "When she needed to?"

Lindsey inclined her head a fraction, holding my gaze.

"And when," I pushed, "was that?"

She looked speculative then seemed to make a decision. "When she started to fall back into her old habits."

This time I was the one who waited.

Another sip of coffee, followed by a small, self-deprecating smile. "Ariel and I had something in common in high school that bound us. We were both anorexic. My parents caught on, and I began seeing a local psychologist who specialized in eating disorders. Ariel's parents were both gone by then, and her brother had no idea what was going on. But once I started to get better, I convinced her to go with me. The woman who was treating me was an angel; she agreed to let Ariel share my sessions for no extra fee. By the time my mother and father found out, I was improving, so they let it continue. Over the course of two years, we both learned how to deal with having an eating disorder." She paused, watching the alpacas outside the window. "I was lucky. Staying well has been easier for me. Ariel

216

had a difficult time."

"That explains it," I said, without think-ing.

"Explains what?"

I ran my hands over my face, suddenly tired. "I keep hearing Ariel wasn't exactly, um, overflowing with the milk of human kindness, if you know what I mean. She didn't like people so much for who they were, as for what they could do for her. She cultivated those who could provide her with something she needed."

Lindsey didn't respond, continued watch-ing the herd. I began to get a sick feeling, like I'd stepped on a puppy. I shouldn't have spoken so frankly.

Then she turned back to me. "I never really thought about it that way. But, of course, you're right. She did exactly that."

"You were awfully nice, letting her come to your sessions. It must have made it harder for you," I said, plunging in further.

"She was killing herself." The simple words, stated so matter-of-factly, gave me goose bumps.

I couldn't help asking, though, "Did you like her?"

"I accepted her. Many people didn't."

"Did you accept everything about her?"

"You mean the men?"

217

"You knew about the high school teacher, then. Owens."

Lindsey's expression clouded. "He should have known better. She acted tough, but she was just a kid. A wildly insecure kid. He lost his job over it, but he should have been prosecuted."

"Did you know she was recently having an affair with a married man?"

She hesitated, licking her lips. "She called me a couple of weeks ago, as a matter of fact."

Interesting. Lindsey hadn't been going to tell me that.

"Did she mention Scott Popper?"

"She talked about two men, both associated with the artists' co-op."

"She was having affairs with both of them?" So she and Jake had progressed beyond e-mails. No wonder Felicia had made that angry phone call.

Lindsey was silent.

"Listen, I know you want to keep her confidence, and I don't blame you. But she was murdered. The police are probably going to show up on your doorstep, asking these same questions. At least, I hope they are, because the people she was involved with right before she died are important, and you have information about them."

Okay, so I wasn't being particularly nice anymore.

With pity on her face — for Ariel and not for me, I hoped — she said, "Yes, she was having affairs with both of them."

"One was a cop, and the other one was a doctor, right?"

Lindsey frowned. "One was a policeman, yes. The other was a mechanic."

"A mechanic?"

"Zak something?"

Oh, wow. Zak Nelson. Not exactly associated with the co-op, but close enough. No wonder he'd wanted to buy one of Ariel's giant canvases. And no wonder Irene seemed to hate Ariel so much; she knew what was going on.

"What else did she say?" I asked.

However, Lindsey was shaking her head. "No. This has gone far enough. I'm sure you're a very nice person, but I don't know you, and I shouldn't be talking to you about Ariel like this. If the police come, fine. But you're not the police, and I'd like you to leave now."

"But —"

"I don't have anything else to tell you. Please. Go."

"All right. Thank you for talking to me," I said. It sounded weak. I could tell by the rueful look on her face that Lindsey regretted talking to me at all. At my insistence she had violated a personal code of ethics.

On one hand, the last twenty-four hours had gleaned a pile of new information about Ariel, some of which might be helpful in determining who murdered her.

On the other hand, I felt like dirt.

Twenty-One

I'd learned a lot about Ariel, things that Robin and Barr might not have unearthed by themselves. I'd sworn up and down I wasn't going to investigate her murder, yet it sure looked like that was exactly what I was doing. Why couldn't I stop asking questions? Did I have some kind of genetic mutation?

Gawd. Well, that was it. Finished. Over. Finito. No more snooping or questioning or even wondering to myself. No more gnawing on the problem like it was a big juicy bone and I was a hungry terrier. Barr had asked me to gossip, but by stealing Ariel's diary and talking to Lindsey Drucker, I'd crossed that line.

Too many people knew I'd been asking questions. Someone had killed Ariel in a very violent manner, and the last thing I wanted was to set them off or make them think I was a danger in any way, shape, or form. After all, it was more than likely I knew the murderer.

Nope, I thought. Stick a fork in me; I'm done.

At least for a few days.

I mean, it made sense to back off and see how things played out. I knew a lot more about Ariel now. Maybe it was enough. I'd learned by now that it was a bad idea to barrel ahead, poking at hornet nests just to see what came out.

Because I already knew the result would be hornets. And I didn't like getting stung.

Our yellow house on the edge of the historic district of Cadyville looked as welcoming as a grandmother's hug. Brilliant azure clematis twined up a trellis to one side of the tiny porch, breathtaking against the butter color of the wall. Lavender bushes lined the walkway, and showy annuals brightened the more sedate perennials tucked all over the small yard. As I walked to the front door, I couldn't help smiling. I was such a homebody, and this was definitely my home. Time for a shower and then back to my normal life.

Once inside the door, though, my cheerful disposition faded. Voices drew me into the living room, where I found Meghan and

Barr, iced coffees in hand, chatting up a storm. As soon as I entered, though, their animated conversation died a sudden death. The looks on both of their faces didn't improve my mood.

"What happened?" I asked.

Meghan glanced at Barr, then said, "Hannah stopped by."

I dropped into a chair. "Again." It wasn't a question.

She nodded. "She seems determined to talk to you."

I exhaled audibly. "Fine. I'll talk to her. Let's just get it over with."

"We have to find her first," Barr said. "And when we do, I want to be the first one to speak with her."

Something ominous in his tone. I peered at Meghan. "What did she say?"

She twisted her mouth and shrugged. "Only that she wanted to talk to you, was in fact determined to talk to you. It wasn't so much what she said, as how she said it."

Hmmm. Meghan had been spooked enough to call Barr.

"Well, I'm here now," I said. "So next time she comes back she can have her wish. I don't know that she's going to be very happy with what I have to say, though." I smiled at Barr. It was not a nice smile.

He stood. "I'm going to try and track her down before she gets a chance to bother you again. I'm sorry about all this, Meghan."

She shook her head. "It's all right. I know you'll take care of it."

I walked him to the door. "I have a lot to tell you about my trip to La Conner."

"Can it wait?" he asked. "I really want to find Hannah."

Great. He was neglecting his job just to track down his ex-wife so she'd stop bugging us.

"I guess," I said. "Or I could tell Robin."

He looked alarmed. "No, let me do that." Bending down, he gave me a long kiss. Then he whispered, "Come over tonight and tell me all about it, okay? We'll have dinner."

I nodded. "What sounds good?"

"Huh uh. I'm cooking for you. But I'm afraid my repertoire is somewhat limited, so you'll have to take what you get."

He was cooking for me? "Deal," I said. This was the first time he'd cooked a meal for me. It was bound to be horrible, but I didn't care. It was a case of the thought that counts.

After showering, I walked into my storeroom refreshed and ready to get back to work. I trailed my fingers along the soaps stacked neatly on the shelves, lingering on the pretty pastel labels, the colored glass bottles. A plethora of scents whirled around me.

I'd recently developed a soap especially for children and babies. It was superfatted with avocado, almond, and jojoba oils, meaning there was more oil in the recipe than the chemical reaction between the oil and lye — saponification — used. This left some of the oils in the soap in emollient form. The result was a mild, moisturizing bar the color of heavy whipping cream. I didn't add any scented oils or colorants, so parents didn't have to worry about allergic reactions with their little ones.

Soon my work island was covered with huge bottles of oil, granulated lye, bowls and measuring cups and scales, as well as stirrers, thermometers, and my safety equipment. I donned the apron, rubber gloves, and goggles and began mixing and pouring. The oils melted together in a big kettle on the ancient stove while I measured water into another giant stainless steel kettle, this one with a pour spout. Gently, I stirred in the lye pellets, careful not to splash any of it outside of thc container.

The thing about making soap was that it

was just dangerous enough that it demanded my full attention. My worries evaporated, and I found myself engaged in the magic of the soapmaking process yet again. I doubted I would ever become entirely blasé about it. At least I hoped not. And right now it made me feel better to create something both beautiful and useful.

Of course, that didn't mean I knew what I should do when I could no longer immerse myself behind the wall of work. The thought of a confrontation with Hannah gave me butterflies the size of dragons.

Talk about overreaction, Sophie Mae.

I pushed the thoughts out of my head and reached for a thermometer.

The lye had heated chemically when mixed with water. When it had cooled to the temperature I needed, I poured the warm oils into the industrial-sized mixer I'd bought from a bakery in Seattle when it went out of business. Then I very, very carefully added the liquid lye and started the beater turning on the lowest speed. The liquids swished sluggishly together.

I moved away from the mixer and removed my goggles, hanging them nearby for easy access for the next stage of the process.

"Are you busy?" I nearly dropped the wooden soap mold I was holding when

Meghan spoke from the bottom step.

"Don't sneak up on me like that," I said with one hand over my racing heart. "What if I'd been handling lye?"

"Sorry. I guess you are. Busy, I mean."

I removed a glove and pushed back a tendril of hair that had flopped over my eyes. "What's up?"

"Ruth's upstairs. Looking for you."

"Can you entertain her for a few minutes? I'm almost done here."

"You got it." Meghan returned upstairs.

I could tell by the texture and viscosity of the soap that it had reached trace and was ready to pour. Donning my glove and goggles again, I turned off the mixer and, with a grunt, removed the bowl and carefully took it to the work island where the wooden molds, each of which held two dozen bars worth of soap, sat waiting. For the first couple I climbed onto a step stool and carefully ladled the thickened mixture into the molds. The last two I was able to pour directly.

It took a little muscle, though. I thought of Chris wielding her hammer and tongs in the forge. She'd be able to pour the whole lot, I bet.

When I had finished, I covered the soap with a light cloth to let it set up, cleaned up my workroom and myself, and headed upstairs.

"How did it go?" Ruth asked.

She, Meghan, and I sat in loungers in the strip of shade that ran along the back of the house. Erin was still at math camp, but Meghan would be leaving soon to pick her up. Out in the yard, the sunshine fell relentlessly on the garden beds. I could almost hear the plants reaching and stretching toward it, determined to procreate. Their biological imperative would benefit our table for the rest of the year. The hens clucked at each other in their pen, and in the neighbor's yard a pair of spotted towhees called to each other. A squirrel ran along the top of the cedar fence, pausing first to twitch his nose at us, and then his tail.

The squirrel let loose with an irritated chatter, then flipped his tail at us one more time and scampered down the fence, out of sight.

I felt kind of funny telling them what had happened in La Conner before I told Barr, but he'd had his chance. Besides, it seemed to fall under his gossip mandate.

Taking a sip of lemonade, I said, "Rocky, Ariel's brother, is twenty-eight, has a wife and twin boys, an inherited tulip farm that doesn't make enough money to survive on, a side business as a car mechanic, prematurely thinning hair, and a lifelong blindness to who his sister really was. Gabi, his wife, is a competent, creative, family-oriented farm wife, doing her best to make do with what she has. She resented Ariel's hold over her brother and the money Rocky gave his sister."

"She's the spinner?" Meghan asked.

Ruth perked up at that.

I nodded. "She has a fabulous stash, and she quilts and sews, too."

"No wonder you like her so much," Meghan said.

Hmmm. "I do like her," I mused. "She's one of those people who, on paper, you have a ton in common with, but there's a lot we don't, as well. Still, I think we could grow to be good friends."

"It's too bad she lives so far away."

"True," I said. "I did find out a few interesting things about Ariel herself, though."

Ruth leaned forward.

"For one thing, she had an affair with a teacher in high school."

"Oh, that poor little thing," Ruth said.

"Ariel's friend from high school would

agree with you. Her sister-in-law, on the other hand, said it was all Ariel's fault and that she deliberately seduced the teacher in order to get a good grade."

"Her friend from high school?"

I told them about my conversation with Lindsey Drucker, including what I'd learned about Ariel's eating disorder.

When I'd finished, Ruth gazed at me with sadness. "She was one messed-up kid, wasn't she?" Her eyes welled, and she looked away, blinking rapidly. Ruth was one of the most tender-hearted people I knew.

Meghan, another bastion of sympathy, nodded her agreement.

"Gabi suspects Ariel was also responsible for the accident that killed her and Rocky's parents," I said.

Both women looked surprised. "Gabi sounds like a very bitter woman," Meghan observed.

Ruth murmured her agreement. "At least when it comes to her sister-in-law."

"Like I said, I think she's doing the best she can."

"This whole situation must be very hard on all of them," Ruth said. "I, for one, think it was very nice of you to take that little girl's artwork up to her family, and I'm glad you met another spinner."

"Say, Ruth?" I asked.

"Yes, dear?"

"You were over at Chris' house the night Ariel was killed, right?"

She met my eyes and slowly nodded. "Along with Irene. Her husband's funeral was the next day, and the three of us have become quite close through the co-op."

"Jake was there, too?"

"For a little while. As her friend and her doctor. She'd asked him for something to help her sleep, and he brought over some samples."

"So he didn't stay long?"

"He left a little after seven-thirty."

Plenty of time to provide Felicia with an alibi.

Ruth looked at her watch. "I have to go — Uncle Thad will be needing his dinner, and he's helpless as a newborn when it comes to feeding himself." She stood, and Meghan and I clambered to our feet as she took her leave.

Back in the house, Meghan collected her wallet and car keys. "How 'bout pizza for dinner? I can whip up some dough and we can all make our own after I pick up Erin."

"I won't be here for dinner. Barr offered to cook for me."

She grinned. "You're kidding."
I grinned back. "Don't wait up."

Twenty-Two

I turned a corner, and the canvas bag of groceries on the seat next to me started to topple. My hand shot out in a classic Mommove to prevent the bag from tumbling to the floor by blocking it with the side of my forearm. Keeping my eyes on the road in front of me, I moved the bacon to make the bag less top-heavy.

Barr might be making me dinner, but I planned on making him breakfast the next morning.

He greeted me at the door, laying a big smacker on me and then taking the bag. When he saw what was in it, he waggled his eyebrows in approval and carried it into the kitchen.

"What is that heavenly smell?" I called after him.

"Garlic sautéed in butter," came the answer from the other room.

There was a big bunch of flowers in the

living room. They sat on a simple, glass-topped coffee table.

The spool was gone.

I felt a little guilty, complaining about it so much earlier. But not so much that I couldn't handle it.

He returned with two glasses and an open bottle of single malt Scotch. The enticing aroma of smoky peat drifted my way.

"What's for dinner?" I asked.

"You'll see." He sat down on the sofa, and I joined him. He poured a finger of Scotch into each glass and handed me one. We clinked them together.

"To new beginnings," he said.

I looked at the coffee table and smiled. "To new beginnings," I agreed. "Thank you for the flowers. And for getting rid of the spool."

He settled back against the corner cushion. "You're welcome. Now give."

I spent the next hour telling him every detail of my trip to La Conner. He listened carefully, only interrupting a couple of times to clarify a point. When I'd finished, I retrieved Ariel's diary from the tote I'd brought that also contained a change of clothes and basic toiletries.

Handing it to him, I said, "I know it was a bad idea to take this. I'm sorry."

But he didn't look upset. "From what you said, it probably wouldn't come into play in any court case anyway. If it does, you're a private citizen. If Robin or I'd taken it without a warrant, then it wouldn't be admissible, but you're you, and while a judge might not appreciate that you basically stole it, anything in it could still be used in court."

"So I did good?"

He glowered melodramatically from under his eyebrows. "It's wrong to steal."

I grinned. "Sorry."

His face relaxed. "Well, okay, then."

"It must make Robin nuts to work with you."

"If it does, the feeling's mutual."

"Uh-oh. Are things okay between you two?"

He shrugged. "Sure. She's not happy about the Hannah thing taking up so much of my time, but then again, neither am I."

"Still don't know where she is, huh." At least she wouldn't try to talk to me tonight, I figured.

"She's nowhere in Cadyville, and we haven't been able to find her in any of the neighboring towns, either."

"Maybe she left after this morning."

"Maybe." He didn't sound convinced. I

didn't believe it, either.

"And Ariel's murder?" I asked.

"Lots of running around, lots of follow up, not much in the way of results. Robin's nearly apoplectic with impatience. But we're making some progress, learning more every day."

Naturally I wanted them to find the killer, but hearing there was a soupçon of trouble in paradise didn't exactly bother me. I nestled my back into the cushions and took a sip of Scotch. Mmm. My favorite: Laphroaig. Barr had thought of everything.

"Do you think Ariel could have had anything to do with Scott's death?" I asked.

"Even if she really did have the mechanical ability to damage his vehicle, he was killed in his patrol car. It would have been awfully risky to sneak into the motor pool to do that."

I sniffed. " 'Motor pool.' It's a parking lot behind the police station, Barr."

"Fenced off, with limited access," he said. "It still would have been risky."

"Did he always drive the same car? Or do they switch around?"

Barr gave a facial shrug. "Same one. And he could have taken it home, parked it in the driveway; many officers do. But he liked to leave it at the station, and drove his truck to and from work."

I took another sip of Scotch and changed the subject. "So who are the suspects in Ariel's murder?" I held up my hand and began ticking them off on my fingers. "There's Chris."

"Alibi," Barr said.

"I know. But right now I'm focusing on who might have wanted Ariel dead, not opportunity."

"What, you think someone hired it out?" he asked.

"How should I know? It's a possibility, isn't it?"

"Strangling someone with your yarn? Sounds more like a crime of passion. Though you may be interested that the medical examiner told us Ariel was struck on the head with a blunt object before she was strangled."

I perked up at that. "Really? Was she knocked unconscious?"

"Possibly, but probably not."

"But she might not have been able to fight back, at least not much. Not that she was very big or strong to start with. So whoever strangled her might not have been that strong, either."

"True. And please don't say anything to *anyone* about the blow to the head. We're trying to keep that under wraps."

I nodded my agreement. "So anyway, we have Chris, because Ariel was sleeping with her husband. And Irene, because Ariel was sleeping with her son."

"Same alibi."

"Right. Then there's Felicia, because she thought Ariel was sleeping with her husband."

"But she wasn't?"

"Apparently not, according to Ruth and Lindsey."

"Okay."

"Then there's Zak," I said. "Because Ariel was sleeping with Scott."

"At least Scott couldn't have done it," Barr said.

"But: Jake could have known about both Scott and Zak. He may have been jealous."

"By giving Felicia an alibi, he's giving himself one."

"Exactly."

"Then there's Daphne, her roommate. Ariel owed her a bunch of money, and it didn't look like she'd pay it back anytime soon. Daphne wanted a new roommate right away," I said.

"That's really reaching, Sophie Mae."

"Yeah, probably."

"What about the brother?" he asked.

"I didn't get any idea that he had a motive. He adored his sister and seems devastated by her death."

"His wife?"

"There was no love lost between Gabi and Ariel, but they live awfully far away."

"It's only an hour drive."

He was right. Why did an hour's drive through the country seem so much longer than the hour's drive to downtown Seattle?

"Okay, put her on the list," I said.

"The friend? Drucker? I'll tell Robin about her tomorrow, so she can follow up."

I shook my head. "She may have more information to give you about Ariel — she clammed up on me all of a sudden at the end of my visit — but I don't see her as the murderer."

Barr took a sip of his drink. "Okay, who else?"

"I can't think of anyone. Can you?"

He sighed. "She'd dated several other men, some of whom were married. But it was all awhile ago. You've hit the current ones. There certainly do seem to be a lot of convenient alibis floating around."

"Somebody's lying," I said.

"Somebody always is."

"Well, this somebody's starving. Any

chance you're going to feed me anytime soon?"

He stood up and offered me his hand. "Come on, woman. Let's get some victuals in you."

The tiny table in the kitchen was actually set with candles and dishes that matched. It was still light outside, but Barr lit the tapers anyway. Then he served shrimp scampi over rice with a simple salad. It was delicious. He had the good sense to buy a ready-made dessert, and the further good sense to make it cheesecake — only my favorite sweet indulgence in the whole wide world. He garnished it with fresh raspberries. As night fell, we snuggled on the sofa and watched an old black-and-white movie on TV.

I was giddy as a school girl on Valentine's Day by the end of the movie and the wine. And I may have even giggled a bit during the activities that followed. Afterward, relaxed in the crook of Barr's arm with a light breeze curling in the open window, I listened to his deep breathing and thought about how happy I was when I was with him. Maybe this living together thing would work after all.

At three a.m. I was wide awake again, thoughts running around in my head like rats in a cage. I found myself reflecting on what Barr had said earlier, before we drifted off to sleep. Ever since he'd told me about the money his uncle had left him, questions had been collecting in the back of my mind. As we cuddled in the dark it seemed easier to talk about, so I'd brought up a biggie.

"Are you going to quit your job now that you have a ton of money?"

"What? Why would I do that?"

"People win the lottery, they quit their jobs. Follow their dreams. I just, you know, wondered."

He'd laughed. "I don't know what I'll do with it yet, but most of it will be invested for when I do quit my job. But I like being a cop, and I like being a cop in Cadyville."

"No changes?"

"Oh, I imagine there'll be a few. Maybe I'll get a new car or something. But if you're worried that I'm going to change my whole life just because I have some dollars to play with, you can stop. It's just money. I'm just me."

I'd also read that a lot of people who won the lottery were miserable and ended up going through their winnings within a few years. Barr was practical and viewed his inheritance as security, though. The guy was solid as a rock.

Sighing with contentment, I pulled the sheet higher. The breeze wafting in the open window held the fragrance of roses as well as a chill. As I began to doze, my mind drifted to the list of suspects we'd discussed earlier. Which one had Ariel angered to the point of murder?

She'd looked so small there on the floor of Ruth's studio space. Hmm. That was kind of strange. Why hadn't she been in her own studio space? She didn't spin. She didn't do anything involved with fiber or yarn, and had never showed any interest in learning. But she'd had that tuft of fiber clenched in her hand; I'd seen it myself. I could see it in my mind's eye now.

It had been green. With a little blue and pink. Like the northern lights. The colors of nature obviously inspired Thea Hawke's choices of color combinations in her hand-painted batts.

Green and blue and pink. Like the stuff Gabi had buried in her spinning basket. Said she'd bought it online.

My eyes opened.

I watched the sky brighten slowly on the other side of the window, from a lighter shade of night to early dawn. The air gradually filled with the songs of early birds looking for their proverbial worms. From beside me came the sound of light snoring. Finally, I slid out of bed and padded out to the kitchen. Barr's laptop sat on the counter.

Thea Hawke Designs had a very nice website, but she referred anyone who was interested in her unique creations to the Cadyville Regional Artists' Co-op. She didn't sell online.

I made coffee and stared out the kitchen window at the backyard. The crows that lurked in the copse of trees across the road joined their raucous calls to the other birdsong. The cacophony made my teeth hurt.

I liked Gabi Kaminski, but she'd lied about where she'd obtained the fiber tucked deep into the basket by her spinning wheel. There was no reason to lie about that, not unless she was hiding something else.

How much bamboo in that color combo had been at CRAC? Ruth would know. And Gabi could have come into the co-op when neither Ruth nor I were there and bought the batt. But that didn't account for the tuft of it in Ariel's clenched fist or why she'd been strangled with my yarn beside a spinning wheel.

Besides, Gabi had come right out and said she'd bought it online. And now that I thought about it, she'd snapped at me when she found me looking at the fiber in that basket. I'd put her less-than-gracious response down to the morning-after grouchies, but perhaps her bad mood had to do with something else — like guilt.

Ariel had borrowed money over and over again from her brother, and it didn't look like that would have stopped anytime soon. Gabi was sick and tired of it. She believed Ariel was a slut, that she had seduced her teacher and made him lose his job.

She also believed Ariel had been responsible for the car wreck that had killed the Kaminski siblings' parents.

In fact, when it came right down to it, Gabi not only didn't like her sister-in-law, she believed she was evil.

Twenty-Three

At six-thirty Barr came into the kitchen, sniffing the air like a hound dog.

"Mmmm. Bacon."

I surveyed him, taking in the bare, lean chest and long legs housed in pajama bottoms. "And hash browns coming up, along with your favorite cheesy eggs."

"A real heart attack on a plate." He sat down at the table. "You must have been up for a while. Why so early?"

I brought him a cup of coffee and gave him a long kiss. "I had some trouble sleeping last night."

"Really? I would've thought you'd sleep like a log." His grin was wicked.

I laughed and turned back to the potatoes browning in a frying pan. "I should have. Woke up, though, got to thinking about things. Do you remember the fiber Ariel had in her hand?"

Behind me, Barr said, "I remember. There

was a lot of that stuff around where you found her. I'm sure the lab folks have it neatly zipped up and cataloged."

I turned down the burner and sat in the chair across from him. Resting both elbows on the table, I held my mug of coffee in front of my face and looked at him through the rising steam.

"Gabi had some of the same fiber. At least I think so. There must be a way to see if they match."

"Really. Is it common?"

"Huh uh. Pretty hard to come by. What you might call limited-edition bamboo roving. Hand painted. Small batches. And," I paused for effect, "only available through CRAC."

"Maybe Mrs. Kaminski got it there."

"She said she ordered it online."

He leaned back in his chair, a speculative expression on his face. "You asked her about it?"

"Well, yeah. But we talked about a lot. Yarn, spinning wheels, drum carders, spindles — tons of stuff. But I didn't see the fiber I'm talking about until the next morning, right before I left." I made a face. "I told her I knew who made it, though."

His jaw set. "That's not good."

I lifted my palms and let them drop. "I

didn't make the connection until this morning." I stood and moved to the stove again.

He grew quiet, staring out the window and slowly sipping his coffee. I poured another cup for myself and leaned against the counter, curious as to what he was thinking but willing to wait.

Finally he spoke, slowly, as if thinking out loud. "I can't see that we have probable cause, not just on your word. It's simply too weak. So no warrant. But if that hand-painted stuff is really that rare, and if we could unofficially get a sample from Gabi Kaminski, then maybe we could put something together for a judge."

"I can go back. Figure out an excuse and go inside and take it. Like I did the diary."

He gave me a look. "I told you that was a bad habit."

I smiled.

"No. I really mean it. And besides, it would be much better if that kind of evidence was gathered by me. Chain of evidence and all. Even outside of the jurisdiction of the Cadyville P.D."

"So what do you want to do?" I asked.

He narrowed his eyes in thought. "At this point I don't really see a choice."

I leaned forward.

"I want you to go back. But I'm going

with you. We can lie and cheat if we have to, but I can be pretty charming when the occasion calls for it."

"Even if you do say so yourself," I teased.

"I bet we can finagle a sample of that fiber out of her."

"By 'we,' do you mean Robin will be going with us?"

He pressed his lips together. "I think this is one trip just you and I will take."

Barr had other work to do that day and so did I, so we didn't leave for La Conner until late afternoon. He drove, and I sat back and acted like I was watching the scenery flow by. The impending task of getting a sample of Thea Hawke's fiber from Gabi hung over my head like the sword of Damocles, making me all tense and jittery. I just wasn't good at prevarication. At lying and cheating. I'd brought that up to Barr, but he'd only smiled and told me my job was to get us into the house, and to identify the fiber for him. He'd handle Gabi. Robin had gone to talk to the Kaminskis alone, so they hadn't met Barr yet.

I decided I'd just have to trust him.

And then I worried about it some more.

If we failed to get that sample, Gabi could

get away with murder. That wasn't acceptable.

If we didn't fail, I would be partly responsible for destroying a family. The twins, Noah and Evan, would be motherless, or essentially so with Gabi in jail. How much worse it would be for Rocky to not only lose his treasured sister to murder, but to learn his wife — his high-school-sweetheart wife — had been the killer. There would be a trial. The scandal in a small town like La Conner would be huge. Rocky's business — both of his businesses — would be affected, if not completely ruined.

I hated that Erin's grandmother, my good friend Tootie Hanover, was out of town. She had no idea what was going on, but I was sure if she did she'd be full of opinions and advice. Advice I could really use right now.

What would she tell me?

I watched the green fields roll by on the other side of the window and remembered back to the last time I'd approached her with a similar question. I'd asked whether murder was ever justified.

Her answer had been an emphatic No.

I knew she was right. And now she'd tell me that I wasn't the one responsible for decimating Gabi Kaminski's family; Gabi herself was. Once again I'd found myself in a situation involving justice and murder. Barr and Meghan might joke, rueful as those jokes were, but maybe the Universe kept dumping me into these situations for a reason. So I'd better grow a backbone and do what I needed to do.

Barr turned onto the Kaminski Tulip Farm's drive at my direction, and I watched for Tut, the German Shepherd, to come barreling out at us. But there was no dog, and as we got out of the car the only sounds of activity around the place were the calls of the birds at the feeders. I began to wonder whether anyone was home. Of course, we hadn't called ahead. Perhaps we'd made the trip for nothing.

So when my knock brought Gabi to the door I felt a bizarre combination of relief and apprehension that almost made me dizzy. The intoxicating scent of freshly baked cookies drifting out to the porch didn't help, either.

Puzzlement furrowed her brow as she pushed open the screen. "Hi, Sophie Mae! What brings you up here again so soon?" Consternation, then. "Oh, don't tell me you forgot something and had to come all the way back."

I scrambled for a response, feeling my smile slide around on my face. "I can't find my watch," I finally said.

Barr shot me a look.

It wasn't exactly a lie. I hadn't been able to find my watch for months, but instead of getting a new one, I'd simply begun to use the clock on my cell phone when I needed a timepiece. It wasn't like I worked for The Man or had a lot of appointments to keep track of.

"Your watch? What does it look like?"

"It's silver." My voice sounded weak.

She gestured us in. "I didn't find it upstairs. We can look again, though."

"Oh!" I said, startling her. "This is Barr Ambrose. My, uh, boyfriend."

He quirked an eyebrow at that.

"Hi, Barr," Gabi said. "Want some cider? It's ice cold."

"No, thank you," he said.

"Sophie Mae?"

"Um, not right now. Thanks."

Her gaze sharpened. Something's not quite right, it said.

Before she could say anything else about the watch, I asked. "Where are the boys?"

Now her smile didn't reach her eyes. "Over at the neighbor's house, for once, instead of Justin being over here. And Rocky had to run into town for some parts."

"Sophie Mae," Barr said. "Could you

show me that fiber you were talking about?"

My heart just about stopped. That wasn't sneaky at all!

Gabi frowned. "Fiber?"

I swallowed, and looked at Barr. "It's by the spinning wheel."

"Ms. Kaminski? You don't mind if we take a look, do you? See, I'm a detective with the Cadyville Police Department, and Sophie Mae was telling me about your, what did you call it? Stash? Anyway, I'm one of the investigators assigned to your sister-in-law's murder."

Gabi's eyes had widened with each word that came out of his mouth, and I could feel my own echoing hers. What was he doing? What had happened to lying and cheating?

He turned to me. "Where?"

Wordlessly, I went to the spinning wheel and pointed to the basket beside it.

"Ms. Kaminski? Would you show us what's in the basket?" Barr asked.

She looked scared, but didn't move. Silence descended on the room, and I could hear a clock ticking somewhere. Then she walked to the basket, picked it up, and dumped the contents on the sofa.

"Thank you." Barr rewarded her with a wide, easy smile.

Warily, she tried a smile in return. "What's this all about? What happened to Detective Lane?"

"She's my partner," he said. "I'm just following up on something. So I hear you're quite the expert spinner."

"Oh, I don't know about expert, but I enjoy it."

He picked up a handful of batts. "Where do you get your fiber?"

Understanding dawned, and Gabi turned to me. "Is this about that hand-painted bamboo you were asking me about?"

"Uh," I said.

Her eyes flashed.

Barr said, "Which one would that be? Is it here?"

I leaned in to look, but Gabi pushed by me. Plunging her hand into the pile of soft fluff, she pulled out Thea Hawke's blue and green and pink bamboo. "I don't understand. Is this what you're here for?"

Barr looked at me, and I nodded my identification. "Yes," he said. "I do believe it is. May I take a sample of it with me?"

She looked nonplussed. "A sample? What for?"

"May I?"

She shrugged. "Sure, I guess."

He teased out a handful, put it in a paper

bag and put it in his shirt pocket. "And where did you say you got this?"

"Ariel gave it to me," she said.

"You told me you got it online," I said.

"I must have been thinking of something else. I don't keep track of where I get every little batt and roll."

"You seem to remember now."

"When your 'boyfriend' started talking about this stuff and Ariel together, of course I remembered where I got it." Her tone was defensive.

"She bought it for you." My disbelief leaked through. Thea's product was expensive, and Ariel was not someone I thought of as generous.

The sound of the front screen door opening made us all turn our heads. "What's going on here?" Rocky asked. Tut followed him inside. The dog froze when he spotted Barr and me, and the fur along his spine ruffled.

Gabi moved quickly to her husband's side. "Sophie Mae brought another detective here. Something about the fiber Ariel gave me. I don't see how it could have anything to do with her death. It's like they think I stole it or something." She looked pointedly at me. "Ariel gave it to me the last time she was up here. Ask Rocky."

He put his arm around his wife and nodded. "It's true. It wasn't the first time my sister brought Gabi presents like that."

Gabi looked triumphant. Barr and I exchanged glances.

"Where were you the night of the twenty-second?" he asked Gabi.

Her head jerked back. "What? I was here, of course."

"All night?"

"Yes!"

Rocky took a step forward. "What the heck is this all about? Of course my wife was here all night, and so was I. I thought you cops were supposed to find my sister's killer, not go around harassing her family."

"Mr. Kaminski —" Barr began. A low growl issued from deep in the dog's throat.

Rocky held his hand up. "You can just get on out of here now. I won't put up with this anymore. If you need us, you get yourselves a piece of paper to make it official, but otherwise you just leave us alone."

Barr nodded. "I understand. Thank you for your time. Sophie Mae?" He indicated the door.

I edged carefully by Tut, terrified he'd take a chunk out of my leg. As I passed by, Gabi said, "I'll be sure and send your *watch* to you if I find it."

Rocky glared at me. "You're not welcome here, you hear me?" Real fury rode his words. I shivered and nodded my understanding.

Barr stayed close behind me, hand on my elbow, and the constant grumbling of the massive dog followed us all the way to the car.

TWENTY-FOUR

"I don't think we're going to be able to make a case against Gabi Kaminski," Barr said.

We were almost halfway home. I felt like an idiot, caught in my stupid lie, and silence had settled over us for several miles. I jumped when he spoke.

"Does that mean she didn't kill Ariel, or that you can't prove she did it?" I asked. "Because if she didn't, you made me look like a real jerk in there."

"Sorry. How was I supposed to know you were going to manufacture a lost watch?"

"But you said we'd lie and cheat!" I protested.

"I said we could if we had to. We didn't have to."

I sniffed.

"Anyway," he continued. "I'm unconvinced she's a murderer. She was extremely cooperative, and her husband vehemently

assured us that she was home all that night."
He cracked the window. "He was pretty
angry that we questioned her at all. I can't
really blame him." Barr didn't look regretful, though. All just part of the job for him.
I, on the other hand, still felt sick to my
stomach.

"Great," I said. "And you have yet another
alibi provided by a spouse." I twisted toward
him in the seat. "But Gabi told me herself
that sometimes she stays up all night spinning and Rocky never knows. She could
have easily left the farmhouse at night
without anyone knowing."

Barr frowned. "How early does Rocky go
to bed?"

"When I was there the other night?
Around nine, I guess. The twins, too. He's
an early riser, and the twins are only six."

"She might have had time to drive down
to Cadyville. It would be cutting it awfully
close, though, to fit in that eight-to-ten
o'clock timeframe."

"But it's possible," I said. "And what
about the way she acted about the bamboo
fiber?"

He lifted a shoulder and let it drop. "Ariel
gave it to her. Brought it up the last time
she visited. Can't prove her wrong. And she
didn't seem too worried when I took that

sample."

"Hmm. I just don't see Ariel dropping the big bucks for that fancy fiber, just to give it to the sister-in-law who didn't even really like her."

"Maybe she was trying to make nice."

Maybe so. Maybe Gabi had been making headway with Rocky, trying to convince him to stop lending his sister money, and Ariel needed to get on her good side.

"Then why was she so upset about us being there?" I grumbled.

"Believe me," Barr said. "I've interviewed a lot of people. That was mild. Rocky was far more upset than she was."

"So that's it? She gets away with it?"

"Well, at some point we might be able to link forensic evidence to her."

I thought he might be humoring me now, but I still asked, "Is that in the works?"

"We didn't find much. I was hoping they'd find evidence under Ariel's fingernails, but there was nada."

"Maybe Gabi came up behind her, and Ariel never had a chance to fight back."

"God, Sophie Mae. Your imagination kind of scares me."

"You'd have this conversation with Robin in a heartbeat, and her imagination would be useful. Just because I'm not —" tall, auburn-haired, fashionable, and a sure shot with any kind of firearm ever made "— a police detective doesn't mean I can't figure a few things out."

We got back to Cadyville around seven-thirty, and Barr went to update Robin on the new information from La Conner. I drove home and spent a mundane evening with Meghan and Erin, watching a movie on DVD, doing my best to push Ariel's murder out of my mind. If Gabi really had killed her, I might have to come to terms with the fact that she'd get away with it.

Great in theory; not so easy in practice. I went to bed early, but slept fitfully, my slumber punctuated with dreams of being caught in a huge sticky web, surrounded by laughing spiders with all too human faces.

The next morning I awoke feeling tired and groggy. I finally forced myself out of bed, showered and dressed, and pasted a smile on my face. Meghan and Erin were leaving for math camp, so I grabbed a cup of strong coffee and went down to my workroom to take inventory.

After making all the custom bath fizzies for the wedding shower, I was low on baking soda. I made notes of some other items I needed and spent some time online, restocking frequently used essential oils and bulk ordering cocoa butter, palm oil, and coconut oil. Then I trundled out to my pickup to run a few local errands.

After a quick stop at the bank, I picked up a twenty-pound container of baking soda from the nice folks at the Cadyville food co-op, who let me order wholesale through them. I also went by the apiary supply store and bought several pounds of unfiltered beeswax; it was amazing how quickly I went through the stuff.

Resupplied, I headed for home. The whole experience with the Kaminskis still sat heavy along my shoulders. I couldn't seem to shake it. Every day Barr had to deal with people lying to him, disliking him, even being afraid of him. Sighing, I signaled to turn onto Tenth Street, wondering how he handled it so well.

I shifted my foot to the brake pedal . . . and nothing happened. My attention snapped back to the present. The pedal sank all the way to the floor, but my truck didn't slow a bit. I tried pumping it.

Zilch. Nada.

Deep breath. Think, Sophie Mae, think fast. And whatever you do, DON'T PANIC.

The speed limit in town was only twenty-five miles an hour, and as usual, I wasn't in enough of a hurry to break it. So it wasn't like I was careening down some winding mountain road, ready to tip off a cliff at any moment. If I had to lose my brakes at all, I probably couldn't pick a better place to do it than meandering through sleepy Cadyville, Washington.

The Toyota was, however, headed down a hill.

I yanked on the emergency brake.

The truck didn't slow an iota.

I tried to downshift.

That didn't work, either.

This might be more than faulty brakes. Another arrow of fear stabbed through my solar plexus. My fingers curled around the steering wheel so hard they hurt, but I didn't loosen my grip.

The slope was gentle, but the pickup's speed was increasing. I eyed the edges of the street, thinking I could nudge up next to a curb. It wouldn't be great for the tires, but it would slow me down. But this street had no curbs. I'd go straight up on the sidewalk, and then into someone's yard. By now I was going fast enough that I might end up in their living room.

There must be other options. Had to be. *Think of something, Sophie Mae. Now.*

A cross street ahead, and a stop sign to go with it.

No choice but to brazen it out. Clenching my teeth, I leaned on my horn and sailed into the intersection. A cream-colored Mercedes approached from the right, and the driver didn't even slow. Narrowly missing my bumper, she leaned on her horn, too, and yelled at me out of her window.

It wasn't a very nice name to call someone under any circumstances, and given my current straits I yelled something equally not nice back at her.

Heart hammering against my ribs, I considered bailing out and letting the truck veer on alone. My hand moved to unhook my seat belt, then stopped. There had to be a better way. Not only would a tumble like that hurt, probably a lot, but a runaway vehicle could do real damage. It could hit a child, for heaven's sake.

There. Pine Street. It wended up a long hill, and if I could make the turn, it would serve the same role as the runaway truck lanes off interstate highways in the mountains.

Turning onto another street would be risky. I calculated the approach, steered as wide as I could, and, teeth clenched, swerved right onto Pine. Rubber squealed against pavement. My sunglasses skittered down the dash and bounced to the floor, and the block of beeswax on the seat beside me slammed into the passenger door. For a moment the truck felt suspended, the wheels on the left nearly leaving the ground. I leaned against my door, as if that would keep it from overturning.

Don't roll over, don't roll over, don't roll over. I muttered out loud to the Toyota, to myself, to the Universe and anyone else who happened to be listening. Panic praying.

The truck made it through the turn, straightened, and began heading toward the hill.

Before Pine began to climb, though, I had another short hill to go down, with Ninth Street at the bottom. Another stop sign. I leaned on the horn again, hoping to warn any oncoming traffic well ahead of their arrival.

No one was coming, and I breezed cleanly through.

Thank God this hadn't happened in Seattle. I'd have been creamed in no time, I thought as the truck reached the bottom of the hill and began to climb.

Perfect.

The Toyota continued up the hill, slower and slower.

Creeping.

Inching to a stop.

I let out a whoosh of breath I'd been holding in my lungs for who knew how long. I was going to be okay. Really okay.

The truck started rolling backwards.

Of course, the brakes didn't work in that direction, either. I swore and concentrated on steering in reverse. Went back through the intersection of Ninth and Pine, and a little ways up the hill I'd just come down.

Again the truck slowed to a stop, and paused, hanging on the verge of movement for a small eternity. My empty hope that the ordeal was over fell away like dust as the truck began rolling forward.

A teenaged boy driving a beat-up Honda came up from behind and veered around me. He gave me a questioning look, but at least he didn't yell or make rude gestures.

And then I was rolling backwards. The seesawing between one incline and the next felt like something out of an irritating slapstick comedy. Finally, the Toyota barely crept along. Slower.

And slower.

And stopped. Really and truly stopped.

Smack dab in the middle of the intersection of Ninth and Pine.

Nice.

Trembling with relief, I unhooked my seat belt and reached for my cell phone.

A horn blared. A really, really big horn followed by the shrieking of brakes. My head jerked up. Fear trilled through me. A semi-truck bore down, trailer slewing as the driver desperately tried to stop. It was going way, way over the tidy twenty-five-mile-an-hour speed limit, and it was about to go over me, too.

In one motion I opened the door and dove out of my little pickup. The grit of the pavement barely registered against my palms as I rolled to my feet and ran. The terrifying crunch of tearing metal sounded behind me. Over my shoulder, I saw the driver of the big rig had managed to slow down, but it still pushed my little Toyota pickup over, crumpling it in slow motion like so much cardboard.

The five-gallon bucket of baking soda in the bed of my truck erupted into the air. The sun shone through the dusty cloud, giving the whole mess a romantic, surreal effect.

The driver leapt from the semi and ran to me. "Oh, God, lady. Are you okay?" He peered at the wreck. "Was there anyone else in there?"

I shook my head, curiously unable to

speak. I looked down at my hands, fluttering at the ends of my arms like leaves in the wind. Oh, wait a minute. No wonder: my whole body was shaking like that.

People began spilling out of houses up and down the street. The eerie ululation of sirens grew louder. I crossed my arms over my chest and eyed my poor little truck, still not quite believing what had just happened.

A patrol car screeched to a stop. An ambulance was next, accompanied by a fire truck. But no one was going to be able to put Humpty Dumpty back together again.

I started to giggle.

The truck driver looked at me with alarm.

"Sorry," I gasped. "It's just so —" The laughter erupted again, cutting off my words. A paramedic hurried over.

"She doesn't seem hurt," the truck driver said, deep concern in his voice. "But she started laughing like that a few moments ago."

"Just a little hysteria," the paramedic said, reaching for his bag.

"Nuh uh," I managed to snort out.

"You'll be okay in a little bit," he said.

"Sophie Mae? Is that you?"

Tears streaming down my face, I turned to see Detective Robin Lane, hands on her perfectly proportioned hips, surveying the scene.

"Oh, yeah," I choked. "It's me." I sniffed and rubbed the back of my hand across my cheek.

She peered at me, then asked the paramedic. "What's wrong with her? Is she on drugs?"

A giggle sneaked out, and I clamped my hand over my mouth.

"Nah, I don't think so," the paramedic said. "It's just a nervous reaction to almost getting killed."

The urge to laugh disappeared completely. I had almost been killed. Oh. Wow.

"What happened?" Lane asked.

For the first time since my old pickup had gone to Toyota heaven, I was able to speak like a normal human being. "My brakes wouldn't work."

Her forehead furrowed. "Just went out? All of a sudden?"

"Completely." I went on to describe what I'd done, and how I had finally brought the little truck to rest. "Then this guy plowed into me." I gestured toward the trucker.

"Hey lady, it wasn't my fault your vehicle was in the intersection like that."

"You were going too fast," I said, my voice

wavering a little. "And you darn well know it."

He stubbed his toe into the ground and looked up at Robin through the fringe of hair that had flopped down on his forehead. I almost felt sorry for him. Almost.

The paramedic poked and prodded at me a little, then pronounced me physically fit. He was recommending that I go to a hospital to make sure when Barr strode up and put his arm around my shoulders.

"Robin called me. What happened?"

I sighed and told the story all over again.

"I'm taking you home," he said. "Stay here, and I'll be right back." He went to where Robin was questioning the truck driver further and spoke to her. She started to shake her head, but he shook his own once, firmly, and returned to where I stood waiting. In seconds he'd bundled me into his car and we were driving away.

"Thanks for rescuing me," I said. "Just drop me at the house, and you can get back to work."

"You dope," he said, the tenderness in his tone belying the words. "I'm taking the rest of the day off."

Wow. Barr Ambrose didn't "take the rest of the day off" lightly. If it took the demise of my vehicle and me almost dying for it to happen, then so be it. I'd sit back and enjoy.

But when I looked over, I saw the muscles working along his jaw. He was really upset.

TWENTY-FIVE

Meghan was appalled when she heard what had happened, and commenced fussing and feeding. The three of us settled into the living room with tea and spice cake. Brodie waddled between us, urging us with his brown eyes, fox-like ears, and occasional corgi talk to share our baked goods while we discussed mechanical issues.

"The emergency brake wouldn't work either?" Meghan asked.

I shook my head. "Nope. And I tried to downshift, but it seemed like it was stuck in gear." I turned to Barr. "Was Scott Popper's patrol car ever checked out, you know, to make sure nothing mechanical was wrong with it?"

"It's still in the wrecking yard. I wanted to get a little more information before calling his accident a homicide," he said.

"There are an awful lot of cars killing or nearly killing their occupants in this case.

There's Scott's wreck. There's what happened to me today. And there's the wreck that killed Ariel and Rocky's parents about ten years ago."

Meghan's brow furrowed. Barr looked thoughtful, then chagrined.

"What?" I asked when I saw his expression.

"I was thinking what happened to your truck today had nothing to do with the murder."

Which murder, I almost asked. I was starting to think we were dealing with more than one. So what was Barr talking . . . hey, wait a minute.

I stood up quickly, and Brodie gave a sharp bark of surprise. "Hang on. Are you saying you think your ex sabotaged my truck?"

Meghan's gaze whipped from me to Barr. "Oh, you can't. She wouldn't. That's crazy."

I began to pace. "Well, your mom said Hannah was a little crazy, as I recall."

Barr held his palms up. "I've never known her to be violent."

Stopping in front of him, I crossed my arms. "But you assumed it was her right away, didn't you?"

He inclined his head a fraction. "I could be wrong. I hope I'm wrong. But I don't

272

like how she disappeared from where she was staying and still keeps trying to talk to you." His eyes flicked to Meghan. "Two million is a lot of money."

I grumbled a word that rhymed with "itch" under my breath. Then cocked my head. "Does she know anything about cars? I mean, would she even know how to do it?"

"I don't know," Barr said. "She could have learned a lot in ten years."

"Oh, no." I rubbed my palms over my face. "You know who else knows about cars? Besides your venomous ex?"

They both shook their heads.

"Gabi Kaminski."

Meghan's head drew back in surprise. "Really?"

"In Rocky's barn-turned-garage, he asked her to give him a clutch-compressor springie thingie or whatever it was. She knew exactly what he was talking about."

Barr's forehead wrinkled while he untangled what I'd just said. "You mean a clutch-spring compressor? Was he working on a transmission?"

"I think so." I waved my hand. "Whatever. But the point is that she knew what it was. I bet Gabi's just as good of a mechanic as Ariel was. She's pretty angry at me. Over the course of the several hours I spent with her and her family, a lot of information about Ariel came out. Then I saw Thea Hawke's roving, told you about it, and had the temerity to come back into her house and point it out to you." I took another piece of spice cake, ravenous after my brush with death. My teeth sank into the moist, cinnamon-scented crumb.

"Well, we can't do anything until we know for sure that your brakes were deliberately sabotaged," Barr said. His expression was skeptical.

"Of course," I said.

"What if it was just an accident?" Meghan asked.

Fat chance.

"I don't know," Barr said. "But we're going to have someone look at it and find out."

"Scott's, too?"

He nodded. "We'd better."

"Well, don't take it to Dusty's Fix-It," I said.

"Why not?" Meghan asked. "Dusty does great work on the Volvo."

"And they have the contract with the city of Cadyville, too. Maintenance on all the police cars," Barr said slowly.

"Oh, wow. Didn't you know?" I drained my tea. "Zak Nelson works there."

We all exchanged looks, and Barr nodded.

"I'm sending both vehicles to the crime lab," Barr said, standing. "I know I said I was taking the day off, but would you be angry if I went and followed up on this?"

I forced a smile. "Not a bit. I want to know if those brakes were an accident, or if someone actually tried to, you know . . ." I glanced at Meghan. "Kill me."

"Because of your investigation," she said, bitterness underlying every word. "I swear, I worry more about you than I do about my own daughter." She stood and turned her ire on Barr. "She promised this wouldn't happen again, and then you had to go and ask her to get involved. Well, I hope you're happy." Shouldering past him, she went into her office.

"Meghan, wait," I called.

The door closed loudly behind her.

I started to go after her, but Barr put his hand on my arm. "Let it be."

"But —"

"She's right. I should have asked you to leave CRAC, not get involved even further with that bunch of snakes."

"Hey, I like it there," I said. "I wouldn't have stopped going just because you asked me."

He gripped my shoulders. "Meghan's still right."

I frowned. "I tried to be so careful."

"Well." He leaned in. "The cat's out of the bag now. You watch your back."

I nodded my agreement. Better late than never.

Barr left, Meghan's one o'clock client showed up, and I took the cordless phone downstairs. Despite my suspicion that Gabi Kaminski had had something to do with my brakes failing, I wanted to follow up on Barr's initial thoughts about the cause of the incident.

I dialed. Waited. "Hello? Is this Mrs. Ambrose? Cassie? This is Sophie Mae. Reynolds. We spoke the other day."

"Hello, Sophie Mae," Cassie said on the other end of the line. "How are you?"

"Well, I'm fine, though I must admit I've been better. That's why I called. I have a question for you."

A pause and then, "All right. Shoot."

I grimaced and plunged on. "Does Hannah know anything about car mechanics?"

"Car mechanics? What on earth? What did she do, offer to change your oil?"

My laugh sounded thin. "Hardly. I'm talking about something a little more sophisticated. Would she know how to cut a brake line?"

There was silence on the other end of the phone, and when Barr's mother finally spoke the bantering note was gone. "I don't think so. Hannah's a tough little thing, and she can ride most anything with four legs, but she knows horses, not cars."

"You're sure."

"Well, we spend a lot of time together, but I couldn't say for sure, no. She has a life away from here. I don't know what all it involves. Not my business."

I couldn't keep the disappointment out of my voice. "All right, thanks."

"What happened?"

Silence on my end this time.

"Sophie Mae, did something happen to your car?"

I sighed. "Yes, ma'am. The brakes went out on my little pickup."

"Are you okay?"

"I am. My truck wasn't so lucky. It was completely totaled."

An intake of breath on the other end of the line. "I'm sorry to hear that. I really am. But why would you think Hannah had something to do with it?"

"Uh, well, Barr kind of said — oh never mind. I shouldn't have called. It's just that neither of us is exactly neutral on the subject of Hannah, and I thought you might be able to, well, you know. Provide some perspective on the situation." The more I talked, the dumber I sounded. But did that stop me from saying more? No.

"See, Barr talked to her, and she said she'd leave town, go home. She left the place she was staying, and he can't find her now, but she's stopped by my house to talk to me twice since then."

"What did she say?"

"I wasn't home either time." I rubbed my eyes. "I just don't know what to think. And then when this happened this morning, we had to wonder."

"Now listen," Cassie said. "Hannah can be a little flighty, but she never struck me as the sort who would really hurt anyone. She'll come back here soon enough. Maybe she just wants to meet the woman who captured Barr's heart so thoroughly. Don't begrudge her that."

"Yes, ma'am," I said. "I'll try not to jump to any conclusions."

"Don't call me ma'am, for heaven's sake. I'll try to get a hold of that girl from this end, see if I can't talk some sense into her."

"Oh, gosh. I don't want to cause any trouble between you and an employee." And the last thing I needed was to make Hannah even angrier.

"Now don't you worry about that. And Sophie Mae?"

"Yes?"

"I'm awful glad you're okay. I haven't met you face-to-face yet, but I'm getting real fond of you already. You take care of yourself, hear?"

"I will. Thank you."

I felt better after talking to Cassie Ambrose. She had a calming, grounding effect. I could only imagine what it would be like in person. But the truth was she didn't know much more than Barr or I did about Hannah's mechanical ability.

My teenaged helper, Cyan, was eager to work after missing a day. Business had been gradually picking up during the previous six months, so when she arrived I dumped a ton of recent online orders on her, armed her with an inventory list, boxes, tape, packing peanuts, and my computer, and told her she could stay as long as she needed to get it all done. She set to her tasks with cheerful alacrity, the Dixie Chicks thumping away on the portable stereo I'd recently added to my workroom.

Since I didn't have a vehicle at the moment, I had to walk to CRAC. I'd promised to watch the retail shop for the four-to-eight evening shift now that we were open again. I wasn't going to let the co-op down just because a semi destroyed my only means of transportation. Not that I wouldn't have changed my mind in a second if Barr had actually taken the day off.

Oh, my poor little Toyota. It had been such a steady and reliable companion for so long. I missed it already. What could I possibly get for the insurance money? It was an old pickup by their standards, and they probably wouldn't give me much for it. Getting a new vehicle, even a used one, would be expensive.

Vehicle failure seemed to be quite the theme surrounding Ariel's murder, but in truth it had nothing to do with how she was killed. Ariel had been hit on the head and then strangled. And *she* sure as heck hadn't been the one to cut my brake line.

But had she cut Scott Popper's? Barr would find out, whether he was the lead detective on the case or not.

Irene was seated behind the register at CRAC, looking bored. She glanced up when I walked in, then went back to the occasional desultory swipe of her pencil across the drawing pad open in front of her.

"Hi." I slung my tote bag under the counter with a dull thump. "Has it been busy?"

She sniffed. "No. You were wrong. No one's come in."

"Well, perhaps no one knows we're open again. It happened kind of fast."

"Maybe."

What an Eeyore. "Are you going to stay awhile, or do you need to get going?"

"I'm waiting for Zak to come get me," she said, filling in the shading on a meaty arm. I glimpsed enough of the rest of the drawing to see she was designing yet another of her female power figurines. "He's late. Again. But then, so are you."

I looked at the clock on the wall. "I was here on time."

She sniffed again.

Oh, brother. What did she have against me, for Pete's sake? I'd never so much as said boo to her before joining CRAC, and my interactions with her since had been infrequent and low key.

"As long as you're here, I'm going to go upstairs and check out some of the fiber for sale."

She shrugged without looking up. Her pencil scratched across the rough Bristol board.

I went up to the shelves and baskets filled with fiber ready to spin. Gabi's stash hadn't been much smaller than this. The raw, uncarded alpaca wool caught my eye, and I thought of Lindsey Drucker, raising animals, spinning, weaving, and living with another artist. It couldn't possibly be as ideal of a lifestyle as it sounded. I mean, could anything live up to being that perfect?

Lindsey was a woman with demons, after all. Demons Ariel had shared, and that she'd tried to save her from.

"Sophie Mae," Irene called from the bottom of the stairs. "Sophie Mae! Zak's here, and I'm leaving. Now."

Sheesh. Give a woman a little time to shop, won't you? "Okay, I'm coming."

I hit the ground floor, and Irene was out the door. Her son turned to follow.

"Zak," I said.

He looked at me over his shoulder. "Yeah?"

"I told Rocky Kaminski about the painting you wanted, but —"

"I know." His gaze jerked to his mother, already halfway across the parking lot, then back to me. "His wife called me. Can I leave the painting here for a day or two after I get it?"

"Rocky's going to sell it to you after all?"

He nodded.

"Okay." I noted the black grease under his fingernails. Was he as handy at *un*fixing cars as he was at fixing them? And how would that translate to strangulation? "You must have really loved Ariel," I suddenly blurted out. The words hung awkwardly in the air between us.

He looked surprised, then ducked his head as pink embarrassment crept up past the rivets in his ears.

I kept my tone mild. "It's nice that you want her picture, is all." I busied myself behind the counter, deliberately not looking him in the eye. Like facing a strange dog, I wasn't sure what I was dealing with here. Best not to appear threatening in any way.

"We were seeing each other," he said.

I risked a glance at him.

"But she broke up with me."

"Really? I'm sorry. That must have hurt."

"Not really," he said.

I stopped arranging and rearranging a pile of Post-its and looked directly at him.

"It was kind of a relief when she did it. Ariel was kind of scary, you know? We had some fun, but she could get really weird and moody and mean. Besides, I kind of like someone else."

I pasted encouragement on my face.

"Anyone I know?"

"Her name's Daphne. She was Ariel's roommate. She's, like, the nicest person I've ever met."

Daphne had some additional attributes which might appeal to a young man, as I recalled. But it was refreshing to hear a boy talk about a girl being nice, and his voice became softer when he said her name.

"The horticulture student? I met her once," I said.

"I guess you must think it's kind of weird for me to want one of Ariel's paintings if she broke up with me, but I did like her, you know. I think we would've still been friends."

"Zak!" Irene's voice floated back to us.

"Anyway, thanks. I'll see you soon." And Zak was out the door.

He'd see me soon? What was that supposed to mean?

TWENTY-SIX

Two hours later, I found out. As soon as Irene left, I added the essential oil blend I'd customized for the co-op to the diffuser on the counter and took a deep breath as the gentle fragrance overrode the stale air. After a while, customers started trickling in the door. I wasn't busy the whole time, but enough people kept coming in that it felt worthwhile to be there. An older couple was in the rear of the co-op looking at some of Jake Beagle's photography when Zak returned.

The front door was propped open to allow the slight breeze in. Zak was a skinny kid and barely filled half the frame. Behind him, I saw an older model blue Suburban turn into the parking lot. I recognized it right away. Zak hurried out as the Chevy pulled into a space.

Gabi Kaminski swung down from the driver's seat. A sleeveless white blouse showed off her tan, as did her denim shorts and leather sandals. She'd plaited her smooth, caramel-colored hair into a neat braid. She and Zak talked for a few minutes. I craned my neck to watch them. He seemed to be doing most of the talking. She gestured widely with one arm and laughed.

"Excuse me. We'd like to buy these." The gray-haired gentleman laid two of Jake's photos from the black-and-white Riparian series on the counter and reached into his pocket for his wallet.

"These are lovely, aren't they?" I asked while darting looks over his shoulder. Zak was unloading something from the back of the Suburban.

"They are indeed."

His wife said, "He's a fly fisherman, and these will keep him company in the den when he can't get out to the river."

I smiled. "Mmm hmm."

Yep: it was the painting Zak had put the note on. I wondered whether Rocky knew Gabi was selling it.

After I took their money, thanked them, and wished them a nice evening, the couple finally wandered out. I followed them to the door, then stepped back almost immediately so Zak could fit the big canvas through the opening. Gabi followed closely behind him.

When she raised her head and saw me standing in the doorway, she stopped like she'd run into a brick wall. Surprise flitted across her face, rapidly replaced with a mask of careful indifference.

"You," she said.

Indeed. "Gabi."

Had this woman tried to kill me? I remembered the sound of crunching metal, the screech of it sparking across the asphalt as the eighteen-wheeler crushed my little truck into the ground. The salt-sting of baking soda lingering in the air. My own fear during the whole ordeal, still on my skin. I tasted it now, in the back of my throat, along with a rapidly growing anger.

And here she was, in Cadyville, right in front of me. I wondered where Rocky thought she was, what he'd swear to this time. Because I was fairly sure he had no idea she'd sold his dead sister's painting to Zak.

I felt my nostrils flare.

Zak's gaze shuttled between us, his eyes narrowing as he tried to discern the flavor of our hostility. He handed her a fistful of bills. "It's all there, Ms. Kaminski. Thanks for bringing it to me. I really 'preciate it."

She began counting the money. "Happy to do it."

"Did you have any trouble finding the place?" he asked.

She looked up. "What? Oh, no. You gave excellent directions."

Sure. Like she'd never been to the co-op before. Probably just one more lie to add to the list.

When she'd finished with the money, she put it in her purse. "I'd better get back. Rocky's watching the boys."

"Gabi," I said again. "May I have a word?"

"I'm not really in the mood to chat right now." She began to turn away.

I kept my voice even and low, though my anger had grown exponentially during their short exchange. "We need to talk."

Ah, those magic words. She paused, then turned back. I could hear her breathing. We both looked at Zak.

"Oh, um, right. I gotta go," he said, no doubt anxious to escape the mounting tension. He gestured toward the painting. "I'll pick this up later, 'K?"

"No problem," I said.

" 'K," he said again. "Bye."

After he'd left, I shut the front door and locked it. I might be locking myself in with a killer, I realized, but I was too angry to care. Besides, it wouldn't have been the first time. Remembering, my hand started to go to where my long braid used to hang down my back, but I stopped and let it drop.

"Thanks again for siccing the cops on me, Sophie Mae. That was real special. I don't know why I ever thought you were a nice person." She stood regarding me with both arms folded across her chest. "Now what's so important that we have to talk about?"

"I think you know."

"Gosh, I'm afraid I don't." Sarcasm dripped from every syllable.

"A semi totaled my pickup earlier today when my brakes went out."

Something crossed her face, then was gone. Guilt? Fear? As carefully as I'd been watching, I couldn't tell.

"Why are you telling me this? It has nothing to do with me, and you're obviously fine if you're here."

"Oh, I'm fine and dandy. However, my brake lines were deliberately cut." Okay, so I was jumping the gun. But she was right there in front of me, and I wanted to see her reaction.

She met my eyes without flinching.

"You wouldn't know anything about that, now would you?" I asked.

She glared. "What exactly are you implying?"

"I'm not implying anything. I'm asking

you straight out. Did you mess around with my truck?"

"Of course not! And you'd better not go around telling anyone that I did, or I'll sue you for defamation of character!"

Oh, brother.

I pushed further. "Guess Rocky must have changed his mind about keeping all of his sister's artwork if you sold that piece to Zak, huh."

Her eyes slewed to the side. "That's none of your business."

Bingo.

But it didn't make her a murderer.

Gabi's eyes narrowed to slits. "What do you want?"

"I want to know if you killed Ariel. I want to know if you tried to kill me." The words flew out of my mouth, propelled by anger at the idea that she'd done exactly those things. Goose bumps rose on my arms. I clamped my mouth shut.

I watched the accusation settle into her psyche. I barely dared to breathe. Gabi, on the other hand, turned pale under her tan and began sipping oxygen through her overbite, almost panting. Suddenly red rage infused her face and she stood, towering over me. I backed away a few steps, then forced myself to stop.

"How can you say such a horrible thing?" she hissed. "I've never met anyone so cruel."

I stood my ground. "Not as cruel as your sister-in-law's murderer."

"Are you crazy? Rocky told you I was home that night."

"Sure he did. But we both know you could have sneaked out when he was fast asleep, and driven down here to meet Ariel. Did you plan to kill her before you came? Or did she ask for yet more money? What did she do to send you over the edge?"

Her lips turned up, then down, as if she didn't know what to do with her mouth. She shook her head. "I'd never kill anyone. I was home that night. All night. Rocky knows that. He'll swear to it."

"And someone saw you messing around with my truck," I lied, looking her straight in the eye. Who's a bad liar? Not me.

It seemed to work. Gabi looked really scared.

But she still didn't tip. "They couldn't have. I was home last night, too."

"And Rocky will confirm that."

"That's right. Listen, I don't know what your problem is, or what you want from me, but I didn't do anything wrong." Her voice wavered on the last few words.

I kept pushing. "Why did Ariel have Thea

Hawke's bamboo fiber clutched in her hand when I found her? Why do you think we came up to see you about that fiber, anyway?"

She blinked. And slumped.

I took the opportunity and walked to the other side of the counter. "Gabi. You know what I'm talking about. You took those batts when you were here. I understand. You couldn't help yourself. You must have been looking at them when you were talking to Ariel, which is why she was by Ruth's spinning supplies instead of in her own studio space."

"I don't know what you're talking about," she mumbled.

"Ariel had a tuft in her *hand.* She must have grabbed it from you when you came up behind her." I said, thinking out loud now. "No, not yet. Because you were holding my yarn."

Her head jerked up. "Your yarn?"

"My yarn. My first sheep's wool two-ply." I couldn't keep the fury out of my voice, consumed with the thought that she'd used my yarn to kill that little girl.

"I have to go," she whispered, backing toward the front wall. She reached behind her back and fumbled with the lock on the door. Turned the knob. It opened.

"I didn't do anything wrong," she insisted one last time and fled.

I followed, but she was already pulling the Suburban out of the parking lot. She left rubber on the asphalt and barely missed hitting a silver sedan with Canadian license plates. The driver honked as she sped away.

The adrenaline seemed to disappear from my veins in a reverse rush. Weariness and inexplicable regret settled on me, heavy as sin, and I had to sit down on the bench located outside the door until I got my bearings again.

A bitter feeling that I'd screwed up crept over me and took up lodging in my stomach. Screwed up royally.

TWENTY-SEVEN

The unusually nice summer weather we'd been enjoying had been pushed out by a low pressure system and glowering skies. I walked quickly, hoping to beat the rain while at the same time gratefully inhaling the cooler air. Thoughts ping-ponged around my brain as if superheated. The more I thought about it, the more I questioned whether Gabi had killed Ariel. All the evidence seemed to point that way, even if she did have reasonable explanations for everything. But her reactions to my accusations were out of sync. She seemed more afraid than guilty. I wished I knew her better, so I could get more of a read on her. If only I could know for sure whether or not she was telling the truth.

As I came up our block, I saw someone on our front step. The closer I got, the more it looked like me sitting there.

Oh, great. Just what I needed.

Hannah Ambrose stood as I approached, her weight on one foot as if she were on the verge of running away.

If I'd had the sense of a gnat I'd have walked right on by, let her twist in the wind long enough to talk herself out of her visit.

But I apparently didn't have the sense of a gnat. "Hello, Hannah."

She looked at the ground. Awkwardly shuffled her feet. "Hi."

This was not the cocky, confident woman I'd met on Barr's front step.

I stopped in front of her. "You here to see me?"

She nodded. "Uh huh."

"Give me a second."

"Okay."

I went inside, shut the front door in her face and marched into Meghan's office. She looked up in surprise.

"Hannah's outside," I announced.

She leaned back. "So? Let her in."

"Really?"

"Or talk to her out there. Either way, I don't know what you want me to do about it."

I grimaced. "Neither do I. All I know is, I don't want to face the music, but the music is standing right on the other side of our front door."

"Go on. You can do it. Then come back and tell me what she said."

I sighed. "Fine."

In the entryway, I took a deep breath, grasped the knob, and flung the door open.

She stood on the bottom step, looking up at me and hugging herself with thin arms. Her short-sleeved cotton camp shirt was wrinkled, as were the Capri pants. She wore an old pair of Keds with no socks. She radiated an aura of disheveled youth and vulnerability.

I didn't buy it.

"Come on in," I said and led the way into the house. She trailed behind like a lost child.

Brodie greeted us in the foyer, and Hannah bent to pet his wiggling little self. He grinned up at her and gave a little yip.

Traitor.

"Can I get you something? Tea? Coffee?" Arsenic?

She shook her head. "No thanks."

So much for putting it off. Whatever "it" was.

"I have some work to do. We can talk while I do it," I said in Hannah's general direction.

"Okay."

Sheesh. What a conversationalist.

We traipsed through the kitchen and down the narrow wooden stairs to my basement workroom.

I didn't know what this woman wanted, or how she had the audacity to come visit me at all, but whatever her reasons, I liked the idea of dealing with her on my own turf. Indicating a stool on the other side of the center island where I worked, I said, "Have a seat."

She sat, craning her neck as she took in the kitchen appliances, the many work surfaces. "Cassie says you're a soap maker."

"I am." I waited for the next question. Talking about soap was easy.

But she wrinkled her nose. "It smells funny in here."

"It smells like rosemary in here." My voice was flat. "Which, last time I checked, wasn't all that funny."

"Oh," she said.

I used a wire grid to cut through one of the slabs of soap I'd poured previously. And waited. Glanced up. Then I picked up a knife and began trimming the uniform bars, smoothing the edges.

She watched the motions of my hands as if mesmerized. I tried to imagine this person cutting my brake line. Trying to kill me. I debated whether or not to confront her about it, very aware of how badly that had gone over with Gabi Kaminski.

Finally, I couldn't take it anymore. "Hannah."

She looked up.

"Why are you here?"

"I . . ." She licked her lips. "Well, I want you to give up Barr."

"Excuse me? Give him up?"

"Yes."

"Like 'give' him to you?"

"Well, I guess it would look like that."

"No. It would be like that. Barr's a big boy, Hannah. Neither of us gets to decide what he does."

"You haven't been together very long. I've known him forever; we come from the same town. We have a history together, and you don't. And even if he won't admit it, he still loves me."

The knife slipped, and I nearly took off my thumb. Very carefully, I laid the blade on the work surface. My hands might have been trembling, but I managed to keep my voice low and even.

"This is ridiculous. I'm not having this conversation with you. You should go."

Raw fury at my dismissal flared in her eyes for an instant. She quickly blinked and looked away.

"I had him first." She sounded like a petulant child. Now tears magnified those big green eyes and made the long lashes shine in a way I imagined would pull at the heartstrings of a lot of men.

Kind of made me cranky, to tell the truth.

"Well, you need to come to grips with the fact that you don't have him now. Coming here and talking to me about it isn't going to change anything."

"But I love him!" she wailed.

Oh, for heaven's sake.

"I'm sorry. I can't give him to you, even if I wanted to." Which I emphatically didn't. After all, I loved him, too. Besides, possession is nine-tenths — well, you get it.

Possession. Did I really think of Barr as a possession?

Of course not.

But he was still mine.

She tried again. "I need him."

More like his bank account. "Hannah, if this is a conversation you should be having with anyone, it should be with Barr." Oh, God. What was I saying?

"I've tried, but he just won't listen."

I couldn't help it. I took the leap. "Did you sabotage my brakes so I'd get in a car wreck?"

She stared at me. "What?" Standing now,

her tone went from zero to sixty in nothing flat. "How *dare* you," she spluttered. "I mean, *God!*"

"Hannah, you need to leave now."

She blinked. "But —"

"No. Really."

Her lower lip crept into a pout. "You're mean."

That, too.

"I'm sorry you're unhappy. And I'm sorry you feel the need to spread it around so freely, but we don't have anything left to talk about."

Her features grew hard and her gaze sharpened. "You won't win. You're only a temporary interloper, Sophie Mae. He's supposed to be with me, and he's going to be, in the end. Whether you do the right thing or not."

"Listen, sister. He's not mine to give. He's his own man, with opinions and affections and desires. I could no more give him away than I could give away the weather. If he wants you instead of me, then so be it."

She smirked.

"But he doesn't," I continued. "He wants me, and there's nothing you can do to change that. Not a damn thing."

"She's right." Barr's voice came from the bottom of the stairs, startling both of us.

His tone was gentle as he said, "Hannah, there's nothing left between us. You know that. Go on home to the ranch. It's where you belong."

"Come with me," she said, pleading.

He slowly shook his head.

She turned and stomped toward the stairway, hands clenched into fists by her side, fingers white. Barr moved aside as I followed her upstairs and through the house to the front entryway. Not once did she turn around, not even as she jerked the door open and exited the house. The loud slam of the door brought Meghan out of her office.

"Sounds like someone left unhappy."

I nodded, thoughtful. "Miss Hannah wanted something, and she didn't get it."

Barr spoke from behind me. "Sophie Mae was wonderful."

"Really?" I asked.

He quoted me. " 'I could no more give him away than I could give away the weather.' "

I rolled my eyes. How corny.

"I think you convinced her," he said.

"What do you think she'll do now?" Meghan asked.

I shook my head. "I don't know."

"I think she'll go home," Barr said.

But I was just as concerned with what she might have already done. Despite her dramatic protestations, Hannah hadn't actually denied sabotaging my pickup.

Meghan, Barr, and I had moved into the kitchen for a late supper of spinach salad topped with chicken, tomato, avocado, and black olives in a warm vinaigrette. Erin and Zoe had made up, and Erin was spending the night over there. Ruefully, I realized I already missed the little imp, and I still lived with her. As she got into her teens, summers would only get busier.

Barr had happened upon his ex and me fighting over him like schoolgirls because he had news. Now he laid it out.

"It's official. Your Toyota was deliberately sabotaged."

Relief washed over me. "Excellent," I blurted out without thinking. After all I'd accused Gabi of earlier, wouldn't it have been ironic if my brakes failed simply because my truck was old and had fallen apart?

Barr lifted an eyebrow at my reaction and took a bite of avocado.

"That was fast," Meghan said, standing at the sink and rinsing her plate. She ate like a bird, and always finished her meals before

302

everyone else. "What about Scott's patrol car?"

"They found some indications that the steering wasn't working properly."

I lifted my chin in an I-told-you-so gesture. "Sabotage?"

He looked uncomfortable, then nodded. "I should have known."

"You did," I said. "At the funeral, you suspected."

"But I didn't do anything about it."

Meghan closed the dishwasher door and turned. "You can't go around being suspicious of everyone and everything, Barr. That would be paranoid, especially in a sedate little town like Cadyville. Didn't you say once that was why you moved here from Seattle in the first place, because you felt like you were becoming so jaded? It looked like an accident, and so you treated it like one."

Sedate little town? Meghan obviously hadn't been paying attention.

Barr didn't say anything. I reached over and squeezed his hand. He squeezed back, then withdrew his fingers from mine. Not interested in being comforted.

Well, at least I could distract him. "Um." I bit my lip. "I kind of messed up."

Meghan came and sat down at the table.

She gazed at me for a long moment. "What did you do, Sophie Mae." Her tone was flat.

I sneaked a look at Barr. He sat back in his chair, eyebrow slightly arched again.

"Er, I kind of accused Gabi Kaminski of killing Ariel."

Meghan's jaw dropped. "You didn't."

I winced. "I'm afraid I did. I also accused her of fooling with the brakes on my truck."

"Before you even knew for sure it wasn't an accident?" Incredulity from Barr. "What were you thinking?"

"It just sort of happened. She brought one of Ariel's paintings down for Zak Nelson, and I knew darn well Rocky didn't know she was selling it, and I kept thinking about how she had a handy answer for everything when we were up there, but I didn't really believe any of them, and that huge truck *demolishing* my little pickup was *scary,* damn it." I took a deep breath and opened my mouth to continue, but Barr cut me off.

"It's okay," he said. "Scary doesn't even cover it, I'm sure. You must have been terrified."

I nodded furiously, swallowing against the lump that had risen in my throat. Barr smiled at me, and I tried to smile back. Didn't dare look at Meghan, or I would have started bawling right then and there.

"Did Gabi say anything incriminating?" he asked in a quiet tone.

When I was able to speak again I answered, "Not really. And I'm afraid I pushed her really hard. Now all I can think of is to try and trick her into confessing. Maybe wave Ariel's diary around in her face and say there's evidence in it. Or I could try blackmailing her, and see if she pays up to keep me quiet."

"Oh, you've got to be kidding," Meghan said. She stood up and walked to the sink, looked out the window at the darkening yard.

"That," Barr said, "is a terrible idea."

I pointed my finger at him. "It could very well work."

He just looked at me. Of course he was right. It was a stupid idea. If I wanted to climb out of the hole I'd dug by shooting my mouth off to Gabi, that wasn't the way to do it.

Meghan turned. "Did it ever occur to you that the reason she didn't confess is because she didn't kill Ariel?" Her voice overflowed with disbelief. "I mean, if you knew for sure she was guilty, you wouldn't have to trick her into admitting it; Robin and Barr would be able to prove it."

I had a fair amount of wonder in my own

voice when I said, "Are you actually implying that there aren't any murderers who get away with it? That there aren't crimes that go unpunished because the police don't have enough evidence?"

She frowned. "Are you saying there aren't people who are convicted despite being innocent?"

I thought of all the suspects in this case and slumped in my chair. Put my head down on the table. Oh, God.

"If you're wrong, you've tortured that poor woman for no good reason." She squinted. "This is a side of you I don't see very often. I'm not sure I like it."

"Yeah," I mumbled. "I don't like it either." I didn't know what to think, couldn't see the forest for the trees. There wasn't any real evidence against Gabi, only my ideas about what might have happened. But she had a viable answer for everything, and simply hadn't reacted to any of my questions in a suspicious way.

All I'd done was make a potential friend hate me for life.

TWENTY-EIGHT

The next morning my alarm buzzed at seven, but I shut it off and went back to sleep. An hour and a half later I woke again, still feeling exhausted. It took me another half an hour to drag my sorry carcass out of bed, clothe it, and wander down to the kitchen.

A wire basket of eggs sat on the counter, and I cracked two small brown ones into a frying pan. Then I assembled a sandwich with the fried eggs on Meghan's home-baked bread, mayonnaise, catsup, dill pickles from the pantry, and a big slice of cheddar cheese. Comfort food from my childhood. I almost moaned as I bit into it, and immediately began to feel better. Two cups of coffee to wash down the fried egg sandwich, and I was ready for work.

I went down to the basement. First I finished cutting and trimming the lye soaps, then laid them in neat rows on my storeroom shelves to cure. So soon after making them, they were still quite alkaline, but the chemical process of saponification continued internally as they sat on the shelf, ultimately resulting in a soap milder than any commercial bar. An added benefit was that cold process soaps like mine still contained naturally occurring glycerin, adding to their humectant and emollient qualities.

Handling the new soap, though most of the time I'd worn gloves, had been hard on my hands. So had all the gardening of late. One of the solutions to what I referred to as "farmer's hands" was the solid lotion bars I made from beeswax, olive oil, and cocoa butter. These little gems were scattered all over the house for Meghan and me to use in the summer. But I'd just run across a lotion recipe on a website that sounded soothing and smoothing, and I wanted to try it. With all the manufacture I did for sale anymore, I didn't have as much opportunity to experiment with new formulas.

I gathered my ingredients and started melting the oils, shea butter, and beeswax together. The recipe called for witch hazel and lanolin, as well as free glycerin and rose water. An emulsifier would be necessary in order to properly blend the water-based elements with the oils. Lecithin would serve as a perfect binder, especially when combined with beeswax. Orange and lavender essential oils would complement the rose water to provide a fresh, light scent.

Using a hand blender, I whipped everything together, then returned every few minutes as the mixture cooled, whipping briefly each time. Finally, I used the blender steadily for several minutes. The result was a pastel, peach-colored fluff that melted into my skin. I rubbed some of it into my ragged cuticles and took a jar up to Meghan, doing bookwork in her office.

"Thanks," she said, and immediately started massaging it into her own hands.

"Sure." I sat down in the chair facing her desk. Through the half-open door, the fountain in the massage room behind her made babbling-brook noises. I closed my eyes for a few moments and allowed the sound to flow over me.

"This smells delicious. I'm half-tempted to take a bite," she said.

"Mmm hmmm."

A long silence, filled only with the serenade of running water.

"I'm sorry," she said, out of the blue.

I opened my eyes. "What for?"

"For coming down on you so hard about

Gabi last night."

My right shoulder rose and fell. "Don't be sorry. You were right. Are right." I shifted in the chair. "You know, the thing that's making me so crazy? There've been two situations we've been involved in where people died, and each time it looked like an accident. But we figured out what really happened." I paused, gathering my thoughts. "Now we have a straightforward murder, and it looks like the killer — whether it's Gabi or not — is going to get away with it."

Meghan shook her head. "You have to give Cadyville's finest some credit. They're still working on finding out what happened. Have a little faith."

"I guess." Even I could hear the doubt in my voice.

She smiled and said, "I know Barr asked for your help, but it's not your responsibility to find out what happened. It's their job. If you can help, great, but you've let this whole thing get under your skin too much."

"I keep *trying* to back off."

"I know. Don't let it get to you, okay?"

I stood up and took a couple of steps to the doorway. "You're right. As always. Thanks for watching out for me."

She blew out a puff of air. "Well, geez. Somebody has to."

■ ■ ■ ■

I'd just finished packaging the last of the custom bath fizzies for the wedding shower when the doorbell upstairs chimed. I hurried up to answer it.

Barr stood on the other side of the screen. "I'll trade information for food," he said.

"Funny man." I gestured him inside. "It's a deal. Tonight's dinner selection has an Asian theme. But first you have to hang out in the workroom while I clean up. Meghan's gone to pick Erin up from math camp."

"I love watching you fuss around down there," he said, and laid a big smacker on me before I could bristle at the term "fuss."

He followed me downstairs and settled onto a stool at the end of my work island. I went back to gathering small cellophane bags together and organizing the short lengths of satin ribbon used to tie them shut.

"Information before food," I said.

He laughed. "It's nothing much." Still, there was satisfaction on his face.

Intrigued, I continued to tidy the packaging materials and tried for nonchalant.

He fingered his string tie, this one a round sand-colored stone with the imprint of a tiny fish fossil in it. "We may have figured out who the killer is," he announced.

Nothing much, indeed.

"Who?" I leaned my elbows on the counter. "Stop teasing."

"We questioned Zak Nelson this afternoon. We hadn't before, at least not in enough depth. After you found out from Lindsey Drucker that he and Ariel had been dating, we decided to go back and have another conversation with him."

"Flatterer," I said. "Does he have an alibi like everyone else?"

He grimaced. "Hard to tell."

I pushed aside the ribbons I'd been sorting. "Meaning?"

"He told us he was at home. But then he changed his story and said he'd seen Ariel on the night of her murder." He paused for effect. "He met her at CRAC."

I sank onto the stool next to him. "Ohmygod. He was there?"

"He insists she was alive when he left."

Something wasn't quite right, but I couldn't put my finger on it. "Did he admit to doing anything to my brakes?" I asked.

Barr shook his head. "Robin asked him point blank. He seemed confused by the question, but then again, he could be a good actor."

"Yesterday Zak told me he'd been seeing

Ariel, but she broke up with him. That he didn't mind because he likes Daphne Sparks, her roommate."

"He told us the same thing. Only he admitted Ariel broke up with him *that night.* The night she was killed."

"Oh, wow. Really?" I frowned, trying to take it all in. "You did say strangulation is a crime of passion. And he could have killed his rival, too. He had the perfect access to Scott's patrol car."

"It's a pretty tidy package," Barr said. "But listen to this: Irene Nelson came in when we were talking to Zak and threw an absolute fit about him answering our questions. Then she told us Zak had been home with her during the timeframe of the murder. She said he'd been at CRAC, but that he'd gotten home *before* eight o'clock."

Shaking my head, I said, "But Irene is Chris' alibi. She can't be both, not unless Zak was with her at Chris' house." I scooped up my neatly arranged packaging materials and took them into my storeroom.

Barr followed on my heels. "When I pointed that out, she said she was lying about being at Chris' house."

"Was she?" I asked. "Or is she lying now to protect her son?"

"Your guess is as good as mine."

We clomped up the stairs to the kitchen. "My guess is that she's trying to protect Zak. After all, Ruth confirmed the group alibi at Chris'. It's too bad. I like the kid, even if he does look like a walking magnet."

The screen door slammed, and a few moments later Meghan and Erin came into the kitchen.

"Hey, just in time," I said. "The rice'll be done in a jiffy, and the chicken and veggies are ready to hit the wok."

Erin looked horrified. "You're cooking chicken?"

"Uh, well, yeah. I thought you loved stir fry."

"Not *chicken*. God, Sophie Mae." She was still shaking her head in disbelief as she went out to the backyard to gather eggs.

I turned to my housemate. "What was that all about?"

"She won't eat chicken anymore. Don't tell me that surprises you." Meghan's tone was wry.

"Ah. Got it. The girls have made her a convert. She's a vegetarian now." I scrambled for recipes in my head that might pass muster with the newly militant member of the household.

"Oh, she's not a vegetarian." Meghan grinned. "She just won't eat chicken."

"I'm not sure whether I'm relieved or disappointed."

"Well, I'm glad you're not going to foist a bunch of rabbit food on me," Barr said.

Meghan laughed. "There's tofu in the fridge for her stir-fry. And I hope she likes it, because she's eating it."

Twenty-Nine

Erin ate her tofu and claimed to love it. After dinner, Barr left to catch up on paperwork at the police station. While we did the dishes, I told Meghan what Barr had told me about Zak.

"I don't think he did it." She reached for the wok and began to rub oil onto the steel interior.

"Really?" I asked. "Tell me why."

"He's a nice kid."

I snorted. "That's what people always say about murderers." Playing the devil's advocate, though I felt the same way she did.

She placed the wok on a stove burner over a low flame to heat briefly, seasoning the metal. "He didn't try to hide where he was, or at least not very hard. It sounds like his mother is more worried about the police thinking he did it than he is."

"Which means his own *mother* thinks he killed that girl, and you don't."

"I'm not Irene Nelson." She pressed her lips together. "She can be a little . . ."

"Granted. Okay, then who did it?"

"You'd know better than I would. After all, you're the investigator."

"I am not! I'm just doing a little . . . extracurricular . . ."

"Snooping," she offered.

I raised my palms. "Fine. Have it your way."

The corners of her mouth turned up. "Better be careful, Reynolds. This is when things tend to get out of hand. But I'm going to bed."

"Goodnight," I said, a little sarcastic bite in my tone. Only a few hours earlier hadn't she said it wasn't my responsibility? "Don't forget to take the phone with you."

She grinned. "Remember when you and Barr talked on the phone every night?"

I had to nod. She was right. At least I got to see Barr; she and Kelly only saw each other every six weeks or so.

" 'Night," she said. "Oh, and tomorrow is the last day of Erin's math camp. It's a half day, and then we have to go pick Tootie and Felix up at the airport."

Tootie Hanover, part of the cruise set. Would wonders never cease?

"Noted. We can coordinate in the morning," I said.

Erin was already in bed, and with Meghan off to the land of nod, it was just Brodie and me. After everything that had happened that day, I should have been exhausted, but I felt like I was wired for sound.

Spinning had helped to relax me the other night. Might as well try it again.

After arranging the wheel, I oiled the moving parts, and attached the bands. Soon I was working my way through a length of off-white sheep's wool. It would be a while before I'd be spinning any more of Thea Hawke's light-as-thistle-down bamboo. The very thought of it left a sour taste in my mouth, after my bad behavior toward Gabi Kaminski. Tonight I even avoided the raw alpaca I'd given in and bought at the co-op. It seemed a good idea to go back to doing something I knew at least a little about.

But the act of spinning was just as soothing as ever. The Zen of it overtook me: the enthralling rhythm of the foot treadle combined with the soft whir of the fly wheel. The wool fairly flew out of my fingers, twisting into a uniform yarn and wrapping neatly onto the spool. It looked good. Really good. Way better than the stuff that had been used to strangle Ariel.

Ruth would be proud of me when I

showed her.

The next morning I walked to the little house Ruth and Thaddeus Black shared and found their mint-green Buick gone from the carport. I knocked anyway. Rustling sounded from inside, and finally the interior door swung open. Thaddeus peered out.

Recognition dawned. He pushed the screen door open. "Sophie Mae! Come in, come in. Glad you dropped by. I'm not getting out as much as I used to, and it's nice to have a visitor."

"Hello, Thaddeus. Is Ruth around? I wanted to show her some yarn I spun last night."

"Nope. Went to the store. That woman shops for groceries every day. I just don't understand it." His cane thumped in exclamation.

"Oh." I couldn't keep the disappointment from my voice.

"She'll be right back, though. Never takes her long. You come on in and wait." He waved me in. The house smelled of fake lavender air freshener. I made a note to bring them some Winding Road gel fresheners, made with essential oils. Some nice soap, too, and bath salts. It was the least I could do to pay Ruth back for letting me borrow her wheel and teaching me so much.

Thaddeus trailed behind me into the living room. "I heard what happened to that little truck of yours. You're a lucky girl."

"Don't I know it."

He nodded. "Sit down for a minute."

I sat. No good trying to get out of a little socializing, and besides, I liked Thaddeus Black.

"Can I get you anything? Coffee, maybe?" he asked, the gracious host.

"I'm fine."

He settled into his own chair and smiled broadly.

I smiled in return. "How's Ruth holding up, with all the trauma and drama over at CRAC?"

"You mean that little girl getting herself killed?" He waved his hand dismissively. "Ruth and I go to a couple of funerals a month."

"This was a little different, wouldn't you say?"

"Well, sure. All I'm saying is that Ruth isn't exactly a wilting vine when it comes to the difficulties in life. She's gentle as a lamb, but tough as nails, too."

"I'm glad she was able to provide an alibi for Chris Popper," I said. "It saved Chris a lot of grief."

"Well now, I didn't realize she had. That was good of Ruth."

Good of her? "But she was over at Chris' house that night."

He nodded. "I remember. Some kind of meeting she had to go to."

"It was a meeting? I thought everyone was over there because it was the night before Scott's funeral."

"Huh. Well, I thought Ruth said it was a meeting about something going on at the co-op. Maybe I got that wrong. And who knows why she hightailed it out of here later."

I blinked. "I'm talking about the night of the twenty-second. The night Ariel Skylark was killed."

"I know which night you're talking about." He spoke carefully, like maybe I was a little slow. "Ruth went to her meeting at Chris', then she came home, and then she got that phone call and had to leave again. I was surprised, because it was almost nine o'clock, and she doesn't usually like to take the car out that late."

"Now, Thaddeus, I don't want you to think I'm questioning your recollection, but what time did Ruth come home from Chris' that night?"

"Oh, couple minutes after eight, I'd say.

I'd just started watching a show on the history channel. You ever watch that channel? A lot of interesting things you can learn from it." He chuckled. "Even if you're an old fart like me. 'Course some of what they call, 'history' I call, 'childhood.' "

But I barely heard him, my brain was so busy trying to assimilate this new information. Ruth had lied, actually lied — to the police, to me, to everyone — about being at Chris Popper's during the time Ariel was killed.

Jake Beagle said he'd left before eight. That gave Felicia an alibi for the time of the murder, and providing her with an alibi meant he had one, too.

Irene said she was at Chris' until Zak got in trouble, and then she said she was at home, with him. Which gave him an alibi, but took away part of Chris' alibi. And now I'd just found out that Ruth couldn't give Chris an alibi, either.

The way I saw it, everyone supposedly had someone else who could account for them during the time Ariel was murdered — but no one really did.

"Sophie Mae?" Thaddeus leaned toward me with concern on his face.

"And you don't know why Ruth left the second time that night?" Tone it down,

Sophie Mae. Way too eager.

Too late. Wariness settled across his face. He said, "I think maybe I've said enough. Maybe I do have the night wrong. After all, Ruth already told the police everything she knows."

Keeping my tone mild, I said. "I'm sure she was very helpful. Did the police talk to you?"

He shook his head. "Why would they? I didn't have anything to do with that whole business." Using his cane as leverage, he stood.

I stood, too, understanding that my welcome was over. "I have a few errands I need to run, Thaddeus. I enjoyed our chat. I'll drop by another time to show Ruth my yarn. Will you tell her thank you for me, for letting me borrow the wheel?"

"I sure will." His voice was hearty, smoothing over any misunderstanding we might have had. The sound of an engine wafted in through the open front door. Thaddeus pointed. "In fact, there she is. You can tell her yourself."

I kissed him on the cheek. "Thanks."

He smiled, at ease again.

Outside, I hurried around to the carport. "Let me get that," I said and lifted the grocery sack from the back seat before Ruth could protest.

"Why, thank you, dear."

"Glad to help. I just came by to thank you again for letting me borrow your wheel, and I wanted to show you some of the yarn I spun."

"I'm always happy when someone converts." She made spinning sound like a cult of some kind. Heck, maybe she was right.

I set the bag on the hood of the car. "Um, Ruth?"

She had already started for the back door that led into the kitchen. Now she stopped and turned. Watched and waited.

"The night Ariel was killed? Where did you go when you left here the second time? After you got back from Chris'?"

For a few moments she considered me. Then she nodded and said, "Let me put these groceries away, and then we'll go downtown and get a cup of coffee."

"But —"

She turned and went inside.

Picking up the bag again, I followed her into the kitchen.

THIRTY

"I didn't want to talk about this in front of Thad," Ruth said.

She sipped her iced latte and gazed at the Cadyville River. We were sitting on a park bench beside the river after stopping in at Beans R Us to get drinks. The afternoon sun was warm on our faces, and the sound of moving water had the usual soporific effect. I'd been patient, waiting until she was ready to tell me what had happened that night.

Now I prompted, "You, Chris, Irene, and Jake met to discuss something to do with CRAC."

Her eyes slewed my way, gauging what I already knew. Looking back at the sunlight sparkling on water, she nodded. "Yes." Another sip of latte.

Carefully erasing judgment from my voice, I asked, "You had a meeting about the co-op the night before Scott's funeral?"

"Yes."

"Must have been something pretty important."

"There was a problem that needed to be solved. We discussed it and decided what to do."

"You're being very vague." Frustration leaked out of my voice. I didn't like the way this conversation was going, didn't like it at all. Dread settled into my gut.

I hesitated, then pushed forward. "What else happened that night? After the meeting."

A long silence, and then a bracing breath. "Jake left first. A few minutes later I left."

Why, oh why, had Ruth provided a false alibi for Chris? With great effort I kept my mouth shut and let her continue.

"I went home," she said.

"And then you left again."

Slowly she nodded. But she didn't speak.

"Why, Ruth?"

Turning to look at me, she said, "Because Chris needed me. She insisted she wanted to be alone, but shortly after I got home, she called. Wanted me to come back. Irene had been getting ready to leave, but then Chris broke down, and she agreed to stay for awhile longer. So I drove back to Chris' house, and we spent two more hours with her, talking some, but mostly listening as she talked about Scott."

That wasn't so bad. I shook my head. "You lied about being with Chris all evening. I don't want that to come back on you. Why did you do it?"

"Right off the bat, that Detective Lane decided Chris had killed Ariel. I knew she hadn't. Irene knew she hadn't. Any gap in our story, and that detective would have arrested that poor woman for something she didn't do."

Relief breezed through me. "You have to tell the police the truth. Tell Barr if you don't want to talk to Detective Lane."

She stood and walked to the garbage can placed a few feet away from the bench. Tossed in her empty latte cup. Came back and stood beside me, looking down.

"We'll see."

"No! Ruth, this is murder. It's a small detail, you going home and coming back, and it probably doesn't affect a thing. But you need to tell them, anyway."

Resignation weighed her features, her shoulders, as she turned away. "I know, Sophie Mae. I know."

"Where are you going?"

"Home."

I stood.

"No," she said. "I need to think."

Not knowing what else to do, I let her go.

Ruth's compassion for Chris was going to get her in trouble. But what had really happened wasn't that big of a deal.

Was it?

Meghan and I had picked up Erin from her last session of math camp — a half-day of awards and cupcakes — and gone down to the airport to pick up Tootie Hanover and her new, ninety-eight-year-old beau, Felix. They'd flown in from Florida after their cruise to the Virgin Islands. They'd looked tan and ridiculously happy, but were understandably exhausted. So we'd taken them directly to Caladia Acres, the nursing home where she and Felix both lived. Tired or not, they were both more energetic and spry than they'd been before they'd started . . . dating?

Now it was late afternoon, and I sat at the retail counter at CRAC gazing out the open door to where Meghan's Volvo sat in the parking lot. She'd been booked with massages all afternoon, so I'd borrowed it. Ariel's painting leaned against the wall by the door where Zak had left it. It was so big it hid half of a tropical-themed batik wall hanging.

Why hadn't Zak picked it up, after going to all the trouble of buying that egregious piece from Gabi in the first place? And it hadn't been cheap. Given his determination to have Ariel's creation and the state of Gabi's pocketbook, I wouldn't have been surprised if he'd paid even more than the exorbitant price her sister-in-law had originally asked.

Had he really killed Scott out of jealousy, and then Ariel when she tried to break up with him?

I thought about the look on Zak's face when he'd told me he'd attached a note to a painting, hoping he'd be allowed to buy it. Then later, what I'd seen as his straightforward honesty about his breakup with Ariel and affection for Daphne Sparks.

Maybe Robin and Barr were right. Maybe he did have both motive and opportunity for not only one, but two murders. But, like Meghan, I liked the kid. When he'd spoken of Ariel, there had been emotion on his face, certainly, but it hadn't struck me as either love or hate. Nothing even approaching such passion, good or bad.

I still thought Gabi had motive and opportunity. Did I want her to be guilty, just to prove myself right? Or was I gun shy about believing Zak was the murderer, after my failure to prove anything against Gabi?

But something was off.

I just knew it.

My, that painting was ugly, wasn't it? I glanced up at the clock. Jake would be here any moment to relieve me. I began to gather my things in anticipation.

Right on time, he walked through the door. His wife followed.

"Hi," I said, not sure how she'd react, since Felicia and I hadn't parted the best of friends the last time I'd talked to her.

"Hello, Sophie Mae. It's nice to see you." A warmer greeting than I anticipated, and I welcomed it. I was growing tired of making enemies of everyone I talked to. Then again, she was an actress, so for all I knew she hated my guts for asking her about Jake and Ariel. It was a sour thought, and reminded me how much my cynicism had increased since I'd become involved in murder investigations.

Jake and I exchanged greetings as well, and I grabbed my bag. "Okay, I'm going to take off now. And as long as I have the Volvo, I'm going to drop this by Zak's house on the way home."

Awkwardly, I lifted Ariel's painting. It would barely fit in the car if I put the back seat down.

"I wonder which end goes up?" I smiled. "Or if it even matters."

Felicia looked away, but not before I caught the look of amusement that flashed across her face.

Jake raised his eyebrows. "You're taking that to Irene's?"

"Don't worry. I won't say anything to set her off."

"I think the painting itself might set her off."

"I'm afraid that's Zak's problem. We can't leave this laying around, blocking items that are actually for sale." I maneuvered the canvas out the door.

"Maybe the back room . . ." Jake's voice followed me out to the parking lot.

"It'll be fine," I called over my shoulder.

I'd never been to the Nelson home before. I wasn't surprised to find Irene's house was painted beige, with lighter beige trim. The front door, on the other hand, was taupe. Even the flower beds were brown, containing only bark and a few small azaleas. She hadn't planted any other flowers.

As I wrestled the splotches of black and white and red out of the car and up the steps, it occurred to me that the addition of all that stark color might actually be an improvement if the interior decoration reflected the exterior.

Zak answered the door. His eyes grew round when he saw what I'd brought. "Hi, Sophie Mae," he stammered out.

"Hi. I brought your painting over."

"Uh, thanks." He peered furtively over his shoulder. "Let's put it in the garage."

"Really?" Maybe he was having second thoughts about gracing his wall with his ex-girlfriend's creative efforts.

Irene came around the corner of the house and stopped cold. "What's *that* doing here?"

"Um," Zak said.

I raised my eyebrows and waited.

"Well?" Irene demanded. She was looking at me, not at her son.

"Oh. Well, I brought this by for Zak . . ." My voice trailed off as anger blazed in her eyes. Anger, and something else.

I'd seen that look on her face every time Ariel's name came up.

She shifted her gaze. "You bought this monstrosity?" she hissed. "After everything she did?"

"Aw, Mom. Ariel didn't do anything. She was just a girl, that's all."

Irene looked pointedly at the canvas his hand rested on. "I won't have it in my house."

And, of course, Zak had known that.

Which was why he'd left it at the co-op until he had someplace to put it. I wondered whether he'd thought that far when he decided to buy it in the first place. Somehow, I doubted it.

Either way, I'd moved the thing out of CRAC. However, it was obvious any hope I'd had of getting more of a read on Zak's guilt or innocence was now dashed by Irene's angry presence.

I watched her, glaring at her son. So much anger under that mousy exterior. Anger at a lot of things, but certainly an abundance of it directed at Ariel Skylark. Anger and, I realized, fear. That was what I'd been trying to pin down.

Irene Nelson was angry, but she was also intensely afraid.

THIRTY-ONE

"Are you going to bed?" Meghan asked. "You're starting to scare me with that thing."

I sat in the living room, glued to the spinning wheel, treadle pumping furiously in the hope that the smooth, neat yarn forming from the messy bundle of raw alpaca on my lap would spark the ordering of my own chaotic thoughts. So far it wasn't working.

"Not yet. I have to do more," I said.

"Have to? You sound like you're addicted."

I loved my housemate, but right then I wanted her to go away and leave me alone. I stopped pumping and allowed the wheel to come to a standstill.

"You don't understand," I said. "I'm thinking. This helps me think."

"And you have more thinking to do."

"Exactly." I began to spin again.

"Right," she said. "Well, goodnight."

" 'Night." I said. Didn't look up.

Keep the strands smooth. Alpaca was exacting, the raw uncarded curls of wool irregular. Challenging. Maybe that was why I wasn't figuring this thing out. Maybe I had to concentrate on the wool too much.

I heard Meghan going upstairs to bed. After some time, a car went by on the street outside. If it hadn't, I wouldn't have realized how quiet the house had become. The wheel whirred. The yarn twisted. Gradually, I got the hang of it. Relaxed into it.

Ariel. Sex. Gabi. Ruth. Anger. Love. Chris. Jealousy. Scott. Hate. Daphne. Jake. Rocky. Irene. Fear. Zak. Lindsey. Barr. Thaddeus. Felicia. Robin.

Death.

Each person involved with this case, all those emotions, tumbled through my thoughts like stones being polished. The rough edges smoothed, allowing the truth to begin shimmering through.

The yarn grew on the spool. Soft and gray. Tidy.

All the strands coming together.

And my gray matter tidied what I knew. Categorized. Theorized. Motivations combined with circumstances, opportunities juxtaposed with temperaments.

An hour and a half later, when the alpaca wool was gone, I had two spools of single spun yarn, ready to ply and set the twist. And I'd figured out a few twists of my own.

This time all the puzzle pieces fit perfectly together. I knew who had killed Ariel Skylark.

Detective Lane had gathered her abundant mane into a sleek, practical bun. She wore black slacks and a white shirt with a minimum of jewelry. Instead of coming across as utilitarian, though, she looked like she was ready to walk down a red carpet to a chorus of oohs and aahs.

It had taken a day for Robin to obtain the arrest warrant for Zak Nelson. This was, she assured us, less due to a lack of evidence than bureaucratic doings. She was convinced he had killed Ariel, and once he was in custody for that crime, she would further investigate Scott Popper's death. She was obviously delighted to be able to close a murder case so quickly, yet another feather in her cap. Despite her lack of interviewing and social skills, she had quickly developed a reputation with her superiors for the ability to efficiently solve any crime that came her way. This reputation meant a lot to her.

Perhaps too much.

Barr had arranged for me to be there when they arrested Zak after I'd laid my theory out to him. I don't know how he did it, and counted myself among the luckiest of women that he would even consider including me, especially as I could tell he had a few reservations. But despite Robin being the lead detective on Ariel's murder case, he was still senior in the department, and they had to work together every day. In any case, she'd acquiesced, however much it went against her grain.

But she didn't exactly welcome me with open arms.

We were alone in the parking lot of the cop shop, waiting for Barr to join us. Robin opened the back door of the patrol car she and Barr were using for this trip and gestured for me to get in. The undercover Impala they usually used didn't have the wire screen to separate the slick, one-piece vinyl backseat (easier to hose out, I'd been told) from the law enforcement up front. This one did.

"Um," I said, craning my neck to see if Barr was coming. "I'm not that excited about small spaces."

Her eyes narrowed. "You know, everything you've done regarding this investigation has caused me grief."

I bristled. "That's not true! What about —"

"Neither of us are riding in the back, so if you're coming, that's where you get to sit. Your choice."

The note of finality in her voice sealed the deal. I slid onto the seat, and she slammed the door. The sensation of being in a cage combined with the lack of interior door handles made my mild claustrophobia flare. Within moments, I found it hard to breathe.

Luckily, Barr joined us then. It was a short trip to the Nelson home, so I did my best to distract myself from the sure knowledge my throat was closing by worrying about the gamble I was about to take. At least, I told myself, I wasn't the reason they were arresting Zak. If anything, I was there to help him as best as I could.

I only hoped my best was good enough.

"You okay?" Barr asked as he opened the door, and I barreled out of the back seat. "You look a little pale. Are you nervous?"

"I'm fine," I said, keeping my tone bright. "Don't worry about me."

Robin gave me a look. "I'm still not sure why you're here, but if you have any ideas about interfering, you'd better think again."

"Yes, ma'am." I saluted.

She rolled her eyes and turned toward the house. Either Irene and Zak hadn't noticed that we'd arrived, or they were inside, waiting to see why we were there. Then I saw a curtain in the front window twitch. That answered that.

Together, we trooped to the front step.

Irene answered immediately, confirming my suspicion that she'd been watching us.

"Officers? What can I do for you?" Her voice shook a little.

"Detectives." Robin barked out the correction.

Irene's pale face lost another shade of color. "I'm sorry. Detectives."

"May we come in?" Barr asked.

Irene's tongue flicked out and ran over her lower lip. "Can you tell me what this is about?" My presence must have registered then. "Sophie Mae? What's going on?"

Barr stepped to the screen door. "Please. We should do this inside."

Wordlessly, she stepped back. The poor woman looked terrified. Single file, the three of us entered her home.

Robin brushed past Irene and strode into the nondescript living room. "Where's your son?"

The fear on Irene's face intensified. "Zak? What do you want with Zak?"

"Ms. Nelson, is he here?" Robin sounded like a drill sergeant.

"Please," Barr said. The one word softened

the tension in the room.

Irene turned to me. "Sophie Mae? What — ?"

I opened my mouth to speak. Robin sent me a look that would have stopped a rhino. My jaw snapped shut.

"Ms. Nelson," Barr prompted gently. "Where is he?"

This time the look Irene directed at me was on par with Robin's. I seemed to be on everyone's shitlist.

"He's in the basement," she said. "He has a separate apartment down there."

"Show us," Robin said.

Slowly, Irene led us to a door and opened it. "Zak?" she called.

Robin pushed her aside and ran down the stairs. Barr was right behind her. For all they knew, Zak was waiting for them with an Uzi or running out the back door. Theirs was a serious, deadly business. Better safe than sorry.

Irene and I followed. She grabbed my arm. "What do they want?"

"They want to arrest your son," I said, and watched the enormity of those words sink in. I pulled my arm out of her grasp and went downstairs. After a brief hesitation, she followed me.

Zak was sitting on a battered recliner in

the main room of the basement. It looked like part living room, with a slumping sofa and the recliner situated in front of a big television screen, and part garage with the half-built motorcycle on a tarp in one corner. A laugh track emanated from the TV. Two guitars and a myriad of concert posters punctuated the pumpkin-colored walls. At least he hadn't inherited his mother's sense of design.

"Stand up, please." Robin's use of the word didn't sound nearly as nice as when Barr said it.

"Uh, sure," Zak said easily, though he looked a little bewildered as he stood and clicked the Off button on the remote.

Robin walked behind him, neatly clasping handcuffs around his wrists before anyone realized what she was doing. Beside me, Irene's gasp caught in her throat.

"Zak Nelson, you are under arrest for the murder of Ariel Skylark," Robin intoned.

She continued on, reading him his Miranda rights. My gaze slid to Irene. Her hands were clamped over her mouth, the whites of her eyes visible all around the pupils above her fingers.

"Are you going to let this happen?" I asked in a low tone.

Zak blinked, confusion coming off him

like a scent. Mother and son stared at one another. Robin droned on.

"You can stop this," I whispered. "They have a lot of evidence. He's going to jail, Irene. Zak's going to jail unless you tell them the truth."

I could sense the intensity of Barr's gaze as he watched us from across the room.

Robin finished her recitation and put her hand on Zak's arm. He still looked bewildered, the fact that he was being arrested for murder seeming to elude his comprehension.

"No!" Irene said in a loud voice. Then in a lower tone. "He didn't do it." She was shaking all over now.

"We'll let the courts decide that," Robin said.

Irene looked at me then. Understanding passed between us. I nodded.

She turned back to the detectives about to march her son out to the patrol car. "But I know he didn't do it." She licked her lips. "Because I did."

Robin glared at me. She began to push Zak toward the stairway.

"Wait!" Irene moved in front of the door to the stairs. "What are you doing? Didn't you hear me?"

"You killed the Skylark girl?" Robin shook

her head. "Right. Just like you were at Chris Popper's house that night. And then you were with Zak here. Lady, you need to make up your mind. But I can tell you that providing so many different stories is going to make it a lot easier on the prosecutor when this case gets to court."

Red fury swept up Irene's face. The fear still shone there, too. How had she managed to get through the days since the murder? She must have been barely holding her life together.

"Ms. Nelson, you need to move," Robin said.

"No. I'm not going anywhere until you listen to me. I killed that little slut."

"Mom, shut up," Zak said. "I didn't kill her, I swear, but you can't take the fall in order to protect me."

Robin sighed. "You will either step aside, Ms. Nelson, or Detective Ambrose here will be forced to move you out of my way."

"I want to confess, and damn it, you're going to listen." Irene was becoming less mousy and more like one of her female power statuettes by the second.

"Come down to the station, then. You can make any statement you want to. But I don't want to have to say it again: get out of my way."

My heart sank. Irene wanted to confess to a murder I was sure she had indeed committed. But who knew whether she'd change her mind, given the chance?

"Let him go." Irene grated the words out. She was almost a foot shorter than Barr's Amazonian partner.

Zak's jaw clenched as the seriousness of his situation sank in. "Mom?" His eyes narrowed, and he slowly shook his head. His voice was soft. "I'm not twelve. Why are you doing this?"

Barr moved to Robin's side, looking grim. She glanced at him. "What?"

He shook his head. "You're the lead on this. But maybe we should listen."

The words were neutral, but I could tell he was afraid we'd lose Irene's confession, too. Robin pressed her lips together. It was not attractive, and only served to make her look petulant.

"I have to tell you," Irene said, her eyes pleading.

Her son blinked in confusion. Robin let out an exasperated breath, and her shoulders slumped a fraction in defeat.

"Okay, Irene," I said. "Tell us what happened that night."

She turned on me. "Shut up, Sophie Mae. You don't know anything."

Well, that kind of hurt my feelings. Obviously I knew something. For example I knew she killed Ariel. And she knew I knew. Irene's constant bitchiness was really starting to get on my nerves.

Barr sat down on the sofa. Robin locked gazes with him, then after a few moments capitulated. She guided Zak to the sofa. "Sit down."

He did, and she slowly and deliberately perched on the cushion on the other side of him. He glanced at Barr, who met his eyes without smiling.

"All right," I said, and reached into my tote bag. Irene's head jerked toward me. "Will you relax? I don't carry anything more lethal than lip balm in my bag."

I fished around, found the tube and took it out. I applied the balm and dropped it back into my bag. Robin pursed those perfect lips of hers and rolled her eyes toward the ceiling. But she didn't know I'd turned on the miniature cassette recorder Barr had let me borrow.

"So let's sit down like civilized people, and you can tell us what happened. Are you game?" I asked.

A moment of hesitation, and Irene nodded. "That's all I wanted in the first place."

"Do you want to sit in the recliner?" Next

I'd be passing around appetizers.

"I'll stand."

I nodded and moved to the recliner, carefully placing my tote by the coffee table. Irene began to pace back and forth in front of the television.

And then she began to speak.

THIRTY-TWO

"I went over to Chris Popper's that night," Irene said. "We were meeting about how to get rid of Ariel."

Zak sat up. "What?"

"Not kill her, just get her out of the co-op. She should never have been a member in the first place, not with our jury process. But Scott had convinced Chris to let Ariel in. That was, of course, before anyone knew he and Ariel were having an affair."

She looked pensively at her son, who nodded. "Yeah, Mom. I already know that."

"But then she started in on you, and even Jake had a crush on her. For some reason she wasn't interested in him, though."

I knew why: Jake didn't have anything she needed. If he had, she would have made a run at him just as she had with Zak and Scott. And now I knew Scott's appeal: he'd been able to get her into CRAC, something Daphne Sparks felt Ariel desperately wanted in order to validate her talent as an artist.

Irene continued. "Things had gotten out of control. She needed to go. But we had to figure out how to go about it."

"What did you decide?" I asked.

"We decided to simply refund her membership dues and ask her to leave. Jake was worried that she'd want to know why. Chris and I wanted to tell her exactly why, but he didn't like that. He was ambivalent about making her leave at all, of course. He felt we were being too hard on her. He left the house in a huff."

"What time was that?" Barr asked.

"Between seven-thirty and eight."

That jibed with what everyone else had said. He nodded. "Go on."

Irene stopped pacing and cupped her elbows in her palms. "Well, with Jake acting like that, a united front wasn't going to be possible. Ruth and Chris and I decided we would approach Ariel in a week or so. After all, Chris owns the building and started the co-op. She has a lot of say about things, more than the rest of us, by default. But Scott's funeral was the next day, and she was grieving and exhausted. We needed to wait."

We all nodded, even Robin.

"So Ruth left next, and a few minutes

after that I did." She passed her hand over her face. "I felt better about things at CRAC than I had in a long time, knowing that girl would be leaving." The hand dropped, and she began pacing again, back and forth in the space between the coffee table and the television. "My way home from Chris' took me by the co-op." She paced faster now. "I saw Zak's car in the parking lot, next to Ariel's little blue car. I couldn't help it. I pulled to the curb across the street and waited."

Now she stopped in front of her son. "I hated that you were seeing her."

"I know, Mom."

"She was going to hurt you terribly. I knew it. She was empty inside, and she sucked the life out of the people around her like some kind of psychological vampire. I couldn't stand that you were in there with her." As she spoke, the volume of her voice increased and her words tumbled over one another.

Her son held his hands up. "But we were breaking up that night. That's why I was there. She didn't hurt me at all. We had some fun, and then we moved on." His voice was steady, but his eyes were full of dread. I could tell he didn't want to hear any more.

"Zak," I said. Everyone turned toward me. Okay, so I was interrupting a murder confession, but I just had to know something. "Did Ariel ever come to work with you, or visit you at the Fix-It?"

"She came by all the time. For a chick, she knew a lot about cars."

"Did she ever come by when you were working on the police cars?"

"Probably. It's not like I kept track, and we usually have one or another of the city's cars in there at any given time." He glared at Barr and Robin. "You guys are rough on those vehicles, and then you don't even bother to take care of them," he spit out. The fury in his tone had nothing to do with maintaining the police department's cars; it was directed at the detectives who sat calmly on either side of him while his mother led up to a horrible revelation.

"I'm sure you're right," Barr said, and flicked a warning at me with his eyes.

I felt sure Ariel had been the one who sabotaged Scott Popper's vehicle, and Zak had at least confirmed that she had had access. Barr and Robin could follow up with him more on that later.

"Sorry, Irene," I said. "Please go on."

The interruption seemed to have calmed her. "I waited outside the co-op for a few minutes. I just couldn't help it. All I knew was that I wanted Zak to come out of there." She took a deep breath. "And then he did. He came out and drove away."

Her pacing resumed. "But she didn't come out. *She* was still in there. And I kept thinking about all the things we'd talked about at Chris', about how disruptive that girl was." Now she sent a pleading look her son's way. "I didn't know she'd broken it off with you. I didn't know." Anguish laced her tone. "Sitting there in my car in the dark, all I could think about was how she needed to go away, and not in a week or so, when Chris would be up to facing her." She stopped speaking for a few moments, but kept striding back and forth. Finally, in a quiet voice I said, "You felt threatened. She'd seduced Scott Popper, ruined the co-op for you, and then went after your son. You didn't know what she was capable of."

Irene shook her head a couple of times, then paused, and stared at me. She slowly nodded. "Yes. That's really it, isn't it? I didn't know what she was going to do next, and I was afraid for Zak."

A derisive noise came from her son's throat.

"You may not have known Ariel as well as you thought," I said to him.

"Are you going to keep interrupting?" Robin asked. "Or can we get this over with?"

I sighed. So much for greasing the wheels of Irene's confession. "So what did you do next?"

"I went inside. It was dark, but I could see something on the floor, to the side of the retail counter." Her eyes blazed. "It was one of my sculptures. The one I call Athena, where she's in the warrior yoga pose?"

I nodded, though I had no idea what she was talking about.

"Someone had knocked it off the table where it was displayed. Her arm was broken. I just knew Ariel had done it, in the dark, too lazy to turn on the lights, and too uncaring to bother picking it up." She gritted out the words. "The light shone down the stairs from above. I knew she was up there. So I took the sculpture upstairs to confront her. And you know what I found?"

We all shook our heads.

"I found little Miss Ariel Skylark going through Ruth Black's things. She was taking some of that pretty, shiny fiber Thea Hawke sells, right out of Ruth's case."

Hoo boy. I hadn't been expecting that. Ruth kept a portion of her stash and fiber to use for lessons at CRAC in a small cupboard in the corner of her work area.

The northern lights fiber Ariel had been clutching in her dead hand when I found her was indeed the same stuff Gabi had in her spinning basket which had sent us on such a wild goose chase. But Gabi had told the truth when she said she got the fiber from Ariel — and I'd been right when I figured Ariel wouldn't shell out the big bucks for a gift like that for her sister-in-law.

Stealing from Ruth Black. Sheesh. The list in Ariel's "con" column just kept getting longer and longer.

"You confronted her?" I prompted.

"Oh, yes. And I told her we'd decided that she had to leave the co-op. That she had a day to get all of her stuff out." Irene pressed her lips together, the anger and fear on her face again as she remembered. "She laughed at me. Said she had no intention of leaving, and that I didn't have the authority to make her. When I insisted Chris was on board with the decision, she got a nasty look on her face. Told me she wouldn't go, and that if we tried to make her, she'd take us to court. Sue the co-op."

"That's ridiculous," Zak said.

"I thought so, too," Irene said. "And I told her that. Plus, if she didn't get her ugly paintings out of the building herself, we'd take them down for her and set them in the alley so she could pick them up. Well, that made her spitting mad, and she came at me."

Her lips opened again, but no words came out. She rubbed her palm over her face and cleared her throat. When she managed to speak again, her voice was quiet. "I hit her with my Athena sculpture, and she fell down." Her eyes welled. "She just wouldn't go *away*. It didn't seem like we'd ever be rid of her. Thinking that made me a little nuts, you know? I saw that hank of yarn hanging over the back of the chair, and I grabbed it and wrapped it around her neck."

She met Zak's horrified gaze, shunted her eyes toward mine and whispered, "I kept it there until she was dead."

Not exactly self-defense, I thought. But an insanity plea didn't seem entirely out of the question. Poor Zak. Poor Irene, for that matter.

I kept my tone gentle. "You hit her with the sculpture first?"

She nodded.

Understanding registered on Robin's face. The official story was that Ariel had been strangled. How could Irene have known Ariel had been struck first unless she'd been there? She slowly rose to her feet.

354

"Where is it?" Barr asked, also standing.

Irene licked her lips.

"Did you get rid of it?" he pushed.

She looked at Zak. "Would it prove that I was the one who killed that girl, and not Zak?"

"I believe it might," Barr said, not committing to anything. But the look he shot my way was triumphant.

"It's outside," she said. "In my workroom. I was going to try and fix it."

And sell it in the co-op, no doubt. Nice way to get rid of a murder weapon — except she could have smashed it to pieces instead. I had to wonder if there wasn't a part of Irene that wanted to get caught.

"So how did you convince Chris and Ruth to give you an alibi for the time of the murder?" I asked, not moving from the recliner. I wanted to get as much on tape as possible.

Irene, looking paler than ever, covered her eyes with one hand for a few beats. Then she dropped her arm and said, "After I realized what I'd done, I panicked and called Chris. I told her what had happened, and she told me to get back to her place as fast as possible. I know I shouldn't have done it, that I should have just called the police and confessed right then, but I did what she said. When I got there, she told me Ruth would be there any minute, and that I should say I'd been at Chris' the whole time, hadn't left at all. That way I'd have an alibi, and both Chris and Ruth could back me up."

Ruth had told me she went back because Chris had broken down the night before the funeral. But when I was in the smithy with her, Chris had told me it was the first time she'd really cried since Scott's death. Now that made sense.

I leaned forward. "Only Chris knew she was lying. You tricked Ruth."

Irene sighed. "She could've said she'd left and come back, but after you found Ariel, she was afraid for Chris. She didn't want her to be blamed. So she fudged a little on the truth — on her own, not because I made her, or even asked her to — in order to strengthen Chris' alibi. But you have to understand, she really thought I'd been there the whole time, so she believed Chris *had* an alibi."

Ruth's heart had been in the right place, but she'd ended up protecting someone who'd actually killed Ariel. Chris, on the other hand, had intentionally aided and abetted. She'd had good reason to hate Ariel, too. No wonder she'd protected Irene.

"Worked out pretty well for you, didn't it?" Robin said, her lips drawing back in disgust.

Defiance flashed across Irene's features. "Until now."

"Show me the statue you hit her with," Robin said.

Irene hesitated then nodded toward her son. He'd run through the gamut of emotions as he'd listened to his mother confess to murder, and now sat stunned on the sofa with his hands still behind him. "Take the handcuffs off of him."

Robin narrowed her eyes, but after a long moment complied, pulling Zak to his feet. Metal scraped against metal as she removed them, sounding loud in the room. He rubbed one wrist, still staring at his mother.

We all filed upstairs behind Irene. Barr smiled his approval when I grabbed my tote bag off the coffee table on the way. We went through the white and beige kitchen to the back door, and outside. A small building stood in the far corner of the backyard. It was little more than a glorified shed. Together we crossed the yard, and Irene opened the door. A table and chair took up most of the interior. Shelves lining the walls held figurines in various stages of completion, as well as neat packages of clay waiting to be shaped into something more. A variety of shiny, clean tools lay in a row on the tabletop. Even here, where Irene made her art, there was little color and no decoration.

She took one of the chunky statuettes down from the shelf and held it out to Robin, who told her to put it on the table. Then she put the handcuffs on Irene and started the whole Miranda thing over again. Zak looked on with a mixture of sadness and repulsion on his face.

Irene met my eyes, and I saw that the fear she'd been carrying around seemed to be gone. Then she mouthed something at me, and nodded. I blinked.

Barr and I went outside. I gave him my tote bag, and he removed the tape recorder and turned it off. "What did she say to you?"

"She said . . ." I shook my head. "I think she said, 'Thank you.' Can you believe that?"

The corners of his eyes crinkled, and his look was tender. "Guilt is a hard thing to carry around."

I thought about things I'd done in my own life. Not murder, but still. "Yeah. I guess you're right."

As we walked toward the patrol car, Barr sighed under his breath.

"What's wrong?" I asked.

"This was such a fiasco, and it could have been avoided if my partner wasn't so pigheaded. Do you have any idea how much paperwork we're going to have to fill out now?"

"Well, at least you got your killer," I said.

"At least one of them."

"Meaning . . . you think Ariel killed Scott?"

He nodded. "It sounds like a possibility. I'll talk to Zak and to the other mechanics at the shop and see if I can find out anything more. It won't make him any less dead, but Chris might like to know what really happened. Might make a difference with his life insurance payout, too."

"Except Chris might be looking at some jail time, too. Don't you think?"

A rueful expression settled on his face. "What the hell was she thinking, covering for Irene like that?"

"My bet? She was thinking that in the same situation, she might have done exactly the same thing. Ariel had a real talent for inciting love and hate. Which one depended on your gender."

THIRTY-THREE

Barr spent the rest of the afternoon at the police station with Irene, processing and doing paperwork and whatever else you have to do when someone confesses to murder. We'd agreed to meet at his house that evening, and as I made the short drive in Meghan's Volvo, I kept replaying the events in Irene's basement in my mind. What kept coming back to me over and over was the look in Zak's eyes as he'd watched his mother confess to murder. As with so many others involved with the case, his life was now changed forever.

I guess I should have been surprised to find Hannah's rental car parked in front of Barr's house, but I wasn't. I was beginning to wonder if she'd ever leave us alone. What had Irene said about Ariel? That it seemed like she would never go *away*.

And look what had happened to her.

The door was open, and I walked right in

without knocking. Hannah stood in front of the sofa. She turned her head, and fury filled her eyes the instant she saw me. She'd cut off her long braid and now sported a short, tousled mop that mimicked my own. A wave of distaste washed through me when I saw it. Words of protest on my tongue, I turned toward Barr, who stood across the living room from her. They died when I saw the expression on his face, at once surprised, fearful, and pleading. The skin on the back of my neck tingled. Tension crackled in the space between them, and I could feel it extending toward me.

What was his ex up to this time?

"Did I interrupt something?" I asked. Couldn't quite keep the sarcasm out of my voice, but I didn't really try, either.

"Sophie Mae," Barr said. "Please don't take this wrong, but I need you to leave. Go home. I'll call you as soon as I can." The pleading in his eyes increased.

I was stunned. "What's going on here?"

"Please," he said.

Hannah shifted, snagging my attention.

And I saw the gun.

She held it easily in her hand. I don't know anything about guns, but it seemed big enough to do some real damage.

I looked at the gun. I looked at Hannah.

She smiled. Then she pointed it at Barr.

"What are you going to do?" I asked. "Make him go back to Wyoming or shoot him?"

She made a noise of exasperation in the back of her throat, and pointed the barrel at me. "Shut up. This isn't about you."

"The hell it isn't."

Barr took a step toward her. She swung the weapon toward him again, and he stopped.

Oh brother.

"Let me handle this," he said, voice low and calm. I had a sudden notion of him dealing with a horse or a cow — or a grizzly bear — using the same tone. "Hannah will let you go. Won't you, Hannah?"

She started to nod, then shook her head once. Her eyes darted left and right, and her shoulders hunched defensively. It was one thing to start waving a gun around at Barr, but another to add a third party, and her rival at that. My presence had backed her into a corner. My neck tingled again at the thought.

Barr was right. I should leave while I still could and let him handle his loony ex.

On the other hand, I had an idea.

"Oh, for heaven's sake," I said, and walked between them and into the kitchen.

Hannah looked confused as I passed. So did Barr.

I opened the cupboard and took out a glass. Ice clattered out of the refrigerator door into the glass, and then I ran tap water into it. Took a long drink.

"Anyone want anything?" I called.

Silence.

"Water?" I opened the fridge again. "There's some root beer in here."

"No thanks," Barr said from the other room.

"Hannah?"

"Uh, no," came the hesitant reply.

"Okay, then," I said, returning to the living room. I walked straight up to Hannah and snatched the gun out of her hand. She was so surprised she didn't resist.

"This time you've gone too far," I said. The edge in my voice could have cut glass.

. Barr was at my side in an instant. I gave him the gun and turned back to his ex-wife. Utter defeat slumped her shoulders, and she stared down at the floor.

She nodded. "I just —"

"You cut your hair."

Silence.

"You can't force someone to love you."

"I know."

"But you can do a pretty good job of making them dislike you. A lot."

Her head snapped up, eyes searching for Barr's. "Do you hate me now?"

A pause, and then he said, "You've got to stop this nonsense. Go back to the ranch. It's where you belong."

"Yeah." She grimaced, and looked between us.

"So go home," I said, "and leave us alone."

She blinked. "I'm sorry."

"Good," I said. " 'Bye."

So I wasn't as easygoing as Barr. Sue me.

And she left this time. Really and truly left.

"What were you thinking?" I couldn't keep the frustration out of my voice as I asked Ruth the question. My spinning wheel whirred, the spokes a blur, and the natural wool roving I was spinning accumulated on the spool at a rapid rate.

"I never should have lied," Ruth said, her voice sheepish beside me. She was also spinning, but her wheel turned slowly.

I didn't look up, afraid I'd lose my rhythm and foul up my yarn. "What did the police say? Are you in trouble?"

"Probably less than I ought to be. It doesn't hurt that I'm a feeble little old lady."

I laughed.

"I have to go to court and testify," she said.

"Against Chris and Irene?"

"Yes." The word was clipped.

I stopped spinning and looked at her. "You don't want to."

"Of course I don't want to, but it's the right thing to do." She calmly fed a soy-silk blend into her wheel. "People can't go around killing people."

I couldn't have put it better myself.

"Well, I have to testify, too," I said. "Chris didn't only protect Irene by lying for her and tricking you into doing the same. She also confessed to tampering with my brakes. They're going to try her for attempted murder."

Ruth's wheel slowed to a stop, and she looked up with a shocked expression. "Chris made you have that wreck? Why would she do that?"

I shrugged. "She thought I suspected Irene, and if Irene went down, so would she. Which is, of course, exactly what happened."

"Did you?"

"What? Suspect Irene?"

She nodded.

"Not at that point. But sometimes guilt can make you a little paranoid, you know?"

Ruth started spinning again. A few minutes later I heard her murmur, "Maybe I won't mind testifying against them so much after all."

People had indeed gone around killing people. Irene had killed Ariel, and it certainly looked like Ariel had killed Scott Popper. Barr had talked to Dusty and Zak, and they'd pinpointed the last time Officer Popper's car had been serviced: the day before his accident. And sure enough, Ariel had been hanging out with Zak that day. They'd even recalled a period when they'd been slammed with work, and she'd had full run of the shop.

Next they figured out what tools she might have used, and Barr had them all fingerprinted. They found two of her prints. But the clincher was that her prints were also found on the rack-and-pinion steering mechanism of Scott's patrol car. They couldn't wring a confession from her now, obviously, and if she hadn't died Ariel probably would have gotten away with the murder. As for her parents' car wreck, we'd never know about that.

And Hannah? Cassie called to assure us that she'd returned to the ranch. Last we'd heard, she was making a play for Barr's younger brother, Randall. If she managed to hook him she wouldn't even have to change her name.

"You've got to be kidding," I said. It was a week later, and I'd thought things were getting back to normal.

"Not even a little bit. Go ahead, turn around." Barr, grinning like an idiot, produced a silk scarf from his pocket.

We were standing in the entryway of the house. Meghan leaned in the doorway to the living room, arms folded.

"Do you know what this is all about?" I asked her.

"Yep."

"And you're not about to tell me," I said.

"Nope."

I looked at Barr again. Still grinning. Well, if it was going to make him that happy. I turned. "Don't tie it too tight."

"Afraid he'll mess up your hair?" Meghan asked.

"Shut up."

He finished tying the blindfold, and put his hands on my shoulders. "Out front."

What on earth?

I stumbled on the front step, but Barr caught me. Carefully he led me down the sidewalk, then we paused and he opened the gate. The sun was warm, the silk was soft against my face, and chickadees called to one another up and down our street. I heard Meghan's steps behind me.

"You didn't buy me a pony, did you? Because I've always wanted a pony, ever since I was a little girl."

"In a manner of speaking," Barr said.

"What? Tell me you didn't go get me a horse or some such nonsense, Barr Ambrose, because I don't know how to ride a horse, and I don't have time for a horse, and I don't even know if I like —"

Barr grabbed my hands before I could rip the blindfold off.

"Will you relax? Geez, sometimes you make it awful hard to be nice to you."

Chastened, I dropped my arms.

"Now come down here," he said.

I did what I was told.

More footsteps behind, and Erin's breathless voice. "Has it happened yet?"

"Not yet," Meghan said.

God, even the eleven-year-old was in on it.

"Okay. I'm going to take the blindfold off now. Hold still," Barr said.

The fabric slid away, and I squinted into the sunlight. We were standing on the sidewalk in front of the house.

In front of a Land Rover.

And not just any Land Rover. It was dark green, an older model, maybe from the nineteen eighties, in perfect gleaming condition. How had he known?

"Oh, my God," I breathed. "It's wonderful."

Meghan laughed.

"Will you take me for a ride?" I asked.

"For Pete's sake, Sophie Mae," Barr said. "It's not mine. It's yours."

I whirled to look up at him.

He smiled. "Look inside."

Bewildered and a little giddy, I walked to the side and peered in the window. In the back seat sat a fully assembled Ashford spinning wheel, like Ruth's. He'd stained it golden pecan, and the wood glowed where the sunlight struck the edge of the drive wheel. Piled around it were bags of wool, puffs of fiber, long snakes of roving, a stack of delicate rolled batts. A handkerchief of silk fiber hung from the rearview window.

I turned and blinked. "You did all this for me?"

There was that grin again. He nodded. "You like it?"

"I love it. Oh, but Barr, it's too much. Way too much."

"In case you haven't heard, I'm a millionaire. That means I get to buy you pretty

369

things if I want to. Ruth helped me pick everything out."

Meghan had that grin on her face now, too. And so did Erin.

"I . . . I don't —" My voice broke. My vision grew watery.

He took a step toward me. "Oh, hey. Don't get all girly on me, now. Don't cry. You hear me?"

I sniffed. Nodded. "Thank you. It's all just perfect."

"That's better. You're welcome. There's just one more thing." He held out a small velvet box.

"The key?" I asked, and opened the box.

A big fat diamond glinted up at me.

Speechless, I watched as the man I loved sank to one knee on the sidewalk. Erin started to say something, but Meghan shushed her.

"Sophie Mae Reynolds, will you marry me?" Barr asked.

I felt my eyes go wide. Next to Meghan, Erin started jumping up and down.

Wow. Oh, wow.

ABOUT THE AUTHOR

Cricket McRae has always enjoyed the kind of practical home crafts that were once necessary to everyday life. Her first Home Crafting Mystery, *Lye in Wait,* focuses on soap making; the second in the series, *Heaven Preserve Us,* features canning.

We hope you have enjoyed this Large Print book. Other Thorndike, Wheeler, Kennebec, and Chivers Press Large Print books are available at your library or directly from the publishers.

For information about current and upcoming titles, please call or write, without obligation, to:

Publisher
Thorndike Press
295 Kennedy Memorial Drive
Waterville, ME 04901
Tel. (800) 223-1244

or visit our Web site at:

http://gale.cengage.com/thorndike

OR

Chivers Large Print
published by BBC Audiobooks Ltd
St James House, The Square
Lower Bristol Road
Bath BA2 3SB
England
Tel. +44(0) 800 136919
email: bbcaudiobooks@bbc.co.uk
www.bbcaudiobooks.co.uk

All our Large Print titles are designed for easy reading, and all our books are made to last.